I0571368

THE BREAKING POINT

THE BREAKING POINT

Copyright © 2020 by Christine Class

All rights reserved. This book or any portion thereof may not be reproduced or used in any manner whatsoever without the express written permission of the publisher except for the use of brief quotations in a book review.

Publisher's note: This is a work of fiction. Names, characters, places, and incidents either are the product of the author's imagination or are used fictitiously. Any resemblance to actual events, locales, or persons, living or dead, is entirely coincidental.

Edited by Kristen Corrects, Inc.

Proofread by Julie Withaeger

Final Proofread by Calee Allen

Cover Art Design by Chriselle Tejera

Interior and Ebook Design by KimPeticolas.com

First Edition Published 2020

THE BREAKING POINT

CECE REEVES

To my mom and dad, who showed me how to find my inner strength. To my family, who never doubted, always encouraged and supported me throughout this journey. To my sister, Lauren, who always stayed up listening to me read my stories since we were little girls. To my beautiful daughters, Kaylin and Leah. Thank you for being so strong and always supportive of me. You are my precious gems.

And to Cammy, Cathy, and Aunt Loretta. Gone too soon but forever in my heart. Until we meet again...

With God all things are possible ~ Matthew 19:26

CHAPTER ONE

Kristin stared at her reflection in the circular mirror that hung over the bathroom sink. With one finger she touched her cheek, now painted black and blue. The bruise from the night before joined the others. She'd once possessed the beauty of a movie star. Her aunt had told her she was a lovely child. Born with beautiful rosy cheeks, perfectly kissable lips, and bright, round brown eyes that allured anyone who gazed upon her. But the last five years had been difficult for her. She didn't recognize the lost woman in the mirror staring back at her. Her eyes had lost their glow. Dark circles had formed underneath them, mostly due to a lack of sleep. Bruises adorned her skin above her eyes and along the jawline. Some were a few days old, and others were just now beginning to heal.

Better take out the white turtleneck, she said to herself. She was planning to go down to the supermarket later. After five years of marriage, she had grown accustomed to the drastic change in her wardrobe. Once a fan of short dresses and snug-fitting blouses that showed off her delicate shoulders, she now wore long-sleeve T-shirts and ankle-length pants. It wasn't because she preferred it that way. It was the only style of clothing that would properly hide the evidence of what everyone had suspected for so long. She had perfected concealing the marks and bruises with makeup. In fact, she thought it quite amusing how much of the allowance Jake gave her was spent on foundation.

In the beginning, her coworkers at the diner would question the marks on her arms and neck. But Kristin played it off as being awfully clumsy. Lord knows how many times she used the excuse of "running into that bedroom door again." Well, she wasn't exactly lying. That statement was true if you wanted to get technical about it. But it was Jake who would push her into that door. Soon, people got the hint when she avoided their stares or pretended to not hear the question. Eventually, they stopped asking. Everyone except Tiffany—her coworker, her best friend.

Tiffany and Kristin had grown close over the last four years waiting tables together. Kristin remembered the first day she worked at the diner—being the new girl. She was surprised Jake had even allowed her to work when she told him she had seen the *Help Wanted* sign in the diner window. But with her need to feel useful instead of being a housewife and his need to bring in more household income with all the financial trouble they were having lately, he reluctantly agreed to it. The first week on the job, the owner, Joe, asked her to shadow Tiffany, a tall, slender blonde with a great big Southern smile, to help her learn the ropes.

She could sense right away that Tiffany didn't take to her too much. In the first week, after constantly dropping plates and glasses throughout the shift, she thought for sure she would lose the only thing that gave her some kind of peace in her life. She had seen Tiffany roll her eyes a couple of times behind her back and get a little frustrated having to repeat where things went and where things didn't.

But when she overheard Joe telling Tiffany that he didn't think she was going to work out, Tiffany had defended her. She'd asked Joe to keep her and said that she would take her under her wing. And that was just what Tiffany did. Tiffany told her it was Kristin's determination to be the best at her job and the kindness she always showed the customers when they walked through the door that had won her over. Not long after that, Tiffany and Kristin exchanged recipes and movie favorites, and they became really good friends. Since Kristin didn't have any siblings, Tiffany had become the sister she never had.

Except there were certain limitations on how much interaction they had. Outside of work, Kristin would hardly ever get to see her dear friend—mostly because of Jake and his demands that she be home right after work to start dinner. But there were times that Kristin could visit with Tiffany at her house without him knowing. She'd tell Jake she was grocery shopping or had picked up an extra shift at work. It didn't help that Tiffany didn't like Jake much to begin with. She knew that things at home between Kristin and him weren't right. She told Kristin that she wasn't one to judge, but everyone deserved to be happy. And if Kristin wasn't happy in the marriage, she should leave while she was still young and had no ties to him—no children. But when it came to Jake, whatever she told Kristin seemed to go in one ear and out the other. And despite how close she felt to her friend, Kristin always denied that Jake had ever hit her. Tiffany didn't believe her, of course, but that didn't matter.

Maybe admitting it to Tiffany wasn't the problem. The problem was with Kristin having to admit to herself she was indeed the stereotypical battered wife in denial. The label alone was too depressing to even think about.

What was the point of testifying to such a horrible truth, anyway? It wasn't like she could leave him at the drop of a hat. It wasn't as easy as Tiffany made it sound. He controlled everything. Jake was the main source of their income, for starters. Of course, she worked her hours at the diner and received her paycheck at the end of the week, but Jake collected every cent she earned. That was the agreement they made in order for her to be allowed to work at the diner. Where her money went, she didn't know, because even though it was supposed to pull in extra income, it still seemed as if there was never enough money to pay the bills. He would never let her in on their financial problems or what was happening in the contracting business. His father had left him the business along with the clear warning, "Don't screw it up!" in a handwritten note Jake was given at the reading of the will."

Kristin turned her focus back to the mirror. Staring at her reflection, she noticed the skin on her bottom lip had split open at the corner of her mouth. There was some dried blood there. That had been the end of their argument the night before. She pulled the purple hand towel from the square brass handle beside the medicine cabinet and ran cool water over it. With the damp corner of the towel, she rubbed at the dried blood. When she was finished, her gaze traveled to her neck. Her skin showed some discoloration, a red handprint wrapped around her throat. Kristin flinched as she recalled how Jake had grabbed her there, squeezing so hard she blacked out.

He had beaten her so badly the night before, she thought her body would shrivel up if someone were to touch even the tiniest hair on her skin. Purplish-blue marks covered her arms, and her back was in crippling pain. She popped open a small bottle of ibuprofen and swallowed two tablets with sips of water she cupped from underneath the running faucet. The tiny nicks on her hands that she got from fighting with Jake flared in pain as the water ran over them. She lifted her gray tank top to look at her torso. More reddish-brown bruises flanked her sides.

Last night she had prayed for her life to end quickly. The heel of his black work boot had jammed fiercely into her rib even though she tried her best to shield herself. But the boot caught both her hands and ribs at the same time.

Yes, Kristin had prayed for it all to come to an end last night. She asked God for an earthquake, another Hurricane Katrina, anything that would stop Jake from using her body as a personal punching bag. She endured so much abuse within the last few years and thought maybe God would do her a favor and take her life last night. But when she awoke this morning to the stench of spilled beer on the bedroom carpet and cigarette smoke throughout the house, she realized God must not have been listening. Or maybe it was the fact that the devil wasn't through having his fun with her. Not yet, anyway.

"Babe?"

His apologetic tone repulsed her from the other side of the door.

"Babe, can you come out? I need to know that you're okay."

"Go away. I'll be fine." She put some ointment on the small cuts by her mouth and the ones around her right eye.

She could hear his fingernails scratch against the paint.

"Ah, love, please don't make me beg. Come out."

"Jake."

"Please, baby. I'm sorry, I don't know what happened to me last night."

"You're always sorry," she mumbled. The battered woman in the mirror glared back at her with great disappointment. She could almost hear the fragile woman say, *It's time to leave him. Pack your bags and leave. I'll help you.*

"Kristin, can you hear me?"

"I hear you."

"You know that I love you."

Was he trying to convince himself or her?

"I'm so sorry about last night… Please come out."

Kristin knew what was waiting on the other side of the door if she did. It was probably some gift. He always bought her gifts, trying to erase the night before—her favorite roses, or maybe her favorite box of chocolate-covered cherries. She had a forgiving nature, and he preyed on it heavily. He had that magnetic charm about him that melted her heart whenever she looked into his eyes. She almost believed his lies that he loved her. Was that the reason she had stayed so long with him? It was getting harder for her to keep lying to herself that he did. Jake was good at manipulating her into doing something she wouldn't normally do, a tactic he'd had much practice with over the years. But this was what she had accepted from him. The few times she did try to stand up for herself, she would get the back of his hand across her face. This had become her reality.

As her aunt used to say, "You made your bed, Kristin, now you have to lie in it."

She opened the bathroom door and walked out. Jake backed away from the door, a pitiful look on his face. He threw his arms around her and hugged her close to his chest, weeping.

He seemed surprised by the bruises on her face and touched the cut above her eye with one finger. When she turned away quickly, he withdrew his hand. He scanned the other bruises on her shoulder and his face saddened. She hugged herself, standing nervously before him in only a white tank top and gray shorts.

"I'm so sorry. Oh my God, what did I do to you, baby?" He kissed her cheeks and ran his fingers through the back of her long auburn hair. "Oh God, baby, I'm sorry." He kissed her lips. It hurt.

He held her tight inside his embrace. She didn't know why she allowed him to. Maybe it was because she had no energy to fight him after the night before. Or maybe it just felt so good to have him show her affection, any kind of affection, even if it wouldn't last long.

"Come with me." He led her by the hand to the brown leather sofa in their living room, where a stuffed white bear sat on the cushion with a bouquet of red roses and baby's breath.

It was the same thing every time. But she accepted the gifts. All of them. What else was she supposed to do? Kristin took the flowers as he placed them in her hands, when really all she wanted to do was slap him with them. She sat on the couch.

"You like them?" He knelt in front of her.

"Beautiful." Her response came softly. She looked down into his hazel eyes.

"No, baby, you're beautiful. I love you. You know that, right?"

"Yes, Jake, I know," she lied, for how could any of this be love? Love was kind, not brutal.

"It's just that sometimes you know exactly how to press my buttons and get me going. I got so upset when I saw the milk carton left out on the counter, and you were fast asleep in bed. It just made me so furious when you know I work so hard to put food on the table, and there you are being so irresponsible." He shook his head. "That's money down the drain, babe. You know how much I enjoy a good cup of coffee in the morning… Anyway, all forgotten. We're going to try to be a little more responsible, right?" He rubbed her shoulders and kissed her forehead. "But please, don't ever think I don't love you. 'Cause I do." He brushed a strand of hair away from her face.

"I'm sorry." As soon as the words came out, she wanted to take them back. What did she have to be sorry for? He was the one who should have been apologizing, but she had become so accustomed to apologizing that there was no point in stopping now. It would only make things worse.

"Let's not think about that anymore. Go take a shower and get ready. I'm taking you out for dinner. We're going to Gino's."

She couldn't understand him. Two seconds ago, he was reprimanding her for leaving a three-dollar carton of milk on the kitchen counter, but now it was suddenly okay to go to one of the most expensive restaurants. It was like he had two different personalities sometimes. It was only okay to spend money when *he* felt it was. But again, she kept quiet, even though she knew that money was tight, the bill collectors calling the house at all hours. But he always said he would take care of it.

Kristin took a shower and got dressed. Jake loved to see her dressed in red, so she picked out his favorite blouse with a pair of black pants. She curled her long hair, letting it fall to frame her face. He loved her curls—he always told her so.

Jake acted like a perfect gentleman that night. He opened doors and pulled out her chair when she went to sit at the candlelit table he'd reserved. She caught a glimmer of the man she used to know. The sweet man who showed her kindness, the man she had fallen in love with so long ago. He made love to her that night as if she were the only woman in the world for him. How sad it was to know that it would only last until sunrise.

CHAPTER TWO

T he next day around noon, Kristin started her shift at the neighborhood diner. She walked in and made her way to the back, grabbing her black apron from the uniform closet. She checked to make sure her pen and pad were in one of the pockets, then tied it around her waist.

Joe was training a new girl on the cash register. "Morning, Kristin. How are you doing?"

"I'm good," Kristin said, squinting in the sunlight beaming through the glass door. She turned around and went to the kitchen to pick up an order.

Tiffany sliced a piece of pecan pie by the counter and served it to a woman sitting on one of the cream-colored padded stools.

"Late night, honey?" Tiffany asked as Kristin passed by her again. "You look tired."

"Something like that," Kristin replied as she called in her order at the kitchen window.

Forgetting that she still had a nasty bruise on her left temple, Kristin had pulled her hair back in a ponytail before starting to clear the tables of dirty dishes. As she made her way towards some tables near the front of the diner, she could hear a small quarrel taking place between a young married couple. The wife was growing impatient about the time it was taking for their lunch to make its way to their table.

Kristin couldn't help but notice that even though the husband was aggravated by his wife's complaints, he spoke gently and never raised his voice above a whisper. Kristin thought to herself, *Wow, you have no idea how lucky you are, lady.*

As she cleared the booth behind the couple, she could sense the wife's eyes were now upon her. Even though she spoke softly, she could hear the wife tell her husband to look over at Kristin.

At that moment, Kristin realized the wife must have seen the bruise by her right temple. She pulled some strands of hair to cover up the bruise and moved quickly to the kitchen to grab their orders.

As Kristin walked over to the customers' table with cheeseburger deluxe plates in each hand, she felt a strong spell of nausea overwhelm her. She abruptly placed the plates down on the table, startling the customers, and fought back the cereal bar she had for breakfast that morning.

"Are you okay, sweetie?" the woman asked. "You don't look so good. Maybe you should sit down," she said, her eyes searching for more bruises around Kristin's face.

"I'm fine," Kristin insisted, feeling the increasing sense of nausea.

"You know, this all looks great," the husband said, looking at the cheeseburger on his plate. "But you know what I've been really craving is one of those tasty almond Danishes that y'all have up on the counter there." He looked at his wife and said, "Had one the other morning for breakfast and it was so good. Could you get me one of those, too?" He then looked up at Kristin with a wide-eyed smile.

"Yeah, sure," Kristin replied quickly, trying to keep down whatever was trying to make its way up.

"Wait, you're not going to write it down?" he asked.

"No." She shook her head and made a dash for the bathroom.

Holding the back of her hand over her nose and mouth, she kicked open the door to the ladies' room. It was right there, surfacing at the base of her throat. She threw open one of the stall doors. Holding her ponytail with one hand, she let loose over the toilet bowl. Everything in her stomach from that morning and probably the night before made its way into the blue toilet water. What in the world did she eat last night? She looked at the orange color beneath her. Was it the penne vodka? No, she'd had that plenty of times before. That couldn't be it.

"Lord have mercy, darling! Are you all right?" Tiffany asked in her Southern drawl, which only came out when she was either alarmed or excited. She entered the ladies' room, holding her nose with two fingers and a few brown paper towels in the other hand. Kristin dusted off her apron and flushed the toilet, wiping her mouth with the back of her hand, then walked over to the sink.

"I'm fine," she replied. She washed her hands, then rinsed her mouth out with some cold water.

"Here, why don't you go sit by the counter for a bit." Tiffany walked her over to a stool. "I'll tell Joe you need a couple of minutes to get yourself together."

Ten minutes later, Kristin was drinking a hot cup of tea while Tiffany cleaned down the counter with a white rag.

"There are hardly any customers this morning," Kristin said, a bit disappointed. There weren't going to be a lot of tips.

"Well, I keep telling Joe to lower the prices. A person can get a Reuben sandwich for two dollars less at the deli next door," Tiffany said loud enough for Joe to hear.

But Joe didn't care. "Then let them go next door," he said in his thick Italian accent, passing behind her to stock up on some supplies. "This is a diner, not a sandwich shop," he added, then mumbled something to himself in Italian.

Turning back to Kristin, Tiffany said, "You know, hon, you need to take it easy on the foundation." She brushed Kristin's hair away from her face. "What's that?" she asked, concerned.

Kristin immediately stood up.

"That bastard," Tiffany said with disgust.

"Please, Tiff, I can't deal with that right now. I need to get back to work."

"What you *need* to do is leave him," Tiffany retorted. "When are you going to realize that man is not going to change?"

"I'm fine. Just didn't get much sleep, tossing and turning all night. I bumped my head on the bedside table in my sleep," Kristin lied. She retied the black apron around her waist and went off to start serving customers again.

"Of course, you did," Tiffany said with sarcasm.

She moved out of Kristin's way, shaking her head at her.

"Danny, where's the order for table six?" Kristin asked. She could smell the bacon cooking on the grill a few feet away before she even reached the window. Her senses were strangely sharper this morning.

"Hold ya horses, lady. It's coming!" he said. He placed the order at the window for her to collect.

Tiffany came up behind her and whispered in her ear, "You're not pregnant, are you?"

"Hey, can I get that almond Danish please!" the husband Kristin served earlier asked loudly, leaning over the counter and appearing very annoyed.

She walked over to the glass box filled with pastries. "One almond Danish coming right up," Tiffany said and handed it to him.

"Pregnant?" Kristin mumbled to herself on her way back to the kitchen. That thought had never crossed her mind. When was her last period? It was just a month ago, wasn't it?

"Yes, pregnant. You know, that thing… when a little tiny being invades your belly for nine months until it's ready to pop out?" Tiffany animated a big belly with her hands.

"No, I can't be." Kristin poured a cup of coffee for another customer, but her mind couldn't escape the thought that she could be carrying Jake's child.

"Well, I think you better take a test to make sure."

Tiffany took the cup out of Kristin's hand and served the customer. Kristin stood there, dumbfounded.

What was she going to do? Tiffany was right. She needed to take a test to make sure. That would explain her waking up lately in the middle of the night to use the bathroom. Then there was this morning—when had she last vomited in the morning?

After work, Kristin drove to the pharmacy and picked up a home pregnancy kit. She had to take the test before Jake came home. If she were pregnant, she wouldn't tell him right away. She would weigh her options carefully. But for now, she just needed to know.

***

Tears flowed from Kristin's eyes as she picked up the little pink and white stick. How could she let herself get into this position? She didn't want to raise a child now. Jake was under so much stress. They couldn't afford a baby now.

She looked down at the small, square test stick, but there was still no result. She put it down and waited to see if another line would appear in the tiny window. The test had said to wait up to five minutes before reading the result. So, she set the little egg timer she had taken from the kitchen and placed it on the bathroom sink. When the timer went off, if two lines appeared, it would mean a baby was on the way. One line in the result window would buy her more time to build up the courage to leave him.

When the five minutes were over, she would have to come to a decision.

As she stood by the sink waiting, she heard the front door open and close. Jake was home. She could hear him muttering to himself, throwing his keys on the hallway table near their coat rack. From his heavy footsteps and the sound of things falling over in the next room, she knew he was drunk again. She heard the television turn on to his sports channel. A few minutes later, there was a heavy rapping on the door.

"Kristin, where's dinner?"

"In the microwave," she replied.

"Microwave? Why isn't it on the table?"

"Cause you're an hour late."

"Don't give me any lip, woman. Have enough of that crap at work," he said, slurring a little. "Come out and heat it up for me, then."

"I can't. I'm in the bathroom."

"Of course," he said sarcastically, then walked away.

She turned her focus back to the stick and glanced at her watch. Three more minutes remained, but she could see a faint second line appearing. She looked back at the door behind her. It was locked, but still, she could never be too sure. Jake could kick in the door at any moment, just as he had done many times before when she was in there trying to escape his fury. They'd installed five new locks within the past year.

Another minute passed before Jake knocked on the door again.

"Kristin, what the hell is going on? I'm starving and I have to take a piss!" Jake shouted through the door, pounding his fist against it.

"I'll be out in a minute." She flushed the toilet to give the impression she had just used it. "If you didn't drink a can of beer every half hour," she said quietly to herself, "then maybe you wouldn't have to piss as much."

"What the hell!" He hammered on the door. "Are you trying to win a pissing contest?" he shouted, walking away again.

He wasn't always such a bully. She thought back to the first time she had ever laid eyes on Jake Summers. She had been living with her Aunt Margaret after losing her parents when she was just seven years old.

Kristin recalled waking up in the middle of the night to the voice of her father calling her name through thick, black smoke that surrounded her bed. Her dad had kicked in the door to her room, scooped her up in his arms, covering her head with a blanket, and quickly carried her out the front door of the house, leaving her with the neighbors on the front lawn. Then he went back in for her mother. She begged him not to leave her, but her brave father ran past a firefighter, who tried to stop him, and back into the house. Kristin watched as the two-story house became engulfed in flames.

Her father never came out. The roof of the house had caved in, and both her parents were lost to the fire forever. All because her father had forgotten to make sure he put out a cigarette before throwing it in the wastebasket. That was probably the reason Kristin never picked up a cigarette, even just to try it. And it was probably the reason she hated the smell of smoke. But as far as Jake was concerned, he wasn't going to stop smoking for anyone, including her.

She met Jake fifteen years later. Aunt Margaret wanted to rent out the basement of their Cape Cod-style house to bring in some income. Money had been tight since Kristin's uncle had passed, leaving her aunt with the financial burden of keeping a roof over their heads. Jake was recommended by a friend of her aunt as the right man to remodel their basement. When he hopped out of his white pickup truck and walked up the three steps to her front door that Sunday afternoon, dressed in blue jeans and a white T-shirt, Kristin's knees almost buckled underneath her. His boyish good looks and charm could make any girl's heart beat a mile a minute. When he introduced himself, Kristin could barely put three words together to tell him her name. He laughed at how nervous she was. He knew how smitten she was with him.

The basement took three weeks to complete. Kristin always had sandwiches and a fresh-made pitcher of lemonade waiting by his tool bag every day, and he ate up all the attention she gave him. It was the first time she had ever pursued a man and not the other way around.

He worked with a friend of his named Collin. They had both worked out of a trailer in the back lot of an old, abandoned warehouse for Jake's dad. But Jake's relationship with his father was a strained one. They were always arguing over money, customers. Jake had wanted to go into business for himself and did jobs on the side, outside of his father's clientele. But his father insisted on him paying back a loan he had taken to buy supplies for the extra jobs. Ultimately, Jake wanted to go into business for himself with Collin, though his father made it difficult. But even when the old man died, he never put that money back into the business his father left him. When she slept over, Kristin would hear Jake talking on the phone late at night about investing money, losing money, and giving money to one of his friends for a new investment.

Kristin shared his ambition to make something of herself and spoke of her desire to become a nurse. She was drawn to Jake like a bee was to honey.

On the last day of the job, Jake asked Kristin out on a first date. They had a picnic by a beautiful lake a few miles outside of town. He was romantic back then, she remembered. That day he packed a basket with some cheese and crackers, two glasses, and a bottle of wine. He laid out a red and black plaid blanket for them to sit on by the lake, and they listened to Van Morrison on his portable radio under clear blue skies. Kristin felt as if she was living a scene out of a romance novel.

It wasn't long before they began sleeping together. The sex was something to talk about. In fact, she'd never met a guy she could connect with so intimately, or who had drawn her in the way Jake had. She fell hard for him, despite the constant warnings of Aunt Margaret, who told her looks weren't everything.

To her aunt, Jake was nothing more than a playboy looking for the next girl to conquer on his list of many. As they continued to date during the months that followed, she could see he was flirtatious with other women.

She observed his roaming eye and how he always chatted up the ladies. But he told her that was just him being friendly, and if she didn't like it, "there's the door." She thought she could change him in time. In her mind, all she had to do was make him fall for her the way she had fallen for him. Then she would be the one Jake would settle down with.

Within three months of dating, Jake asked Kristin to move in with him. She thought this was a sign that their relationship was progressing. Later, he told her it was because he had to drive her home every night after their passionate lovemaking, then get up early for work the next morning. It was an inconvenience for him, and he told her it just made sense they lived together. She had some doubts about moving in with him so soon, but Jake was great at persuading her to do something even if she didn't really want to at first.

Her aunt strongly protested. She begged Kristin not to move in with him. But despite her warnings, Kristin didn't listen and, against better judgment, moved into his small studio apartment. A couple of months later, when his dad died of a heart attack, she and Jake moved into the family house his father had left for him in his will.

Three months after she moved into the house, he proposed, and even though Kristin had many doubts, she married him anyway a month after their engagement.

It was around six months after they had married when the abuse began. She could remember the shock of the first time he had put his hands on her throat. That was when Kristin saw a side of Jake she never knew existed. *You never know someone until you live with them*, she once heard someone say. Boy, was that person right. Jake had been getting annoyed with her late-night nursing classes; he felt that she wasn't giving him the full attention at home he deserved. She always had her nose buried in her books. And he disliked anything that took her focus off him.

But that one spring evening had changed Kristin's life forever, and she never looked at her husband the same way again. She remembered the events like it was yesterday. It started with her dozing off in her pharmacology lecture when her professor tapped her on the shoulder.

"Mrs. Summers, do you find this material boring?"

Kristin woke to see Professor Tillsdale tapping the end of a long, thin wooden stick he used as a pointer for the blackboard in his open palm.

"I'm sorry, Professor?" Kristin asked, confused. Professor Tillsdale was known for being lenient with the deadline for papers. But when it came to students falling asleep in his class, he considered that intolerable.

"Can you please answer the question?" he asked, rather sternly.

"I'm sorry, Professor, I'm afraid I didn't hear it." Kristin looked at the textbook in front of her. There was dead silence as the other nursing students looked on at their interaction.

He bent over and whispered into her ear, "Maybe it's because your eyes and ears were closed when I asked it. See me after class, please." He walked to his desk in the front of the classroom and continued to lecture.

At the end of class, the students grabbed their backpacks and rushed out the door to get home. Pharmacology was the most boring course in the program, at least in Kristin's opinion, but it was still an important one. Kristin walked over to Professor Tillsdale to apologize. Before she could, she got another lecture, but this time it was about her future in the nursing program.

"Mrs. Summers, you are one of my brightest students in the class. But lately, you haven't been doing so well." He looked into his black book, where he recorded the grades for all his students.

"I know."

"You received a fifty-five on your last test, and you didn't hand in yesterday's assignment. If you don't get at least a ninety-five on the exam next Tuesday, I will have no choice but to fail you."

He closed the book, stood up, and pushed in his chair before walking around his desk, rolling up the long sleeves of his gray sweater. He took a seat on the edge of the desk. Kristin fidgeted with her fingers, still embarrassed that he had caught her asleep earlier.

"Kristin, is something going on at home? You seem distracted these last few months. Some days you don't even show up to class."

"I'm fine, Professor. I'll do my best to get a higher grade on the next exam. I promise," Kristin said. She threw the strap of her heavy book bag over her shoulder.

"You better. I would hate to see you have to repeat this class, or even the program, for that matter." He popped open his black briefcase on his desk, placed his grade book inside with some papers, and locked it. "Get it together, okay?"

He exited the classroom, leaving Kristin alone. She looked at her watch and ran to the bus stop outside the school. She only had two hours before Jake came home, and the bus ride was over thirty minutes long.

Kristin was still cooking dinner when Jake walked in that evening—and she could tell he was agitated. She welcomed him home and attempted to kiss him on the lips, but he gave her his cheek instead. After popping the cap off a beer bottle he took from the fridge, he retreated to their bedroom in silence, staying there until dinner was ready, only emerging from time to time to get another beer.

The tension in the air was thick. Jake was now on his fifth beer. He lifted the bottle to his lips, took a sip, and with a sly grin asked Kristin how her day had been.

"It was okay. There were a lot of questions the class had because of the upcoming exam on Tuesday. So, the lecture ran longer than expected tonight." Kristin munched on a piece of steamed broccoli.

"Seems to be the case these days. You're always running just a little bit late. Aren't you?" He shuffled around in his seat, setting the beer down on the table. He looked around the house. "Did you clean up today?" He picked up his fork and knife and started to cut away at the steak.

"Cleaned this morning, before I left for work." Kristin raised the glass of soda to her mouth, taking a sip.

He abruptly threw his knife and fork onto the plate. "I can't eat this. It's overcooked and tough!"

Kristin sensed things were about to take a turn for the worse. "I could make you something else," she offered.

"You know, I'm starting to think your classes are much more important to you than me and your duties here at home. Where are you getting the money from for these classes, anyway? 'Cause I haven't gotten more than two hundred dollars from your last paychecks."

"I'm getting financial aid. The counselor at the college helped me find scholarships specifically for students who were orphaned. My essay won me the scholarship," she said.

"Well, that's just great. Expecting me to do cartwheels or something… at least your parents were good for something," he said with derision. Jake went on, "Don't think for a second you're irreplaceable around here, because you're not." He waved his fork at her and took another sip of his beer. "Hell, man, I get hit on at every job I go to these days. You don't know how lucky you are to have me. Every woman north and south of Parsons County would give their right arm to be in your shoes. Yet I come home to this bullshit!"

He took another bite of the steak, then spit it out onto the plate. Angrily, he threw his beer bottle at the portrait of his dad hanging in the middle of the wall. The glass of the frame shattered. Beer dripped from the photograph and streaked the lemon-colored walls. "Damn it! Look what you made me do."

"Why don't I make you a sandwich, babe?" Kristin offered, trying to calm him down. It was the first time she had been afraid since the fire that took her parents.

"A sandwich? Did you really just say that?" He looked off for a moment, rolling his eyes, then looked at her as if she had three heads instead of one. She felt the alcohol was making him behave like this. He had thrown back five beers since he had come home. "A sandwich? I worked twelve hours on a job today and you want to offer me a sandwich? I don't want a goddamn *sandwich*! I want a juicy *steak*! That's why I spent forty dollars at the butcher yesterday for a prime cut. But *you* want to offer me a sandwich!"

He stood up and kicked over the dining table onto its side. The steaks flew off the square, blue dinner plates, along with the bowl of steamed vegetables Kristin had placed at the center of the table. The plates shattered as they hit the floor. Ice and soda skated across the hardwood floors as Kristin's glass rolled toward her feet.

Kristin slowly got up from her chair. She had never seen him like this before. Quickly, she moved past him and into the kitchen to get the dustpan and broom that stood at the side of the stove.

"*Now* you want to clean, hmm?" Jake questioned, his voice sarcastic. He looked on as Kristin bent down to clean up the mess.

"Look at this." He moved some of the food around with his foot. "I'm sick of this crap. I'm sick of *you*!" He was sometimes hurtful and maybe a little mean when he was drunk, but this night he was nasty.

"I'm sorry," she said, not knowing exactly what she was apologizing for. What did she do? She thought that apologizing might help. But it didn't.

"Yeah, you are one pathetic, sorry excuse for a woman. Can't get anything right. How the hell do you screw up a perfectly good steak? That's what I'd like to know."

Kristin turned her back to him and continued to sweep up the pieces of the broken plates and food into the dustpan.

"Hello, McFly? Anyone home? I'm talking to you." He reached out and smacked her on the back of the head like she was a disobedient dog that didn't answer to its master quickly enough. Kristin looked at him in shock. He had never hit her before.

She dropped the broom, rubbed her head for a moment, and then picked the broom back up. He was drunk. It was just better to clean up the mess and leave him out there to sleep off the beer on the couch. Kristin couldn't stand it when Jake called her McFly. He had heard the name in a movie once and said that the name fit her perfectly. He knew exactly how to make her feel stupid. But she allowed him to. She never defended herself.

"I'm sorry, Jake. What can I do?"

"Well, my money is not going to be wasted. So, someone is going to have to eat that, and I tell you right now it's not going to be me." He pointed at the steak lying on the floor.

"You can't be serious." She looked up at him. He was being completely ridiculous. There was no way she was going to eat anything that had fallen on the floor.

He bent down over her and roughly grabbed the bottom of her chin in his hand. "That's your dinner tonight, doll. Enjoy." He turned the table back over on to its legs.

"I'm not eating that," she replied firmly.

"So, you think you're going to throw my hard-earned money in the trash? I don't think so." He stood beside her now. "Pick it up and eat it."

"No." She couldn't understand how the man she loved had become so cold toward her. She swept the steak and vegetables along with the pieces of the broken plates into the dustpan and stood up slowly.

"No?" Jake turned sideways to look at her.

She tried to move past him to throw what she had swept up into the kitchen trash. "Come on, Jake. I'm not eating that."

"Yes, you are, *Kristin*." He grabbed her arm and whirled her around to face him. "Even if I have to shove it down your throat, you're eating that."

"No, I won't. What is wrong with you? Why are you acting this way? I'm throwing this out and I'm going to bed."

"No, you're not. You're going to eat that!" he shouted, nostrils flaring.

"No, I'm not." Kristin stood defiantly.

Jake cocked his hand back and smacked her hard across the face, sending Kristin backward against the glass china cabinet in the corner. It hit her like a bolt of lightning—at first, she wasn't sure what happened. But the ugly truth blossomed in her mind. Stunned, Kristin got quickly to her feet and fled down the hall toward the bedroom. Jake ran behind her and grabbed her by the back of her hair, shoving her into the room before she could lock him out.

"Where do you think you're going, huh? You think you're so much better than me with your snobby nursing classes?" He held on to the chunk of hair he had grabbed and hurled her toward the queen-size bed. "I got news for you, baby, you're not."

Kristin's head hit the table next to the bed. She had never seen Jake in such a crazed state before. She was still in shock that he had hit her. This wasn't the Jake she knew and loved. It was the drinking, she told herself. It had finally taken control of him. She knew someday it would.

She saw him reach for his belt buckle and, with one swift motion, pull the belt out from his trousers. No, he wouldn't dare use that on her. She stood up and moved away from the bed.

"Please, Jake. Don't do this. I'm sorry about the steak. It won't happen again. Please don't," she pleaded and tried to get to the door. But he mirrored every move she made.

"Now you're sorry, huh? You're too focused on those stupid classes that you can't do anything right at home! Take your clothes off!" he ordered, unbuttoning his pants and dropping them to the floor.

"What?" She couldn't believe he was serious. "No, Jake, not like this. Please." She pleaded with him, but he wouldn't listen. All she could see was hate steaming out of every pore.

"I said take your clothes off!" he insisted, moving toward her and shoving her back toward the bed.

"Jake, you're drunk. Please…"

"Don't tell me what I am!"

He slapped her across the face a second time. She stumbled backward onto the rose-colored sheets. With both hands, Kristin scooted back toward the headboard to get away from him. But he grabbed her hard by the ankles and pulled her toward him at the foot of the bed. She tried to push him off her, but he was much stronger than she was.

"If you can't make me dinner like a wife, then, believe me, you're sure going to please me like one!" He ripped open her blue blouse with his hands. She slapped at his face with her hands, but he caught them and pinned them down with his knees. She cried out and finally managed to withdraw one hand from underneath him, scratching him with her fingernails.

It was like a wild beast had possessed him. He leaned over her, dragging her panties down around her ankles with one hand and trying to force himself inside her. Kristin fought as hard as she could to keep her legs together. She scratched and pounded on his shoulders with her free hand, squirming beneath him. But he wouldn't stop.

"Get off me! You're hurting me! Please stop!" she cried out. But it was pointless—he only ignored her.

"Shut up! You're nothing, you hear me! You're nothing without me and never will be. School is over, you hear me? You're through with nursing. You're gonna stay home and be the wife that you're supposed to be to me. And when I get home, my dinner will be on the table the way I like it!" He struggled to open her locked thighs.

"Stop it!" she cried out. But the look in his eyes was of a madman she had never seen before. There was no doubt about it—he stared into her eyes with such intensity—he was indeed going to rape her. He grabbed her by the throat, choking her, then released his grip.

No matter how much she pounded on his chest, he was stronger than her. Jake responded to her fighting by striking her, one hard slap above the ear. Her ears rang, and slowly, as he got what he wanted, she felt her body start to give up.

It will soon be over, she said to herself as she kept her eyes on the numbers of the alarm clock display. Jake grunted in pleasure while Kristin cried silently, her insides screaming out for him to stop. Finally, it was over, and he collapsed onto her stomach.

The next morning, he woke to find her sitting against the headboard, cradling her naked body. She couldn't walk for the next few days and had to use an old cane left behind by Jake's dad. She had tried to make an appointment with the doctor, but Jake wouldn't drive her in fear of what she might tell the physician, and she had no money to call a cab because he wouldn't give her any.

The bruises would heal and fade over the next week, but the anguish she felt in her heart, the hopelessness she felt, would remain. She had become one of those women that she only heard about or saw on one of those made-for-TV movies—the battered wife. She hadn't slept a wink that night. But with all the alcohol in his system, she was sure he'd slept just fine.

Jake came home with flowers or gifts for her every day for a week to show how sorry he was for what he had done. But he told her she had to make a choice between him or school. Foolishly, Kristin gave up nursing. She was convinced that if she did, then the events that had taken place that night would never be repeated. But she couldn't have been more wrong, for it was only the beginning of many more nights like that to follow.

Kristin snapped out of her memories as Jake banged impatiently on the bathroom door again.

"Kristin, I swear to God, if you don't let me in there, you're going to regret the day you met me!" Jake yelled on the other side of the door.

She looked down at the small pink stick on the sink. The results were in. Slowly, she raised the test to her eyes to get a closer look and took a deep breath. Two lines.

You're too late. I already do.

CHAPTER THREE

The next morning, Kristin was in the kitchen, making herself a cup of coffee and shaking her head. Jake had drunk himself into a stupor before passing out on the living room sofa. As she sat down to drink her coffee, she noticed some papers on the breakfast table: collection letters on credit cards Jake used to buy new tools when he started up his construction business with Collin. Collin had come on board as Jake's partner after he inherited the business. Jake did not discuss business with her, but judging from all the past due notices on the table, things weren't going as well as Kristin thought. As Kristin went through more of the notices, she realized he was taking cash advances against the credit cards to keep things afloat.

Jake walked into the kitchen and snatched the papers out of Kristin's hand.

"What are you doing with this? Stay out of my business!"

"Don't you think it is my business as your wife to know when we are behind on our bills?" She turned in her chair to look at him as he placed the papers in his tool bag. He zipped the bag closed.

"Oh, because you're my wife, you need to know everything now. Why the sudden interest? You were never concerned about how the bills got paid before!"

"Because you told me the money I give you from my paycheck goes to paying them. I just want to know how we are doing financially. Bill collectors have been calling the house a lot more now than they did before and—"

"So, don't answer the phone then. I've been the one taking care of the bills for the last five years. Stop poking your nose where it doesn't belong."

He went over to the kitchen cabinet, took out his favorite mug, and poured himself a cup of coffee.

Taking a long sip, he said, "You know I keep telling you to let the water boil longer. I don't know if you're dense, but every morning I'm drinking lukewarm coffee." He placed his mug on the table, then took a seat. Opening the newspaper, he flipped it over to the sports section.

"It's hot enough for me," Kristin mumbled, passing her fork through the runny yolk in her plate.

"What's that?" he questioned, raising his eyes at her.

"Nothing. I'll leave it on longer tomorrow morning."

He closed the newspaper and put it down on the table. "I don't think I ask too much of you. A hot cup of coffee in the morning and a hot dinner on the table when I come home from work. Is that seriously too much to ask?"

He stood up and grabbed his jacket off the back of the chair. "What are you going to be doing today?" He turned back to look at her as he buttoned up his winter jacket. It was a chilly December morning. Christmas was right around the corner.

What am I supposed to do? she thought sarcastically. Every cent she earned went to him to help pay their bills. She had given up school and damn near lost her job at the diner because he always needed her home early. So, she was pulling three shifts a week if she was lucky. Thank God she had a very understanding boss.

Jake had controlled every aspect of her life. It was like having a tight leash around her neck.

"Hello, McFly? I'm talking to you." He snapped his fingers twice in her face.

"I have a doctor's appointment this morning. Can't seem to get over this cold."

"Fine." He leaned over to give her a kiss on the cheek, but she leaned back in the chair. "What's the matter with you? I can't kiss you now? Is it because I came home late last night? I told you not to wait up for me. What's the problem, Kristin? Jimmy wanted to have a couple of beers and time slipped away from me."

Kristin looked down at her plate. She really didn't care anymore what he did when he wasn't home. For one, she didn't trust him. He was always coming home late and "having beers with the guys after work." At first she'd protested about his late-night outings, until she got a good smack for having a loose mouth and not knowing her place as a wife. At least that's how Jake put it. She had suspected there was another woman. Hell, there were probably more than one. She was always hearing about Jake with other women, but she never actually caught him in the act.

The latest rumor had been a week before, while she was grocery shopping. Kristin was heading to the counter for some pork chops when she heard

Ms. Walker, who lived up the road from them, tell the butcher she had seen Jake on Grand Street the night before with his arm around Annie Jenkins. Annie Jenkins was notorious for messing around with married men. When Ms. Walker saw Kristin standing behind her, she shook her head in pity and walked away. Kristin was so embarrassed that she turned around and headed in the opposite direction.

Jake was always coming home late and jumping straight into the shower to get the stink of cheap perfume off of him. It was only a matter of time before she caught him in the act. Maybe then, if she had proof, it would be exactly what would push her to the edge and make her leave him. She didn't understand the magnetic hold he had over her. It was like no matter how much he hurt her, she could never leave him. It wasn't even the sex, because it wasn't enjoyable for her anymore. Sometimes, she faked an orgasm just so he could get off her and it could be over. Other times, she'd just lay there waiting for him to finish, which seemed like an eternity because the booze made it so hard for him to perform.

"I'm just not feeling well." She picked up her plate and placed it in the sink to be washed later.

"Well, go see the doctor and ask him to give you something. Tell him to give you something for your appetite too. 'Cause, I mean, have you stepped on a scale lately?" He slapped her outer thigh. She turned around, folding her arms, and braced against the sink. "I don't want no roly-poly to come home to late at night. Then you'll be wondering why I don't want to touch you anymore."

He flashed her a wide grin. "I'm serious. When I'm at work, you should try doing some crunches or even leg lifts."

Kristin shook her head. Did he even hear the words that came out of his mouth? Did he look at himself with his receding hairline and pointy chin?

"Don't get mad at the truth." He picked up his coffee mug from the table and took one last sip. "Well, I'm off. Dinner at six." He kissed her on the cheek, his lips like ice. It was amazing how the man she had once been so madly in love with was the same man she couldn't stand to be around or feel his skin against hers.

Jake pushed his way through the screen door and headed to the white pickup parked in the dirt pathway in front of the house.

Kristin turned around and began to wash the dishes in the sink, watching from the kitchen window as Jake threw his tool bag into the back of the truck and then drove off. It was beginning to snow.

She wouldn't go in to work today. Tiffany would cover her shift at the diner. After putting away the laundry, Kristin decided to take a cab down to the clinic. She wasn't about to wait for a bus in this weather. She knew the wait would be long before she saw the gynecologist, but she had no choice. She was a bit nervous, for she hadn't been to a gynecologist since she got her period when she was thirteen years old. Aunt Margaret had taken her. But Kristin remembered it was the most embarrassing experience she had ever had. Having someone poke around down there was never fun. She knew she was supposed to go every year, but Jake's motto was, *If it ain't broke, why fix it?* But this was different—she had no choice but to see the doctor. She had to confirm the results of the home pregnancy test.

After a thorough examination and a pap smear, Dr. Anderson said, "Well, Mrs. Summers, you're about twelve weeks along in your pregnancy."

He was a tall, skinny Asian doctor and extremely pleasant. He looked at the monitor as he performed the ultrasound. After capturing the shot on the little gray monitor, he printed out a snapshot of it for her to keep.

Kristin sat up, feet dangling off the table, as she stared down at the tiny sac embedded in the black and gray picture she held in her fingers.

"Congratulations." The doctor smiled and opened the doors of a glass cabinet in the corner. "Here you go. A one-month supply of prenatal vitamins. I'm going to write a prescription so that you have it filled before these are done. It's important that you take these for the health of your baby." He took out his prescription pad and scribbled a few words down. Ripping off the first page, he handed her the paper.

"Thank you, Doctor." Kristin took the prescription from him.

"Drink a lot of water. If you notice any spotting, it's quite normal in the first trimester. If you notice heavier bleeding, call the clinic and have me paged. Saltine crackers are good for nausea in the morning. We will have a follow-up visit in a few weeks to see how the pregnancy has progressed. But for now, just take it easy. No heavy lifting. This trimester is crucial for the development of the fetus. Don't forget to stop by the front desk to make your next appointment." He patted her on the shoulder and sent her on her way.

So, it was true. Kristin was in as much disbelief at the doctor's words as she was when she saw the double lines in the little square window of the pregnancy test. Now how was she going to break the news to Jake? Would he be happy or upset that there would be another mouth to feed? Would he finally stop drinking, knowing she was now carrying his child? A million thoughts ran through her mind.

The snow had stopped, so Kristin decided to wait for the bus. She rubbed her belly and thought of her child running around with his friends one day. She knew she had to do everything to protect the life that was growing inside her womb. If anything good could come out of being with Jake, it would be this child. Suddenly, her life had meaning after all.

CHAPTER FOUR

"Get up! Get your ass up!"

Jake grabbed a chunk full of her hair and yanked her from the bed onto the floor. Her arms flailed about, grabbing hold of the foot of the bed. But he pulled her hair even harder, forcing her to let go. Tangled up in bedsheets, she tried to free herself from him, but his grip only became tighter. Her scalp was on fire. The pain was too much; she could not bear it.

"Jake, stop!" she pleaded with him as he pulled her off the ground by the hair, rushing her down the hallway, manipulating her as if she were his puppet. What did she do? After dinner, she had cleaned up and put away the dishes as she always did. Everything was in its place the way he wanted it. Had she turned off the television before retiring to bed? She had forgotten to do that once, and he'd ranted on about how expensive their electric bill would be when next month's statement came in. Then, as always whenever he was angry or stressed out, he turned to drinking and playing a game of soccer with her ribs after blackening both her eyes.

"Jake, let me go. Ow-Ow-stop!" she shrieked even louder. "What did I do? I don't understand!"

"Liar! I knew it was only a matter of time before you did this to me!" he fired at her.

"Stop! What are you talking about? Please—stop—you're hurting me." She pulled at his fingers repeatedly, trying to release them from her hair. But his only response was shoving her down onto the black-stained hardwood floors. Her body hit the floor with a loud thud.

"Why are you doing this to me?" she implored, afraid to look up at him, staring at the tops of his black boots.

"Get up! Get the hell up!" He yelled louder and louder.

"No! No! No!" She guarded her face, afraid he would swing at her. But instead, he grabbed her by the hair again, yanking her through the opened door of their bathroom. The floorboards cut away at her flesh as her legs kicked the air. She knew the moment he got her in the bathroom, it was only about to get worse.

"You think I don't know what you've been planning?" he asked, letting go of her hair as she cowered near the toilet.

"What are you talking about?"

"SHUT UP! ALL YOU DO IS LIE TO ME. WHY ARE YOU LYING TO ME, KRISTIN?" He bent over and grabbed her by the throat, pulling her off the ground. Her legs kicked beneath her as she grappled at his rough and calloused hands. She couldn't breathe.

Just as she was about to see black, Jake threw her back onto the cold, tiled floor, and she slammed her jaw against the bathtub. Kristin clutched her stomach as she felt a sharp pain in her lower abdomen.

"What are you talking about? What did I do?" she cried.

"What did you do? WHAT DID YOU DO?" He slammed her head against the lid of the toilet bowl. Blood trickled down the corner of her eye. She had cut it on the plastic lid when it cracked.

"Always playing the victim, huh, Kristin? Get up!"

But Kristin couldn't stand up. She was in too much pain. Cowering by the bathtub, afraid of what he would do next, she watched the monster rage on as he reached into his back pocket for something. He took out the pregnancy test stick she had buried in the bathroom garbage, where she'd thought it would be undetected. But as he bent down in front of her so he could meet her at eye level, she realized how wrong she'd been. She was paralyzed with fear.

In a calm voice, he said, "I was looking through the garbage this morning for a paper that I had written a number on for work. You can imagine my surprise when I found… this!" He waved the used stick. She could see the words *Early pregnancy test* written on the back of it.

Kristin jerked her head away, afraid he was about to swing at her.

"Why didn't you tell me you were pregnant?" He waited for her to answer. When she didn't, he barked at her, "Why?"

Sweat broke out above his brow, and he wiped it away with the back of his hand.

"Jake, I was waiting for the right time to tell you. You were under so much stress with work lately. I didn't want to add to it," Kristin said, her voice shaky.

"Didn't want to add to it?" He placed both hands on the side of his head and began pacing back and forth. Then he turned back and looked at her, still cowering next to the bathtub. "You were planning to get rid of it, weren't you? You wanted to kill it!"

"No! Jake… I wouldn't do that!" Kristin cried.

"LIAR!" He got in her face, his hot breath assaulting her cheeks when he parted his lips to speak. She could smell the stench of cigarettes and beer on his breath.

Grabbing a loose cigarette from his jeans pocket, standing up now, he lit it up in front of her and took a drag before he stated, "You know my mother wanted to kill me when she was six months pregnant. She shoved a wire hanger up inside her to do the job." He demonstrated on himself with an invisible hanger in one hand. "When that didn't work, she threw herself down the stairs from the outside porch. Broke her arm, but for some reason, I was stilllll kicking." He grinned and took another drag.

Kristin grabbed her knees and buried her head between them. The inside of her mouth was bleeding, and she massaged her jaw with one hand. She closed her eyes tight. Maybe if she wished hard enough, she could wish herself out of there somehow. There was a brief silence, then she heard the door close, but she didn't dare open her eyes. Why couldn't the earth just open underneath her and swallow her alive?

Then Jake spoke once more. Raising her head so that her chin rested on her knees, she opened her eyes to see if he was still in front of her. Her body trembled. The bathroom floor was cold and hard underneath her as she sat there in her turquoise nightgown.

Jake had put out the cigarette in the bathroom sink and now sat with his back against the door and his legs stretched out in front of him. But he wasn't looking at Kristin. Instead, he stared up at the ghostly white ceiling, as if it held a big crystal ball that he could see into his past.

"Yeah, she really had it in for me. Then one day, Dad came home and found her wigging out on the bedroom floor. He took her to the hospital… Did I ever tell you I was born three months early?" He looked down at Kristin, who did her best to stifle her sobs, then turned his eyes back to the ceiling. "Yeah, lucky me. My mom hanged herself a few days after I was born, but Dad… Now there was a real winner for you. Whenever he was upset about something—and man, that was basically all the time—he'd take me down to the basement to 'toughen me up.' That's what he called it. Teach me how to defend myself if I got picked on in school—except I was never able to hit back. Always putting me down… saying I needed to grow a thicker skin."

Jake lowered his head and stared blankly at the tops of his black boots. "That's why I'll never shed one single tear for that man. Never have. The business was the least he could have left me after the bastard died. And even then, he had to add one last jab with that note he left me. He always had to have the last word. Didn't he? But I'm gonna show him. *My* business is going to have three times more clients than he ever saw. He'll be rolling over in his grave."

He glanced over at Kristin, who was still trembling.

"Jake, I'm sorry I didn't tell you."

He got up and squatted down in front of her. "You think I don't know what you want to do to my baby? You think I'm a loser, don't you? That's why you want to kill it! Always trying to make me pull out when we have sex. That way, you can find someone better than me and run off with him."

"Please, Jake… I was going to tell you, but you didn't come home right after work," Kristin managed to say in between sobs.

"STOP LYING TO ME!" He smacked her across the face. Kristin covered her face with her hands. Her jaw was pulsating.

"Stop it, Jake! Stop hitting me!"

"What are you gonna do about it? You want to punch me, Kristin? Go on, then. Here." Jake turned his cheek toward her, but Kristin only sobbed more heavily with her head down, holding her knees, rocking back and forth.

Jake looked her up and down. "You're pathetic, that's what you are really—pathetic. You got something to say to me, Kristin? Huh?"

Kristin knew he was waiting for an apology, so, meekly, she replied, "Jake, I'm sorry I didn't tell you."

"I won't let you kill my baby." He pulled at her arm so she could look at him. "Did you hear me? I swear to God, Kristin, I'll kill you first!"

The doorbell rang. Kristin and Jake looked at each other, confused. Jake released his grip and immediately went to find out who was at their front door. Kristin stood up and walked out slowly into the hallway, keeping out of sight. She could see two shadows on the beige wall in front of her.

"Good morning, Officer," Jake said, holding the door open with his broad back.

"Morning, sir. I'm Officer Gavin with the Parsons County Police Department." A man in uniform, much taller than Jake, peered into the living room from where he stood.

"Parsons County, huh? You must know Darrell… Jay—"

"Yeah, yeah, yeah," the policeman cut him off, appearing annoyed. "That's nice to know. We had a call of a disturbance at this address. Is everything okay?"

"Ah, well, there must be some misunderstanding. It's just me and my wife here. I assure you everything is fine." Jake paused, thinking of some excuse. "Ah, you know what it might have been? We were just watching one of those horror films on TV and there was this part where the slasher jumps out. I think my wife might have screamed then—you know how women are."

The officer glanced down at his watch, then back up at Jake. "What kind of horror movie is on at ten o'clock in the morning?"

"I mean… I had put on a DVD," Jake stuttered. "It's an old movie, but it gets to her every time."

"Ah, huh," the man said, not believing a word of Jake's story. "Do you mind if I talk to her for a moment?"

"She's inside, using the bathroom," Jake replied all too quickly.

"Mind if I come in and take a look around?" he asked, inviting himself in without waiting for Jake to reply.

"Sure." Jake followed behind him, but the officer periodically kept checking over his shoulder, not giving his full back to Jake.

Now that the uniformed officer was inside, he observed his surroundings with a careful eye. The black, 42-inch flat-screen television was off, as was the DVD player on the glass stand underneath.

Kristin went back to the bathroom and closed the door, hearing the officer walk around the living room. She pressed her ear against the locked bathroom door.

The officer walked up to Jake and looked him straight in the eye, taking off his hat and holding it to his chest. Jake rolled a cigarette between his middle finger and thumb, just dying to light it up.

"Do you mind getting your wife, Mr.…?"

"Summers, Officer. Jake Summers."

"Yes, well, do you mind getting *Mrs.* Summers for me?"

"Well, she's really not feeling well. Morning sickness… we're expecting our first child."

"It'll only take a minute. Promise I won't take up too much of your time." The officer looked over Jake's shoulder at the hallway.

"Okay," Jake replied, reluctantly.

"Thank you."

Kristin walked over to the mirror, staring at her reflection as she turned on the faucet. With her hands, she washed away some blood from the corner of her mouth. Opening her mouth wider in front of the mirror, she pulled her top lip up to reveal a chipped tooth. Rinsing her mouth with some of the water, she thought about how lucky she was that the officer had stopped by when he did. *God knows how far Jake would have gone if he hadn't shown up.* She spat out the bloody water from her mouth, watching it mix with the fresh water, then circle down the drain.

Putting on his best impression of a concerned husband, Jake rapped lightly on the bathroom door and spoke in the sweetest voice possible.

"Hey, babe? There is someone out here that would like to have a word with you. Can you come out here for a second?"

"One minute," Kristin replied, following the same act. There had been numerous calls made by the neighbors. She was surprised they even bothered to call. Usually, Jake was able to get rid of the officers before they stepped onto the porch. But this time, she guessed his charm didn't work as well as it had in the past. He wouldn't be able to offer Officer Gavin a beer and send him on his way. She splashed some cold water on her face and patted it dry. Her eyes were puffy from crying, but it would have to do.

Jake walked back to the living room and waited with the officer for Kristin to join them.

A few minutes later, Kristin found herself standing in front of the officer. Underneath his badge was a nine-digit number.

"Good morning, miss. I'm Officer Gavin." The gentleman stretched his hand out for Kristin to shake.

Kristin could feel his eyes take her in, and she held her neck instinctively to cover up the redness, even though she knew he had already seen it.

Withdrawing his hand, he asked Kristin, "May I ask how you got that?" He moved her hair away from her face and looked over at Jake, who was sitting on the black leather recliner behind him, trying not to notice what he was doing.

"Oh, I'm a little bit of a klutz. I came out of the shower and banged my head on the bathroom cabinet," she said, doing her best to not look him in the eyes. She was afraid he would be able to see right through her.

"I see," he said. Taking a notepad with a small blue pen from his back pocket, he jotted down a few words. "Well, if I were you, I would get rid of that cabinet. It's only going to continue if you let it stay there."

Kristin knew from the way he looked at her that he wasn't referring to the cabinet. Her eyes looked upon Jake, who still sat on the leather chair with a wide smile on his face.

"Yes, sir." Kristin moved her hand to her temple now, self-consciously.

"Mr. Summers, I suggest you don't watch any more horror flicks at ten in the morning. I've already come here once. If I have to come back again, you're leaving with me… in handcuffs." He stared at Jake hard until Jake opened the door for him to leave.

"Got it. Thank you for your concern."

The officer took a step out onto the front porch. He turned back to look at Kristin, who stood by the little brown foyer table, and told her, "If you need anything, everyone down at the precinct knows me as Frank, or just ask for Officer Gavin."

Jake turned and looked at Kristin, smiled, then looked back at the officer. He watched him pull out of the driveway, then shut the door.

"I'm Officer Gavin… blah blah blah. People need to mind their damn business." He slammed the door shut and turned around to Kristin, who still stood by the hallway table. "What are you waiting on? Go into the kitchen and get started on breakfast. All this drama in the morning made me hungry." He then retired to the sofa to watch the morning news.

After breakfast, Jake went into town. Kristin paced in front of the living room windows. She had to leave him. The officer was right. Things weren't going to change if she didn't leave Jake.

She picked up the phone and dialed Tiffany. Her mind was racing, and she needed to talk to someone.

"Tiff, it's me." Kristin cradled the phone to her ear. She kept her eye on the driveway from the kitchen window just in case Jake decided to turn around and come home for some reason. "The police came to the house—Jake found out I was pregnant, he found the stick in the garbage, he got mad… Oh God, it was really bad."

"Girl, slow down. I can't make sense of anything you're saying to me. You're talking way too fast. Start over," Tiffany said.

Kristin took a deep breath and admitted to her friend, after years of denying it, that Jake had beaten her and had been beating her all through their marriage.

"I'm glad you finally said something. I knew it, but I didn't want to keep pressing you about it. The question is, what are you going to do about it now?"

"I have to leave him. I don't know why I tried to lie to you before about what was going on. I'm sorry. But I must leave him. Can you help me?" she asked.

"Of course, Kristin. Tell me what to do."

"Can you pick me up in an hour?"

"I'll be there."

Kristin walked into the bedroom they had shared for the last five years. She had painted the room red and white when she had moved in with him, thinking she could decorate it and give it a romantic feel. She had in mind a bedroom that was something from the days of Shakespeare. She loved Shakespeare. But there was nothing romantic about anything in that room.

She looked at her bed with the chocolate sleigh headboard and thought back to the nights she lay there on the mattress crying herself to sleep after being beaten for whatever reason while he made fun of her. He would leave her then finish off his beer on the living room sofa. The floor underneath her bare feet felt cold. All the nights he had refused to take no for an answer and would rape her right there on the floor. One night he was so drunk that he couldn't get it hard enough to stay inside of her. She begged him to stop because he was hurting her with his finger. Frustrated by her whining and to prove a point at how painful it could be, he used her curling iron. She never complained again when he wanted it. Not after that night. The bedroom was cold, but it wasn't the temperature that had made it that way. It was all the memories from being in that room with him.

Opening her old, beat-up brown suitcase that she had used to move out of her Aunt Margaret's house, she threw in everything that could fit. Whatever wouldn't fit, she would come back for later. But right now, she had to get out of there before she chickened out.

When Tiffany pulled up into the driveway in her Subaru, Kristin didn't utter a single word. She hopped in and threw her suitcase into the backseat, and Tiffany sped away from the house.

Kristin was relieved when they finally reached Tiffany's house. For some reason, she had thought they would run into Jake while heading there. It was crazy, she knew, but she was scared out of her mind of him finding out about her plans of escape before she was far away.

As Tiffany led them into her living room, Kristin could feel a warmth that she had never felt at home

"Have a seat." She gestured to the dark-blue sofa. It was soft and comforting as Kristin sank down into the plush cushions. She looked around. Tiffany had added some new art on the wall opposite the couch. Kristin always felt at peace whenever she came over to the house. It was such a different feeling from her own home. There were other paintings on the silver-gray walls and a bunch of photographs on the coffee table. A tall bookcase stood in the back of the room.

"How about a cup of tea?" Tiffany asked from the kitchen, taking the kettle out of one of the cabinets and setting it on the stove.

"I'd love a cup of tea," Kristin said, even though she knew she was supposed to stay away from caffeinated drinks for the baby.

Tiffany lived alone. Her husband, who had died of lung cancer a few years back, had left her the small two-bedroom house. Tiffany never regretted a single moment of being married to him. Her only regret was that she never had the chance to have children with such a wonderful man. She had told Kristin she often thought of moving because she could still feel his presence throughout the house and next to her when she slept at night. But then she asked herself, how could she leave the happiest place she had ever known?

Kristin was truly sad that she never had the chance to meet Adam when he wasn't bedridden with cancer. He died about a month after she started working at the diner. She would have loved seeing Tiffany and him together in earlier times. Maybe seeing the way he treated Tiffany when he was healthy would have given her motivation to leave Jake years ago.

"Did you do something different? The house looks different for some reason." Kristin smiled as her friend handed her a hot cup of tea and took a seat beside her.

"Can't believe you even remember what it looks like. You've only been here about three times since we've known each other. Thanks to your controlling husband. But no, I haven't done anything different, maybe moved some furniture around."

Kristin smiled at her dear friend. She loved her so much. Tiffany was more like a sister to her than a friend. The bond they had developed over the years was strong, far stronger than the one between Kristin and Jake.

"Does Jake know where I live?" Tiffany asked.

"Not that I'm aware of. But if he wanted to find out, he would. I don't want to impose on you. I can find somewhere else to stay."

"Don't talk nonsense. I was only thinking of your safety. I can handle Jake," Tiffany said and walked over to an oak desk in the corner of the room. She opened a drawer, grabbed a shiny red wallet, and took some money out.

"Here, I want you to have this." She handed Kristin a wad of cash and a small silver cell phone she took out of her jeans pocket.

"What? Tiffany, I can't take this from you," Kristin said, amazed at how generous her friend could be at times.

"Yes, you can. This is an old phone of mine. It's a flip phone. I added a line to my account for you to use. It's already activated. This is your number." Tiffany handed Kristin a piece of paper with nine digits written on it. "Memorize it. Only give it to people you need to give it to."

Tiffany scrolled through the main menu and showed Kristin how to place a call and how easy it was to send and receive a text message. In all her life, Kristin had never owned a cell phone—Jake had never allowed Kristin to have one. But then again, aside from the diner and the little errands she ran here and there, she was always home, so in his opinion, she didn't need one. He claimed it was an unnecessary expense, even though he didn't feel the same about having one of his own. He told her he needed one for work. But she was sure that wasn't the only thing he used it for, as close as he kept it to him.

That phone went everywhere Jake went. He'd even take the cell phone to the bathroom with him when he took a shower. She recalled trying once to look through it when he was asleep, especially after hearing the rumor about him and another woman, but he had put a password lock on the screen. *It was just as well that he did*, she thought back then. It was better she didn't know what was on that phone.

When you snoop around, sometimes you get more than you bargain for. Another thing her aunt had told her. How she missed her Aunt Margaret. She had lost all contact with her after the marriage. Then, a man had called her house one day while she was working at the diner and passed a message along to Jake. Over dinner that evening, Jake casually brought up that her aunt had died in her sleep—like it was nothing. There was no emotion on his face or in his voice when he told her. She couldn't comprehend his lack of compassion or sympathy for her, even though he knew how much she loved her aunt.

Before Kristin could even ask about the funeral, he told her that there was no way she was going to go to the funeral of a woman who had despised him from the moment she laid eyes on him. And if she did, she would pay for it. Kristin excused herself from the dinner table and went to her room, muffling her cries with a pillow. The guilt she felt for not visiting her aunt was only exacerbated by Jake's refusal to allow her to attend the funeral. So, Kristin stayed home when they buried her Aunt Margaret out of fear that Jake would make her pay for it physically if she defied him.

Kristin was brought back to the moment by Tiffany waving her hand in front of her face. "Hello, you listening?" Kristin nodded yes. "If you can't reach me on my cell, you can text me by following the steps I showed you. It's a bit tricky with the letters and numbers but you'll get it. Just promise me you won't go back to him."

"I'm not. I promise… I don't know how to thank you. You're a good friend."

"Don't need to thank me. I'll talk to Joe at the diner when I go into work tomorrow morning. For now, I think you should stay here until we figure out what to do. Don't go to work, because he'll find you there. Okay, let me go whip something up for us to eat for lunch. That baby must eat." She patted Kristin's stomach affectionately and went to the kitchen to prepare lunch.

Kristin stared out the long square windows of Tiffany's house where sunlight poured in. It was calm and peaceful here. She could get used to living in a place like this. Her home had felt more like a prison.

She didn't know how long it would be before Jake found her. But at least tonight, she would sleep a little easier knowing that, for now, he couldn't hurt her.

CHAPTER FIVE

Three months passed. Tiffany had spoken to Joe at the diner and explained what was going on with Kristin. He was sympathetic, offering her full pay for as long as she would be out. He considered her like a daughter, knowing that she had no parents and no one else to turn to for help besides Tiffany.

Jake had been by the diner every week of the first month that Kristin had been away from home, hoping that she would eventually show up to work one day. But she never did. On the last Friday of that month, frustrated and annoyed, he demanded Tiffany tell him where Kristin was. But he got no information from Joe, Tiffany, or anyone else that worked with her. Pissed off, he left and didn't return. Tiffany told Kristin she was surprised that he had never thought of following her home from the diner after work to see if Kristin was there. But Kristin had a feeling that Jake had known where she was all this time—and that for whatever reason he was leaving her alone, it wouldn't be too much longer before he popped up again.

To repay Tiffany for her hospitality, Kristin did what she could to help out around the house. She cooked the meals and cleaned up while Tiffany was at work. She was excited at the belly bump that was becoming more prominent with each passing day. Tiffany had bought her a book on what to expect during pregnancy, and Kristin felt she could handle what lay ahead. But what she wasn't looking forward to was the labor. Tiffany assured her that she would be right by her side.

When the doctor told Kristin at her four-month checkup that she was having a boy, she was ecstatic. Jake would have been too. For some reason, as much as she hated what he had done to her in their marriage, she still missed him. Tiffany told her it would take time to get used to him not being around. She showed her how to use the computer and internet so she could occupy her free time. Kristin read up on pregnancy, and almost every night she surfed the internet looking for the perfect name. There were two names that she liked very much—Tommy and Lucas.

As the fifth month came around, she gained five pounds. Tiffany assured her it was all baby weight. Kristin didn't care, as long as the baby that woke her up at night kicking inside her belly was healthy. She loved feeling him move around inside her, and she couldn't wait to finally see him. Things were going wonderfully for her, and she even thought about the possibility of returning to nursing school after her son was born. Her life was starting to get back on track.

Then one evening, things started to change. Kristin heard the door close as Tiffany came home after work

"Hey, Tiff, I'm in the kitchen! I made a lasagna. You know I've been thinking about naming him Tommy. What do you think?" She took out the pan of lasagna and set it on top of the stove.

Tiffany walked into the kitchen, her face pale. Closing the oven, Kristin walked over to the table where Tiffany stood.

"What's wrong?" Kristin asked, concerned.

"There was a delivery today that came to the diner."

"Delivery?" Kristin invited her friend to sit down at the small round table in the kitchen.

Tiffany took a seat and her hands shook terribly. "Need a drink. Can you pour me a scotch?" she asked, taking off her jacket.

Kristin hurriedly fixed her friend a scotch from the bar in the den then returned to the table.

"Tonight, a package came for me at the diner…" She paused, taking a gulp from her glass of scotch.

"And?" Kristin's eyes widened with curiosity.

"It was a big black box. Inside, there was a dead cat."

"What?" Kristin sat back in her chair, stunned. "What do you mean a dead cat? Are you sure it wasn't a toy? You know how these dumb kids always like to play practical jokes on people around here, so they can take a video of it and post it on the internet. Maybe they were hiding in the back of the diner with their phone, recording the whole thing when you got the package."

"Kristin, no. There were no kids. And it was a real cat. It was all black and the eyes were still open… oh God… and the jaw was clenched. It was the most dreadful-looking thing I have ever seen." Tiffany closed her eyes.

"Are you sure this was for you?"

"Yes, the label had my name marked in black sharpie."

"Oh my God, Tiff."

"Kristin, there's more. On top of the head was a handwritten note." Tiffany chugged the last of the scotch in her glass.

"Are you serious? Did you call the police? I think we should call them right now." Kristin walked over to the cordless phone on the counter. She picked it up and was about to dial 911 when Tiffany took the phone away from her.

"Sit down, Kristin," she said, placing the phone down as they both took their seats again.

"Why? We need to let the police know what happened. It could be one of the guys you were dating. You have to let the police know about this," Kristin insisted.

"Kristin, it's not anyone that I've been seeing…"

Sinking back into her chair, Kristin looked at her friend. She knew that whatever Tiffany was about to say, it wasn't something she would like hearing.

"How do you know this?" Kristin asked.

"Because the note in the box said, '*If she doesn't come home, you're next!*'" she replied, holding her friend's hand.

"Are you trying to say Jake did this?"

Tiffany nodded. "I think so."

"No. Jake might be crazy, but he would never do something like that." But as the words fell from her lips, she wasn't too sure. She had seen the look of a sinister man behind those hazel eyes more than once when he was raging. *Maybe he could do something like that.* Her leaving him may have pushed him over the edge.

"Kristin, it's Jake. I know it. The police came to the diner and Joe filed a complaint. They took the letter and asked me some questions after they saw my name on the box. They are trying to find the courier who delivered it. The cashier, Stephanie, had to sign for the package, but there was no sender labeled or even a receipt. Kristin… the police have Jake's name. They're going to go by the house to see him tonight. I told them that you were staying with me and why. I'm sorry, but I had to. I'm worried he might come after you, come after me. You're not safe here anymore."

Kristin sat baffled as Tiffany relayed the events that took place earlier. But even though her body was present, her mind wasn't. It was somewhere else. *Jake brutally murdered a cat?* She could see maybe one of his new shady-looking business associates doing that, but not Jake.

She had seen Jake talking to a guy one night outside their house. She remembered being awoken by bright lights that glared through her bedroom blinds and had noticed it was a few minutes past midnight. She heard voices coming from her driveway and had peeked through the blinds to see Jake talking very seriously to a tall Latino man. She heard Jake refer to him as Miguel, and something about the man made her skin crawl.

She asked Jake later that morning at breakfast what it was all about. But Jake told her, as always, to keep out of it and that it was his business. So maybe it was that guy, Miguel, that did it. The question was why? Why would he get involved, if it were him? She could imagine that guy doing something like this, but not Jake. Not her Jake. She'd spent five years with the man and never had she ever seen her husband behave cruelly toward animals. But if she were wrong about him, there was no reason he wouldn't kill her. What if he really did try to kill Tiffany next? She couldn't let that happen. This was her mess, and she shouldn't have allowed anyone she cared about to become involved in her twisted relationship with Jake.

"Kristin?" Tiffany nudged her to get a response.

"Huh?" Kristin looked back at her friend.

"We have to get you out of here. It won't be long before Jake finds out where I live and comes looking for you. He could have followed me home tonight for all I know. We must get you to a shelter or somewhere safe."

"No, Tiffany. You've been more than hospitable and generous to me. But I'm not going to allow you to put yourself in danger for me. And there is no way that I'm going to a shelter."

"Kristin, you are not allowing me to do anything that I don't want to. You're my friend. I'm not going to abandon you when you need me the most."

"Tiffany, if Jake is behind this, he could really hurt you. I would never forgive myself if something happened to you."

"You can't be serious. I know you're not thinking of going back to this idiot. Right? Tell me that's not what you're thinking."

Before Kristin could answer, the phone rang, making both of them jump in their seats.

"Hello," Tiffany quickly answered the phone. "Yes... ah huh... okay, but are you going to..." Tiffany rolled her eyes then said, "Yes, Officer, I understand. Well, thank you for calling."

"What?" Kristin asked as Tiffany hit the button to end the call.

"They picked up Jake for questioning and are holding him overnight. But unless you make a formal complaint, they will have to release him in the morning. The courier was paid in cash, and the police interviewed the messenger who delivered it. He said he received the package from a young woman. But the name she gave the messenger doesn't check out. So, they are still trying to figure out who sent it. But you and I both know it was Jake."

Kristin knew the right thing was to press charges against Jake, but she just couldn't do it. She was too scared of what he would do to her if she did. She didn't want to go to a shelter, for she was too embarrassed to tell other people what had been happening to her. Even though she knew that the women there would be able to relate to what she was going through, she wasn't ready to talk about it with anyone or tell stories about her husband's physical abuse to other women whose lives were just as dysfunctional as her own. One thing that she wasn't ready to do was live a life in hiding.

"Kristin, this is not the Jake you married. You and I both know that. He's not all there. To send me a dead ca—" She paused to take a breath, shaking her head fiercely as if she were shaking away the horrible image from her mind. "He needs to be behind bars or in a psychiatric ward."

"Tiffany, he just lost his head is all. I'm sure he's not thinking clearly. We're not even completely sure that he was the one who sent it."

"Damn, Kristin! Why are you defending this man? Do you like being his personal punching bag? Don't you get that you deserve better? Think about you and the baby. You need to go down to the station and tell them what he did to you that day. Tell the police what he has been doing to you the past five years so they can arrest this fool," Tiffany demanded.

"I can't! He is still my husband! He's my husband!" Kristin lashed out at her friend.

"Yeah, and you're nothing more than his doormat!" she fired back at her, regretting it the moment those words left her mouth. "Kristin, I'm sorry. I didn't mean that."

Kristin rose from her chair without responding and walked into the guest room that Tiffany had made up for her. She slammed the door behind her. Tiffany didn't follow. After tonight, she had to admit even she was scared of what Jake's next move would be.

The next day, Kristin borrowed Tiffany's Honda Accord. It had been Adam's before he had passed away.

After much deliberation, Kristin drove down to the police station to find out exactly what would happen if she did file charges against Jake. When she walked in, she was surprised at how big the station house was. It took up two floors. But then again, she really didn't know what the norm was since she had never been inside one before. Walking up the stairs to the first floor, she noticed there were only a few officers behind the desk, helping patrons with their complaints.

"Can I help you?" asked a short, chubby-cheeked gentleman in a green and yellow uniform, stapling some papers together. He placed the stack of papers in a black box then gave her his full attention. The name on his badge was Officer O'Neil. A real Irish name to match the red hair and green eyes.

"Is Officer Gavin in?" Kristin asked.

"Actually, you just missed him. He should be back in another hour. Is there something I can help you with?"

Kristin gave a brief summary of the abuse she had been dealing with at home, the incident that happened on the morning Officer Gavin had shown up at her front door, and the delivery at the diner. She told how scared she was for not only her life, but for the life of her unborn child. He listened carefully, but nothing she said seemed to shock him. *He must be used to hearing things like this on a regular basis.*

"Well, for starters, the Tiffany Martin case is being headed by Officer Gavin. So, you should speak to him if you have any information you think might help him. But I'll give you the general rundown of how things work. First, you would have to start by filing a complaint. Even though you file the complaint and press charges against him, it still must be corroborated— meaning after the arrest. If there is not enough evidence to support your complaint, the charges can be dropped. I'll tell you now, from what you are telling me, it's not going to be easy. It's a little hard to prove because you have never pressed any charges against him before. You never even went to the hospital on the times you claim he beat you so badly and broke your ribs. If you had, there would have been pictures taken and the hospital would have put in their own report. Even when Officer Gavin showed up at your house to respond to a disturbance call, you told him that you were fine."

Feeling somewhat defensive, Kristin blurted out, "I was scared… I didn't know what—"

"Look, if you want to fill out the complaint form, I'll take a statement from you."

"What happens then?"

"We'll file the complaint and take an affidavit. The next step would be placing him under arrest. After that, it goes before the judge, who could issue a temporary order of protection restricting your husband from coming any-where near you. But if the judge feels there is no evidence to support your claim, then your husband will be released. If the judge grants you an order of protection and your husband violates the order in any way, you would call the police and he would be immediately taken into custody. It's a lengthy process." The police officer handed Kristin a complaint form.

Kristin wasn't exactly sure she appreciated the tone he used with her. It was almost as if he was encouraging her to *not* file the complaint. She took the paper from the officer's hand.

Taking a seat on the wooden bench underneath a few small box windows, she started to fill out the form with a pen she had taken out of her bag.

"Ma'am?"

She raised her head. Officer O'Neil was waving her to come back to his desk. She got up and walked over, and he leaned forward so that the other officers around them couldn't hear their conversation. A younger officer who was sitting at a desk behind Officer O'Neil glanced up at Kristin then back down at his computer screen.

"Listen, I know your husband. You're Jake Summers's wife. He's a nice guy. He's worked on my house and done work for some of the officers on this floor dozens of times. Why don't you see if you can try to work things out with him before you go dragging the police into this? I was there last night to question him with Officer Gavin. He's just upset over you leaving him. You know we all can turn into monsters when we're hitting the bottle a little hard. Find him some help and go get counseling together. Both of you guys will be just fine. Trust me." He looked down at Kristin's pregnant belly. "Believe me, in your condition, it's better to have the father around. Think about it."

He walked toward the back of the room, leaving Kristin feeling foolish for even coming into the station in the first place. She looked down at the paper and wondered if she should even bother filling out the rest of the form after what he said. She waited for the officer to come back to the desk, but he never did. Kristin stuffed the form in her black tote bag and left the police station.

It all made sense why the officer didn't seem to push her on filing the complaint. He was a friend of Jake's. So, everyone in the community knew Jake and loved him too. That was just great. How was she going to leave him or even press charges now when there were officers like O'Neil who would surely have his back? He acted like the perfect husband who worked hard to support his family. But no one knew the real Jake she knew behind closed doors. People only saw the Jake he pretended to be. How could she change their perception of him?

The officer was right—she never went to the hospital or called the police on the nights he had beaten her senseless. But she couldn't, or else he would have beaten her even more. Even when she had broken ribs and could barely breathe, he told her that everything heals on its own in time. What was the point of doing anything now about it? No one would believe her.

As Kristin drove away from the station, she felt heavy-hearted. She had already lost the battle she had yet to begin. When she turned on to Forest Lane, two blocks from Tiffany's house, she noticed many people were out on this sunny spring day with their families. People were jogging and riding their bikes like they didn't have a care in the world. She craved that kind of happiness.

The cell phone Tiffany had given her began to ring, interrupting her thoughts.

"Mrs. Summers, this is Officer Gavin. Was that you I just saw drive away? Were you looking for me?" the officer asked.

"No, Officer, I just stopped by to ask some questions. How did you get this number?"

"Your friend, Tiffany Martin, gave it to me. But did any of your questions have to do with the ongoing investigation of her case?"

"Yes, sir."

"Well, I'm running the investigation. What would you like to know?"

"I just wanted to know if you caught the person who delivered the package."

"Well, we received a handwriting sample from your husband with his lawyer's approval. It cleared him, but I think we both know who sent that package to your friend. People can be cunning. Listen, Mrs. Summers, I have a feeling that you have a lot of mixed emotions regarding this case. And I can surely understand why. Why don't you come into the station and we can sit down and talk about it?"

"Officer, I really would rather just forget about it right now."

"Can I speak frankly, dear?" he asked her.

"Sure."

"A man is only going to do what you allow him to do to you. You know, not every officer at the precinct is a friend of Jake Summers. There are still some of us who take the law seriously despite who our friends are in Parsons County. Look, there is a domestic violence women's support group that meets down at Christ the King's Baptist Church. It's not that much of a drive, closer to town. They meet there on Wednesday evenings at seven. There is also a National Domestic Violence Hotline that you can call if you need someone to talk to about what you're dealing with at home. I would be happy to give you the number if you just hold on for a second."

"No, that won't be necessary. But I thank you for your thoughtfulness."

"You're not alone, Mrs. Summers. I want you to know that.

"I'll keep that in mind," Kristin said and quickly ended the call.

She pulled up into the garage adjacent to Tiffany's house and sat behind the wheel for a minute before getting out. Officer Gavin was right. She had no one to blame but herself for the predicament she was in. She rubbed her stomach. *I must stay strong.*

CHAPTER SIX

Kristin couldn't believe how time was flying. Now in her sixth month, she started to look in the newspaper for places to live. Since Jake hadn't come by the diner again to look for her and things were quiet, Tiffany insisted that she continue to live with her. Kristin agreed to stay with her until her son was born, but she wanted to start over fresh—have a place of her own that she could make a home. Tiffany understood and told her she would help her in any way she could.

She never dropped off the complaint form or went back to the police station after that day. She didn't know why. Maybe it was because she felt that she really didn't need to revisit the issue since Jake had left her alone for so long. She wondered if he realized that they just weren't good together. Or was it because he had found another woman, maybe one that he was rumored to have been sleeping around with? She didn't know why he hadn't continued to seek her out, but she wasn't complaining.

According to Tiffany, Officer Gavin said the investigation into the mysterious delivery was still open with no leads. Kristin promised herself that if Jake showed up to harass her when she went back to work after the baby was born, then she would file the complaint. But for now, she would enjoy the peaceful life she had grown accustomed to and raise her baby the best she could as a single mother. She honestly believed that. She needed to believe that she could make it on her own.

Joe had been so good in paying her over the last six months for the time that she had been away from work. Tiffany refused to take a penny and told her to save it, and Kristin now had over a thousand dollars saved. Tiffany had suggested she open a savings account with the money she had been saving. But Kristin was afraid that somehow Jake would find out from the friends he had in the community, and she didn't want to stir things up or make him angry for any reason. She had lain low for the last few months, only going out when she went to the doctor or down to the supermarket, then straight back home. That was how she maintained the peaceful life she was living now, and that was how she wanted it to stay. At least, until the baby was born.

One morning she walked out of the supermarket, pushing the shopping cart into the parking lot. The baby was kicking up a storm. She paused for a second to take a deep breath and rubbed her belly, standing under the warm sun in a pink maternity sundress that Tiffany had bought for her. Pants were starting to become extremely uncomfortable for her to wear, even the maternity jeans she had ordered online using Tiffany's computer. It was getting much warmer lately. But it was fantastic that she didn't have to worry about any marks on her body or people asking questions and prying into her private affairs.

As Kristin moved past other shoppers pushing their carts to and from the supermarket, she spotted a white pickup truck parked in the space beside Tiffany's Honda Accord. Her heart started to race. It looked a lot like the truck that Jake drove. But it couldn't be him, could it? She always made sure to go at different times during the day when she knew he was at work. Every time she shopped for groceries, she would change the route she took to get there and to get back home.

As Kristin approached the car, she could see that the truck's engine was running. She looked at the license plate and froze. The muscles in her stomach tightened. She read the thick black numbers and knew there was no doubt—it was him.

He had left the engine running and the driver's side window was down, but she couldn't tell if he was lying down inside or hiding as he waited for her to emerge from the market. Slowly, she walked up to the side of his truck, her heart beating faster with each step she took. She glanced into the driver's window, but there was no one sitting behind the wheel or on the seat. Thinking that he might have gone inside, she unlocked the trunk to the Accord and started to pack away the grocery bags.

As she removed one of the bags from the shopping cart, a shadow stretched on the ground behind her. Startled, she turned around—and there he was, standing behind her in a black T-shirt and faded blue jeans. Kristin looked up at him as he took one last puff of his cigarette and flicked the butt onto the ground.

"How are you?" he asked, smiling at her.

He grabbed one of the shopping bags to help her and placed it in the open trunk beside the others.

"I'm fine. I really can't talk right now. So, can you please move out of my way, so I can do what I need to do and get home?" She did her best to avoid looking at him.

"Home, Kristin? What, Tiffany's house?"

So, he did know where I've been all this time, Kristin thought to herself.

"Home is where I am. So, you're not home if you're not with me." He shuffled his legs and sat on the car's bumper, blocking her from loading any more groceries.

"Jake, please don't. I don't have time for this. I need to put the groceries in."

"Why are you in such a hurry? I just want to talk to my wife for a minute. You're still my wife, Kristin, last time I checked. I'm still your husband." He showed her his wedding ring and then tried to grab her hand, but Kristin immediately pulled away. "Baby, I miss you. I can't eat. I can't sleep. I feel like I'm going out of my mind in that house alone without you." He played with a strand of Kristin's hair.

She responded by pushing his hand away from her face and taking a step backward. *Here we go again. It's time for loving Jake to show his face.* He was putting on the charm, the way he watched her and the way he smiled at her. She could clearly understand why women were so taken with him.

"I really have to go," she said, becoming more frustrated. "So, can you please move so I can finish putting the groceries in the car?" Those hazel eyes were piercing as he towered a foot over her.

"Okay, fine." He said, running his fingers through his short, jet-black hair. He moved out of her way as she loaded the rest of the groceries into the back of the trunk, slamming it down hard. Before she could get into the car, Jake was at her side, with his hand on the handle of her door.

"Just hear me out for a minute. I know you're not interested in anything I have to say. But damn, can I just get one minute?"

"One minute. Go," Kristin said, annoyed and looking at her watch. She didn't know why she agreed to even that. What could he possibly tell her that he hadn't told her a million times before? How sorry he was, how it would never happen again? She figured she would just let him speak, but she was not prepared for what he would tell her next.

"Thank you. Look, I know I haven't treated you well." He looked at her, but she wasn't really paying attention. She stared blankly at a car pulling out of a spot as he rambled on.

He pulled at her hand gently and tilted his head to see what her focus was on. "You said you would listen…"

Kristin turned her head back to look at him.

"I've quit drinking, Kristin." He had her attention now.

"What?" she asked, now focusing on what he was saying.

"I'm in a program and I'm getting help for it. I know that's why you left me. That's why I went to get help. For you and our baby."

"That's not why I left you, Jake. It didn't help matters that you drank, but you know very well that's not the only reason. I left you because I'm not going to allow you to use my body as an outlet for your frustrations whenever you want. I have to start thinking about my safety and my baby's safety," she fired back at him.

Jake reached out and placed his palm on her belly. "It's my baby too, Kristin… Please come home. I'm better now. I swear things will be different this time. Our child needs to have a father around."

Kristin couldn't believe her ears. Was he telling the truth or feeding her lies as always, just to get her back? How could she believe anything he said?

"What about the cat that was delivered to the diner?" she asked him, leaning against the car, a shopping bag still in her hand.

"What? You think I had something to do with that? Come on, Kris, I can't believe you would actually think that low of me. When the cops came by to question me about it, I couldn't believe they were serious, but I was cleared with the handwriting sample. Come on, babe, you know me. I may be a jerk sometimes, but I'm not crazy enough to kill some poor cat then have it delivered to your best friend. I don't even hunt," he said. Kristin looked away.

He stood a bit closer to her and grabbed hold of her hand. She looked up into those eyes of his again.

"Kristin. You know me."

He rubbed her belly with his hand. She tried to push it away, but he playfully swatted her hand away and rested it on her stomach. He then got down on his knees in the middle of the parking lot and placed his lips over the pink sundress that covered her stomach. He looked up and smiled at her.

"How do I know you're even telling me the truth?" She looked down at him.

Rising to his feet, he said, "Okay, look at this." He took a pamphlet out of his jeans pocket. "This is a pamphlet from the AA meetings I've been going to. I brought it with me in case you didn't believe me. You see there where it says Parson's Community Center on top?" Jake pointed at the leaflet and handed it to Kristin to look it over. "We meet every Monday and Wednesday at eight p.m. Even got me a sponsor, Jack Ryder. He's a great guy. You would like him a lot. Down to earth and he understands the pressures that I've been under. 'Cause he was right where I was."

Kristin opened the pamphlet and saw a few writings along the edges of the pages. Some numbers were scribbled under the program's mission statement, and Jack Ryder was listed as one of the sponsors on one page. His name was circled in red ink with his number written underneath.

"You see, I'm not lying to you. Not about this." He held her face in his hands. "I love you, Kristin. I promise I will never lay my hands on you again. Please just come home with me."

"I can't—I don't know, Jake. I've had a lot of time to think about things. The way things have been in our marriage, how you treat me. I'm not happy, and I don't think you are either. I think—"

"All I'm asking for is for you to give me a chance to prove to you that I'm not the same man I was when you left me. I'm not the drunk you've known these past five years. I've changed, I know I have. These past six months have been hell without you. I left you alone so I could work on me. I knew you were staying with Tiffany months ago, but I didn't want to bother you until I felt I got myself straight. I'm a different man now. All I want to do is take care of my family, you and the baby."

Shaking her head, she replied, "I don't know."

"Please, just give it a chance. If you don't see a change in me, then you can leave me. You can walk out the door and I won't stop you."

"You promise?"

"Yes, I promise. Please come home, love."

Kristin looked up into his eyes again as he circled his arms around her waist and kissed her lips. She was conflicted inside. She wanted to have a family, but could she trust that he would live up to his promises? But he had shown her the pamphlet, and the fact that he even went to get help was a step in the right direction. Maybe Officer O'Neil was right. Maybe all Jake needed was to get some help for his drinking. Maybe now that he was, things would finally be better between them.

If not, then by agreeing to come home, she had just made a horrible mistake.

"Okay," she replied, doubt circling in her head.

"Thank you." Tears filled his eyes. "Thank you." He hugged her close to him.

CHAPTER SEVEN

It was the seventh month of her pregnancy, and Kristin was back at home with Jake. Tiffany was furious, of course, and told her she was insane to even think of going back to him. She felt betrayed by Kristin, especially after the cat incident. But Kristin assured her that Jake was getting help and things were going to be different. She even gave Tiffany back her cell phone because Jake had bought two new phones, one for her and a brand new one for him. He said he would die if anything happened to her and the baby, and that the moment she felt contractions, she was to call him or text him. There was no way he would miss the birth of his son.

Tiffany warned that something wasn't right about all of this. That Jake would say whatever he could to get her back, but that she doubted he changed. She told Kristin to keep her eyes open. But Kristin had seen a completely different side of him the last two weeks. She didn't want to doubt that anything about the change in him was less than sincere. He had kept his promises so far. Not once did he lay a finger on her since she came home, and as far as she could see, he was attending his AA meetings regularly. He would even call her from the meeting when they had refreshment breaks.

She even noticed a change in how he behaved with her. He was much more affectionate at home. Was it because business seemed to be doing so well lately? Since Kristin had been home, there had not been one call from a bill collector. She also couldn't help but notice that he had a lot more cash on him and around the house, but she never questioned it. She was just happy that the once cold and bitter atmosphere she had lived in was finally warming up.

But then that same business associate of Jake's from that night in her driveway started to come around their home more regularly—Miguel. Sometimes, he was accompanied by another man who Jake also referred to as his "business associate." There were times they had popped up when even Jake was surprised to see them.

When Miguel had been formally introduced to her by Jake, she'd immediately gotten chills.

He had been sitting in the living room with Jake and the other business associate, Robert. She had come in with a pitcher of iced tea and Jake's favorite snack, jalapeno poppers, and offered them some. Miguel stood up, taking the tray from her hands, undressing her with his eyes as he did from that day forward every time he saw her.

He stood about six feet tall with a stocky build and caramel skin. His dark-black hair was curly and fell to his shoulders. It almost seemed like the tan he had was painted on him, it was so perfect. Every time he came by the house, he always wore a shirt that seemed too small. It outlined his well-sculpted chest and abs. He also wore tight-fitting jeans that hugged his rear end. He was definitely Latino; his accent confirmed it as he greeted her. He was possibly in his mid-thirties. Whenever he was around, Kristin felt more than uncomfortable, and she would remain in the bedroom until he left. He made her feel as if she were not wearing clothes whenever he looked her way and smiled.

The other business associate, Robert, was no comparison. He seemed less threatening and was only a few inches taller than Jake, who was about five foot nine. He was also of Latin descent but looked as if he might be in his early twenties. He had short brown hair and a much fairer complexion. She noticed he always wore a loose-fitting shirt and beige Dockers.

As much as they were business associates, Kristin could not understand why Jake always held late-night meetings with them in their kitchen and not at his office. They would often stay in the kitchen talking until the wee hours of the morning about packages they were expecting and who was going to deliver what. But Kristin could never decipher exactly what was in the packages they kept mentioning. Part of her suspected that Jake might be involved in something illegal. But that idea was quickly put to bed after she tried to question him about it. He told her to mind her business, and when she saw that he became a little annoyed, she decided it was better not to bring it up again. She didn't want to rock the boat.

But then beer started to appear in the house again. Jake insisted it was for Miguel and Robert even though Kristin would see him take one out of the fridge for himself now and then. Still, she didn't say a word. She couldn't dare tell Tiffany—all Tiffany would say to her was, "I told you so." If she didn't ask questions or push any buttons, things would remain calm between her and Jake. So, she kept the blinders on—until one evening when Jake wasn't home, and the phone rang.

"Kristin, it's Collin. Have you seen Jake?"

"Isn't he at the office with you?"

"No, he hasn't been here all day. I've got clients on the phone complaining about work not getting done on time. You know, I'm getting tired of these disappearing acts. If he doesn't know, we have a business to run here. Been covering his ass for the past two weeks. I mean, I can't manage this all by myself. This only works if both of us are here. Phone is ringing off the hook… There is just too much not getting done. Ever since he's been hanging out with Dumb and Dumber, he's always leaving early, or I can't reach him. If something doesn't change, this business is going to go under. And I have half of my money tied up in this—"

"Collin, I will tell him when he gets here that you called," Kristin said. "Okay?"

She hung up the phone, unable to deal with anything stressful. She was already having early labor pains, and at her last checkup, the doctor had said to avoid as much stress as possible.

The phone rang again and Kristin picked it up, annoyed. "Collin, I told you that I would—"

"I'm sorry for calling so late, ma'am. My name is Jack Ryder… Hello?"

Kristin recalled the name being vaguely familiar, but she couldn't remember why. "Ah, yes, can I help you?"

"Is this Kristin?" he inquired.

"Yes, that's me."

"Hi, I've heard so much about you," the man on the other line said happily. "I'm your husband's AA sponsor. I was calling because Jake has missed two weeks of meetings. I was wondering if everything was okay. Because it's not like him. I haven't heard from him and was worried something might have happened. When I try to reach him on his cell phone, I always get his voicemail."

"Well, that would make two of us," Kristin replied sarcastically.

"I beg your pardon?" Mr. Ryder replied.

"Sorry. I mean, Jake isn't here, and I'm not sure when he will be home. But I will be sure to give him the message that you called."

"Okay, thank you. Have a nice evening," he said, and she placed the phone on the receiver.

Kristin felt that all-too-familiar dull pain in the pit of her stomach she got whenever she was nervous. How could Jake go back on every word he had said to her that day in the parking lot? For two weeks, he had been lying to her, saying that he was going to his AA meetings and lying about being at work till four in the morning. Who were these business associates of his? What kind of business associates were they?

Jake walked in the door.

"Babe, I'm home," he said, walking into the kitchen to take his food out of the microwave. He gave her a quick peck on the cheek.

She could smell the liquor on his breath.

"Have you been drinking?" Kristin asked, looking at him as he took out a fork from the drawer and sat down with his plate of food.

"No, I haven't been drinking." Jake started to eat the meatloaf and mashed potatoes she'd made for dinner.

"Jake, I smelled it on you when you leaned in to kiss me just now."

"Okay, so I had one drink with the guys after work. Rob and Miguel wanted to unwind for a little at O'Brien's, and they bought a round of drinks. I swear, one drink. Nothing serious. I'm still going to my meetings."

"You were at work tonight?"

"Yes."

"And you're still going to your meetings." Kristin sat down at the table with him.

"Yes, Kristin. What, you don't believe me?" He put his fork down and looked straight into her eyes.

"No, Jake, I don't believe you," she said bluntly.

"Well, I guess that's on you," he said and got up to get a beer from the fridge.

"I don't believe you because tonight Collin called here looking for you." He watched her, twisting the beer bottle cap off and throwing it away into the garbage can a few feet away.

"And?" Jake asked, shaking his head in mock fear.

"Collin said you haven't been at the office for a few days. That business is not doing well. He said the clients are calling, complaining that the jobs are not getting done on time." The words came out quickly. She didn't even pause to take a breath.

"Oh, give me a break. What does he know? Says I wasn't around for a while." He scoffed. "Damn, woman, I've been at the office every day busting my ass with those guys, trying to get work done. I told you that. But you don't believe me. He probably gets there when I'm leaving. We don't have to be there at the same time, you know. Collin is a big boy."

"So, he's lying then?" Kristin asked, not believing anything he was telling her.

"Yes, he's lying," Jake stated in a tone that suggested he couldn't believe she doubted him.

"So, is your sponsor lying too? Is Jack Ryder lying? Because he says that you haven't been at an AA meeting in two weeks, which is kind of strange since you called me last Wednesday from your break. So, if you weren't at your meeting, then where the hell were you?"

Ignoring her questions, Jake stared at her hard. "So that's what you do when I'm not home. You stay on the phone talking about me with my business partner and my sponsor? Are you serious?"

"I want to know what's going on. Who are these guys that you are hanging around with lately? They don't look like people who care much about the construction business."

"They are business investors Kristin, they—"

"Investors—really, Jake?"

"What the hell is this? The Spanish Inquisition? Jeez, I can't even come home to eat my dinner in peace. This is ridiculous!" Jake stood up from his seat.

"What kind of business are you doing with them, Jake? Is it anything illegal?"

"Do you really think that I would be that stupid to jeopardize the safety of you or my child you're carrying? Come on, Kristin!" Jake gripped the back of the chair with both hands.

"Jake—"

"Just stop this. I'm not doing anything illegal. Those guys are helping me keep a roof over our heads, pay our bills, and keep my business running. If everything keeps going smoothly, we'll have enough to retire on in a few years and enough in the bank to send our kid to college. Maybe even more. Haven't you noticed that the bill collectors have stopped calling? That's because I've paid most of our debts off already."

"Jake, I just want—"

"Drop it, Kristin, I mean it. I'm going to bed. I've lost my appetite." He picked up his plate, threw his dinner in the trash, and then tossed the plate into the sink.

Kristin had wanted to press more about the subject because he really hadn't answered any of her questions. But the baby was one month away. She was too afraid that if she pushed any harder, things would go back to the way they had been. She didn't want to risk that. At least he wasn't beating her now—and she wanted it to stay that way.

CHAPTER EIGHT

It was a Monday afternoon. Jake was still at work, or so he had told Kristin—she never knew what was true anymore. Miguel had stopped by the house uninvited.

Without greeting him hello, Kristin stated coldly, "Jake isn't here. You'll have to come back later."

He took in her long slender body, with the exception of her very pregnant stomach, in a long denim skirt and white cotton T-shirt. His eyes rested on the cleavage of her full bosom.

"Well, I'll just come in and wait for him, then," Miguel replied, making his way past her and into the house, almost pushing her and her protruding belly out of his way. He seemed a bit annoyed as he sunk down on Jake's leather chair. Kristin slowly sat down on the sofa opposite him. She knew it would take a minute for her to stand up again, with the extra weight she was carrying. But she wouldn't dare ask him for help when she did.

"Is the business okay? Why are you here? Where's your partner, Rob?" Kristin asked nervously. She looked at the clock. Where the hell was Jake?

"He's probably with your husband. You know, leather sucks in the summer. It can get pretty sticky if you're wearing shorts or a skirt… pasting onto your skin." He looked at the curves of her leg that peeked through the slit in her skirt.

Kristin sat up straighter and moved the slit underneath her, so that the skirt covered both legs. She looked at him with his hands folded behind his head, leaning back on the recliner, making himself comfortable.

"I'm going to the kitchen to get something to drink. Would you care for a glass of water?" she asked and grabbed onto the arm of the sofa to give herself a boost. Practically waddling with the heavy weight pressing against her bladder, she walked into the kitchen. She just didn't feel safe in the same room with that man.

"A beer would be great!" he shouted from the couch.

She opened the fridge door and bent down to see what she had to offer him. There were some beers Jake had bought earlier in the week, but she would be damned if he would be drinking with her alone in the same house. "All out of beer. How about that glass of water?" she shouted back.

"I see a beer right down there," he whispered from behind her, startling her. He placed his fingers over hers on the door. She could feel his breath on the back of her neck and his body pressed against the back of her skirt. She could also feel he was aroused.

Pulling a beer out of the fridge, she turned around and practically shoved the bottle into his chest.

"You don't seem to like me too much." He stepped back and twisted off the cap, taking a long sip.

"Actually, you have it wrong. I don't like you at all," she replied candidly.

"Honesty; I like that in a woman. You're smart. I'm not a very good man," he said, then muttered a few words in Spanish before saying, "but then... there are things you wouldn't like about your husband if you knew them."

"What is that supposed to mean?" she asked, even though she really didn't want him to answer that.

"I'll let him talk to you about that." He gave her a wicked grin. Gazing down at her stomach, he asked, "When is the baby due?"

Kristin remained silent as he stared at her, smiling.

"You know, I find pregnant women sexy." He took a sip of his beer, licking his moist bottom lip.

Jake walked into the house with Robert. The two were deeply engaged in conversation.

"Kristin, where you at?" he called out for her.

"In the kitchen," she answered, relieved he was finally home.

Jake walked into the kitchen with Robert at his side and immediately stopped at the archway where the hallway met the kitchen. Kristin could see the tension written all over his face when he saw Miguel standing close beside her.

Seeing the expression on Jake's face, Miguel chuckled.

"Relax, man, we were just talking," he said and patted him on the shoulder. He gestured to Robert to follow him into the living room.

But Jake remained unmoved, standing by the archway, looking at Kristin with such disapproval that he had her convinced that she had done something wrong. He moved past her and grabbed a few beers from the still-open fridge, then walked away.

Kristin stayed in the kitchen while the three of them chatted with one another. At times, they would speak so softly, almost in a whisper, that she had to really focus on listening to hear what they were saying. Miguel was incredibly upset, swearing more than usual as he spoke to Jake. But Jake kept trying to assure him that things were going to be fine. That all he needed was more time. *More time for what?* Kristin couldn't comprehend what was happening. He told them that he would find it one way or another.

Then Kristin heard Miguel threaten her husband. He told him he was lucky that he even agreed to work with Jake. He also mentioned that Jake should be grateful that Kristin was home and that it was all thanks to him. Kristin shook her head, not understanding. But it all began to make sense when she heard Jake's response.

"You were responsible for that dead cat going to her friend? You're one sick, twisted—" Jake tried to say before Miguel cut him off.

"She's home, isn't she? You should be thanking me," Miguel laughed.

"I almost went to jail for that stunt you pulled. I never once told you to do that!" Jake protested angrily.

Kristin's blood began to boil. She wanted to go in there and raise hell, but she knew in her condition it was safer for her not to get involved. She continued to listen. There was silence for a few moments before Kristin heard the front door slam. She ran over to the kitchen window only to see Miguel's black Nissan Armada reverse out of their driveway with Rob sitting in the front passenger seat. Rob flashed Kristin a smile, and she quickly stepped away from the sink.

"Like what you see?" Jake asked, walking into the kitchen, catching Kristin the moment she moved away from the window.

Turning about to face him, she asked, "What was that about?"

"I should be asking you the same question." He took a beer out of the fridge.

"You promised you wouldn't start drinking again. But every time I turn around lately, you have a beer in your hand."

He drank his beer, not really giving any consideration to what she had just said. "I guess we all fail at keeping our promises to each other. Don't we?" He walked into the living room and turned on the television. Sitting on the couch, he watched old reruns of *The Honeymooners* until he fell asleep.

***

The next morning, Kristin woke up in horrible pain. She felt something wet and slimy between her legs. She raised the covers off her legs, and in the middle of the bed was a big wet stain mixed with some blood. She screamed at the sight. It was too early for this to happen! There were still two weeks left before the baby was due.

She called out for Jake as she got up off the bed. Slowly, she made her way from the bedroom to the living room as blood and water dripped down the sides of her calves.

Jake wasn't on the sofa. Where was he? She called out again for him, but there was no answer. *He must have left for work already.* It was already a quarter after nine. She grabbed the cell phone he had bought her and dialed his number. But there was no answer. She sent him a text, then another. Still nothing.

The pain started to come more frequently. She didn't know what to do. How would she get to the hospital? She thought of calling a cab but knew the car service where they lived wasn't reliable. The only person she could count on was Tiffany.

Reluctantly, she dialed her number even though she knew that Tiffany was still mad at her.

"Tiffany, it's me, Kristin. I'm in labor." Kristin spoke slowly, almost holding her breath as another wave of contractions came over her.

"Where's your adoring husband?" Tiffany inquired sarcastically.

"He's not here. Tiff, I'm freaking out. This isn't supposed to be happening for another couple of weeks."

"Just calm down. I'll be right there. Hate that son of—"

Kristin disconnected the call.

Within ten minutes, Tiffany and Kristin were on their way to Parsons General Hospital. Tiffany coached Kristin in the car with the breathing exercises she had taught her a few months ago to help focus on her breathing instead of the pain. She had gone through this once before with her sister. As Kristin took short breaths in and out to take her mind off the horrendous pain radiating from her lower back to her stomach, Tiffany kept telling her that they would be at the hospital soon. But for Kristin, it seemed like an eternity.

Tiffany called for help as she pulled up front. A nurse came running to the car door with a wheelchair, and Tiffany helped Kristin into it.

Halfway down the hall, Kristin screamed. The labor pains were much stronger and were coming a lot faster than before. A doctor standing nearby lifted Kristin's bloody nightgown to check her cervix.

"Nurse, get her to labor and delivery. She's dilated at ten centimeters. This baby is coming now!" He gestured to the nurse that he would be there soon.

Kristin was propped up on a bed with pillows behind her back and her legs wide open in stirrups. Tiffany continuously tried to reach Jake on his cell, but there was still no answer.

"Where's Dr. Anderson?" she asked Tiffany, who was holding her hand.

"Kristin, I told the nurse to page him."

A nurse overhearing the conversation spoke up. "Dr. Anderson is away and won't be back till Monday. But Dr. Martinez has been with us for a long time."

"Don't worry, Kristin, you're in good hands. Now, we're going to push. It's time, okay?" said the skinny, masked doctor in blue scrubs and a face mask between her legs.

"You can do this," Tiffany assured her friend, holding on to her hand.

"Where's Jake?" Kristin asked, out of breath as she moaned in pain. The contractions were right on top of each other.

"Don't think about that. I'm here. Come on, we're doing this together," Tiffany said encouragingly.

"On three, you're going to bear down and push as hard as you can. Okay?" the doctor ordered. "One, two, three, push!"

Kristin pushed with all her might. She could feel something inside of her rip through the lips of her vagina, but she kept on pushing. She felt burning and the most incredible pain she could have ever imagined. But she knew once it was all over, it would be worth it—and that was what kept her going, even though she felt she was going to pass out at any moment.

"Good, Kristin. The head and shoulders are out." The doctor kept her informed of what was happening below. "Okay, Kristin, one more good push. One, two, three, push!"

Tiffany now sat on the bed, moving behind Kristin to keep her sitting up. She held on to Kristin's shoulders and said, "You can do this. One more push and you're going to see that baby."

Kristin grabbed Tiffany's hand tighter. When the doctor said push, she pushed down so hard she felt her face turn red.

"You have a boy!" the doctor announced happily and handed the newborn over to the nurse to be cleaned.

"Did you hear that? Open your eyes, Kristin. You did it!" Tiffany hugged her friend from behind. "You did it!"

Kristin stretched out her arms as the nurse placed a beautiful baby boy, wrapped in a blue and white hospital blanket, into her arms. He had a head full of light-brown hair, and as he opened his eyes, Kristin could see them. They were light blue, but she had read in a pregnancy book that could change as he got older.

Kristin kissed her son's forehead. "Hi, baby. Oh my God, I've waited so long to see you, darling. You're so beautiful. I love you so much."

Kristin kissed his tiny little round nose and cheeks and held her pinkie out for him to latch on. This tiny, beautiful little being who had rented her womb for the last nine months had finally arrived.

"We have to take him for some bloodwork. But we'll bring him back to you," the nurse assured her and wheeled her tiny little angel in an incubator out of the room.

The doctor continued to deliver the afterbirth. Then, after being cleaned up and moved to another bed and room, Kristin was soon resting peacefully.

An hour later, Tiffany checked in on her friend to see how she was doing, bringing flowers and a blue teddy bear. She even had a tiny helium balloon that said *Congrats! It's a boy!*

"How are you feeling, Mommy?" Tiffany asked with a smile.

Kristin looked over at the window where Tiffany had placed the flowers, balloon, and teddy bear. "Oh my God." She laughed.

"Well, I thought I'd go crazy in the gift shop, but then I thought I'd buy a few items now, then take you shopping for clothes when you're up to it."

"Tiffany, I really don't know how to thank you."

"Don't mention it. So how are you feeling?" Tiffany sat down in a chair opposite her.

Kristin sat up a little in the bed. "A bit of pain, but I'm okay. Have you heard from Jake?"

"Nothing yet," Tiffany said, checking her cell phone then placing it back in her purse.

Kristin couldn't understand it. How could he miss this? How could he not want to see his own son? His office was only a ten-minute drive to the hospital. She knew he had to have gotten all ten of her voicemails and her text messages by now, as well as the ones that Tiffany had sent him. But there was no call and no text from him.

***

A little while later, Kristin woke up from a deep sleep at the sound of a baby's cry. The painkillers the nurse had given her earlier after Tiffany had stopped by must have knocked her out. She looked at the empty infant bed beside her. Her son wasn't there. She was about to reach for the nurse call button when, out of the corner of her eye, she saw a man standing by the door cradling her son in his arms.

"Jake?" she called out. It was a little dark now in her room. The sun had gone down.

"Yeah, it's me." He held their son with one hand and flipped on the lamp by her bed.

"Where were you?" Kristin asked, a bit groggy. "You missed it!"

"Shush… Look at this little fellow with his tiny little fingers and toes." He played with his son's hands and feet. "Kristin, he's so damn beautiful."

"I was waiting on you to pick out a name. I was thinking about Tommy?"

"Tommy, I like it," he said, not taking his eyes off his son. "Hi, Tommy." Jake smiled at his baby boy, placing his pinkie in Tommy's hand to grab on to.

Kristin wanted to ask Jake where he had been the entire time while she was giving birth to their son. She wanted to know why he never returned any of her calls or texts. But suddenly, it all seemed so unimportant as she watched Jake play with their son. She didn't want to ruin the moment. They were now a family. Tommy was finally here.

CHAPTER NINE

Tommy's birth was a true blessing for Kristin. It seemed to have also inspired Jake to be a better human being, and he spent every free moment doting on Tommy. After Kristin had expressed her concern about having strange men around her son, Miguel and Robert now only visited Jake at the office.

For the first six months, it was quiet. Kristin took a million snapshots of Tommy, from his first bath to the first time he crawled. She couldn't believe how fast he was growing. She wanted to freeze the precious moments she spent with her baby boy.

Things with Jake weren't exactly great, but at least for the last six months, he stayed out of her way due to the fact he was preoccupied with work at the office. But when he started coming home early, Kristin suspected business wasn't doing so well. Plus, he was receiving calls on his cell phone and at the house from random people she had never heard him mention in the five years they had been married. One day, she overheard him on the phone, screaming to one of the guys at the office how most of his clients were leaving him to go to a competitor that was charging half his price. He even threatened that if it continued, he would start laying off the men to compensate for the money he was losing.

Collin was disgusted by Jake's lack of consideration for the men who had worked for them for so long. When Jake ignored his requests to sit down with him to find an alternate resolution instead of the layoff, he asked Jake to buy him out. Kristin learned all this when Collin called for Jake at the house to find out the status of the final paperwork to transfer the partnership over to Miguel.

"Collin, I'm so sorry," Kristin said.

He sighed on the other end of the phone. "There's no need for it. Jake is the only one to blame in all of this." He also told Kristin that Jake better never find himself on Miguel's bad side because he wouldn't be as forgiving as he had been throughout their relationship as partners or as friends. "Kristin," he said before hanging up, "steer clear of Miguel and Robert. If you're smart, you'll take your son and leave Jake."

But for some reason, she couldn't. Kristin wanted a family, and she wanted Tommy to have a father, not just a weekend dad in his life. If she knew her place, things could work out for them, she told herself.

Yet things continued to get worse. After Collin left, Jake's business started losing money. One afternoon as Kristin put Tommy down in his crib for a nap, Jake walked in angry and drunk, livid about losing another important client. Kristin could hear how angry he was from the moment he walked through their front door. He called out to her and she found him pacing beside the dining room table.

"Can't believe this shit! Randy Sykes just told me he's going to have someone else work on his bedroom extension if I don't knock two hundred dollars off my fee. He tells me this after I just paid for all the materials. I can't believe this! What am I going to do?" he asked Kristin, but she didn't respond. She was caught off guard that Jake was even discussing this with her. Usually, he told her to mind her business whenever she asked questions about it.

His eyes moved to the small pile of mail Kristin had left on the dining table for him to look through. Tearing open an envelope, his eyes quickly read the notice.

"Just great! Another bill that we're late on!" He crunched up the notice into a ball and threw it into the corner of the room.

"But he can't do that. You have a contract, right?" Kristin asked.

"No, McDummy, I don't have a contract with him because I've taken his word for the last ten years! We don't deal with contracts, me and him." Jake glared at her behind bloodshot eyes.

Kristin's eyes widened in fear. She had seen that look before.

She touched his arm lightly and said, "I'm going to go make you something to eat." She headed to the kitchen with Jake following right behind her.

"Come here. You think I'm a loser, right? I bet you're thinking, 'what a loser I married,' right?" He grabbed her wrist to turn her around to face him. They stood next to the kitchen counter, where Kristin had taken a plate out to make him a sandwich.

"No, Jake, I don't think that at all." She took her hand away from him, trying to remain calm.

"Yes, you do. I know you. I can see it written all over your face. Jake the loser—my husband—the pathetic loser!" He started to raise his voice.

"Jake, quiet, you're going to wake the baby."

"Oh God forbid we do that, right! God forbid we wake your precious Tommy." He picked up the plate and threw it across the room, breaking it to pieces.

Trying to keep things from escalating further, Kristin placed her hand on his shoulder and said, "Calm down, okay. I know things are rough. But we're going to get through this."

He pushed her hand away and spat at her. "Oh, shut up, Kristin! Stop trying to make everything better with your kind words and soft touches. It's not helping, okay! Get through this?" he mimicked her. "How the hell do you know what it is we need to get through, when all you care about is that damn baby in there!"

"How could you say that? Jake, he's your son."

"You sure about that?" he asked, the corner of his lips forming half of a smirk. He went to the fridge to take out a beer.

"I don't have to listen to this." She turned to walk away from him and headed to Tommy's room to check on him. She was sure he was up by now, moving around in his crib.

"Oh, yes, you do." He grabbed hold of Kristin's arm and squeezed it so hard, it was starting to cut off the circulation.

"Get off of me, Jake." Fear rose inside her. *Here we go again*, she thought.

"What were you doing that day when I found you alone with Miguel in the kitchen?"

"Nothing!" Kristin fired back at him. The old Jake had resurfaced.

"Nothing?" he asked sarcastically.

"No, nothing happened!" she cried out, trying to shake her arm free as his nails started to dig into her skin.

"I don't believe you. He told me you came on to him. He told me how you asked him to touch you. You like it better when he does it, is that it?" Jake squeezed at her left breast with his free hand.

"Jake, stop it, you're drunk."

"I know I'm drunk! Hell, you're the one that makes me drink!" He shoved her against the kitchen counter.

She looked at him as he watched her, anticipating her next move. She was scared, but she knew if she didn't get out of the room, he was going to hurt her.

"What did you let him do to you, Kristin?" He flicked his tongue at her and grabbed her groin.

"Just stop it." Kristin pushed his hand away. He responded by grabbing her hands and pushing one knee between her legs. She struggled against him. The beer he held slipped out of his fingers and fell to the floor. He looked down at the spill, and Kristin shoved him back, making a dash for the bedroom, locking the door behind her. Jake banged insistently against the door for her to open. Tommy woke up and started to wail.

"Open the door, Kristin!"

"Stop it! You're scaring Tommy!"

"Open the door or I'm coming in there."

But Kristin wouldn't unlock the door. She was afraid, for she knew things were only going to get worse. She stood behind the door as Jake tried to ram it open with his shoulder. Tommy cried even louder now.

"Kristin! Get out here or I'm coming in."

Kristin's body trembled. She walked over to the crib to soothe Tommy, who was lying on his side in his red onesie. She rubbed his back in circular motions as he wailed.

"It's okay, baby. Mommy is here." She bent over and kissed his soft chubby face.

Outside, Jake was still trying to ram the door.

"Okay! I'm coming out," she screamed, and the banging stopped.

Kristin threw open the door, ready to face the music, but Jake wasn't on the other side. If she didn't go to Jake, he would come to her. Slowly, she walked down the long hallway to the living room.

Jake sat on the sofa with his black pants around his ankles and another beer bottle in his hand. His penis was exposed.

"Come over here," he demanded.

She walked over to him slowly, not knowing what to expect.

"Strip," he ordered her, and she obeyed.

She stood in front of him, trying to cover her naked body with her hands.

"Wow, pregnancy really did a number on you. The only thing it did for you was give you bigger breasts. Your stomach is saggy." He slapped his hand against her belly. She flinched from the sting. "Your thighs are thicker. Damn, I can't even get hard looking at you anymore."

Kristin felt humiliated. One by one, tears flowed from her eyes. She knew they were only words, but words hurt just the same.

"Get over here and get on your knees. You know what I want, so come here and take care of me like a wife is supposed to. *Now*, Kristin." She did as he demanded, knowing things would be much worse if she refused him. Better to endure the humiliation and degradation of the act rather than the pain of his brutality.

When he finished, he threw her off him as if she was some cheap prostitute. Kristin ran to the bathroom naked and threw up, then collapsed onto the bathroom floor. She could hear Tommy crying for her, but she couldn't move. Her naked body curled up into a fetal position on the cold floor.

"Kristin! Stop that baby from crying!"

The nightmare had started all over again.

CHAPTER TEN

Tommy's third birthday had arrived, and Kristin held a small gathering for him at the house. Tiffany was in charge of picking up the cake the day of the party, which she was more than happy to do. Kristin had spent a month picking out the right colors for the cake and had selected a picture that she had taken of Tommy when he was nine months old. She remembered taking that photo like it was yesterday. He was holding on to the edge of the sofa cushion as he took a step toward her, one arm stretched to grab the camera out of her hands. The look on his face was so adorable that she'd just had to capture the moment. He was only wearing his diaper. But it was the cutest picture she had of him, and that was what she told the baker she wanted on the top of his cake along with his favorite red Hot Wheel. Everything had to be perfect. Of course, he wouldn't know the difference, but she wanted to remember it.

Jake was still at work, and Kristin didn't know if he would even make it home to celebrate Tommy's birthday. At this point, she couldn't care less if he showed up. They had coexisted like strangers in the house unless he decided she had done something wrong, and in some way, he would make her pay the price. She didn't even try to stop him now.

Tiffany opened the front door and called out for Kristin. Other people from work had gathered in the living room around the birthday boy, who was playing on the floor with his toy cars.

"I'm in here," Kristin answered from the kitchen. She was getting the rest of the mini crescent dogs out of the oven and placing them onto a silver serving tray. She'd put them on the coffee table for the guests, along with a big bowl of potato salad.

Tiffany entered the kitchen with a long, rectangular, double-layered cake in her hand. "God, the baker gave me such a headache when I went there to pick it up. He wrote Tommy's name wrong three times," she said, placing the red-and-black frosted cake on the counter next to the birthday candles. Kristin smiled at her friend, who looked pretty with her bouncy curls falling about her shoulders. She was dressed in a beige camisole and white jean shorts.

Without thinking, Kristin pushed some of her hair back, not realizing she was revealing the shiner that Jake had given her the night before.

"That bastard!" Tiffany exclaimed as she moved closer to her friend.

Kristin quickly pulled her hair back around the frame of her face to cover the bruise.

"I can't believe you're still allowing this to go on." Tiffany shook her head in disbelief.

Kristin walked over to the fridge to get a pitcher of iced tea and added more ice to it. "What am I supposed to do?" She placed the pitcher back in the fridge.

"Fight back—damnit! Fight back!" Tiffany said bitterly.

"It will only make things worse for Tommy if I do," Kristin explained.

"How could it? Do you want Tommy growing up thinking it's okay to beat up on women?"

Those words hit Kristin like a bullet through the heart. The idea of Tommy treating his wife the same way Jake was treating her was too horrible to even imagine. She could see the gentleness behind his brown eyes, and she never wanted that to disappear.

"How's my little baby boy?" Jake walked in through the front door, sweeping Tommy up in his arms as Kristin entered the living room with the tray of mini crescent dogs and potato salad. She placed them on the coffee table, then returned with a pitcher of the iced tea from the fridge. Jake did not even acknowledge her and continued to make his way around the room.

Joe, her manager, walked over to her and complimented the salad she had prepared.

"You make one mean potato salad, hon. Has a bit of a kick to it. What did you put in it?"

"A little splash of tabasco," she replied with a smile. Her eyes followed Jake around the room as he continued to ignore her.

Jake greeted Kristin's friends, flirting shamelessly with some of the women from the diner. A few of them seemed a bit uncomfortable, but reluctantly carried on a conversation with him. Kristin knew they only tolerated him because they were friends of hers.

Jake finally turned around to see Kristin standing in the corner with a grimace. Acting surprised that she was in the room, he walked toward her. "What's the matter?" He turned back to look at the women he was just chatting with. "Oh, that? Come on, Kristin, I was just being friendly." He kissed her cheek. "I was just looking for you." He turned away.

Kristin mumbled under her breath, "I'm sure you were."

"What was that?" he asked, then stood beside her, watching Tommy run around the room with some of the waitresses' kids who were playing with him.

Kristin began to collect the used paper cups and plates from her guests.

Jake called out to her, "Get me a beer, Kristin, when you go into the kitchen!"

She ignored him as he walked over to Tommy and picked him up in his arm, tickling him under the neck. Tommy stared at his father adoringly.

As Kristin continued to collect more paper plates, Jake called out again to her.

"Kristin—beer!"

She gestured with her hand to Jake to hold on. "Give me a minute. I'm doing something right now." She was afraid that giving him a beer would lead to another then another. She could just imagine the drunken stupor that would soon evolve from that, embarrassing them both. She walked back to the kitchen to place the candles on the cake.

"What did you say to me?" Jake rushed into the kitchen, grabbing the matches out of Kristin's hand before she could light the candles.

"Give them back to me!" Kristin yelled at him.

"You're going to talk like that to me in my house? In front of our guests? Have you lost your mind, woman?" He grabbed her around the throat and started to choke her. Kristin pulled at his hands. He was cutting off her air and her vision was becoming blurry.

Seeing Kristin in trouble, Tiffany pulled at Jake's collar.

"Get off her, you bastard!" She continued to tug at him. "Joe, help! Come quickly!"

But Jake ignored her, smacking her in the forehead with his free palm. He still had his hand wrapped around Kristin's throat. Tiffany watched in horror as Kristin's blood rushed to her face and became swollen.

"Joe!" Tiffany screamed.

Scurrying into the kitchen with two men by his side, Joe immediately ripped Jake off Kristin with some help. One of the men who came into the kitchen with Joe gestured for Jake with both hands to fight him. But Jake only laughed at them.

Kristin coughed, trying to fill her lungs to catch her breath. Her hands held both sides of her throat.

Tiffany ran to her side. "Kristin—Kristin! Are you okay?" Tiffany held her friend around the waist as Kristin continued to cough.

Hunched over with her hands on her knees, her eyes on the ground, she took three deep breaths as Tiffany rubbed her back in circular motions.

"Get off of me!" Jake pushed one of the guys off him, and they all backed away from him.

"Come home with me," Tiffany begged Kristin.

"Take her!" Jake shouted at Tiffany to show he didn't care. "But my son stays here! You hear me? You're not taking my son anywhere!"

Kristin watched as Jake wiped some blood off his lips. She looked at Tiffany, who waited for an answer from her.

"I can't. I can't leave Tommy."

Tiffany shook her head. "Don't you see this man is going to end up killing you? We'll come back with the police in the morning to get Tommy."

Jake moved toward Kristin, eyeing her hard. "We'll be long gone! So, go right ahead!"

Joe stood in the middle of Jake and Kristin.

"What are you going to do, shorty?" Jake asked, amused at Joe's brave attempt to protect Kristin. "I think you better get the hell out of my face before I tear you to shreds."

"You're not going to touch her as long as I'm standing here."

Jake stepped up to him, but the two other men suddenly surrounded him in a threatening manner. Jake turned around and walked out of the room.

The guests, who were bustling in conversation only minutes ago, now glared at Jake. They had heard everything.

"The party is over! Grab your things and get the hell out of my house—now!" he screamed at them.

All of Kristin's guests scurried toward the door as Jake barked at them to leave. She remained in the kitchen with Tiffany, Joe, and the other men. Tiffany kept shaking her head at her in frustration.

"I can't leave. He'll take Tommy, and I'll never see him again," Kristin explained.

Jake walked back into the kitchen. "You all better leave before I call the police and have them remove you personally. And just in case you're wondering, I *do* know people on the force." He walked over to the cake and looked at Kristin. "This is what you bought for my son? Garbage!" He smashed his fist into the center of the cake. Locking eyes with Kristin, he licked the back of his red-and-black frosted hand, grinning at her before walking away.

"You're really messed up, man. You seriously have issues," one of the men said to Jake.

Kristin collapsed to the kitchen floor, sitting with her back against the wooden cabinets, crying as she held her face in her hands. She couldn't believe Jake could do such a thing. Tommy didn't even get the chance to blow out his candles or hear everyone sing "Happy Birthday" to him. All her guests had been thrown out of her house. She was humiliated once again.

"Don't let the door hit you on the way out," Jake said sarcastically as he picked Tommy off the living room floor and headed with him to the bedroom.

"Kristin, I know you're scared," Tiffany said. "But you must come home with me. You can't stay here. I promise you we will get Tommy in the morning. Even if Jake tries to take him, he won't get that far. Trust me. The police will have cops all out looking for him."

"Don't you see? I can't. Besides, he has friends at the police station. They think he's a saint… I'm not leaving my son alone with him."

Tiffany sighed, defeated. "Call me in the morning."

"I'll be okay," Kristin reassured her friend, hugging her.

"Come on, Tiffany, he's going to call the police if we don't leave. We're only making it worse for Kristin by staying here longer," Joe said, and signaled to the men to start leaving.

Kristin cleaned up the kitchen after they left, throwing the cake into the trash can. She knew it was only a matter of time before Jake would put Tommy down in his crib and "deal with her," as he often told her he would.

CHAPTER ELEVEN

The next morning, Kristin had some trouble climbing out of bed. She lifted her pajama shirt and could feel the welt on her hip.

Flash! Tommy crying in the crib.

Flash! Jake had her face down on the floor, her legs spread eagle. With intense rage, he took her body, entering her from behind. The louder she cried for him to stop, the harder he gave it to her. After, he got up and grabbed his clothes like nothing had happened. He passed out on the couch, leaving Kristin bleeding on the floor.

Kristin blinked her eyes, trying to erase last night's events from her mind. She didn't even remember how she got into bed. Maybe he had brought her there. She rubbed her hip again, moaning as she stood up.

Tommy wasn't in his crib. Had Jake taken him like he had threatened he was going to? She leaned forward on her bed slowly, grabbing her blue robe. She moved toward the kitchen as she threw it on. They both sat at the kitchen table, with Tommy in his highchair eating cereal from his little plastic bowl.

"Look who's up? It's Mommy." Jake stood up and walked over to Kristin, placing a kiss on her forehead. "Sit down, I'll make you a cup of coffee," Jake said, guilt-ridden.

"I'm okay."

"Well, you look like crap. So, sit down and have a cup with me. By the way, I have a surprise for you."

"Sa-prise." Tommy clapped his hands together.

"Yes, Tommy. Daddy has a big surprise for Mommy." He patted Tommy on the head.

"What sort of surprise?" Kristin asked.

"Here, finish your cup of coffee. Then we're gonna go outside for a bit."

"Jake, I'm not even dressed."

"Doesn't matter. We aren't going far."

After coffee, Jake told Kristin to close her eyes and took her out onto the front porch as Tommy played with his cars in the living room. Kristin didn't know what to expect.

"Okay, open your eyes," he said.

There, parked beside his old pickup truck, was a brand-new, shiny, bright-red Toyota Camry.

"You're favorite color, right?" He took her by the hand and led her toward the car.

"Yes, but, how did you...? I mean, I thought you were having problems at work. Where did you get the money for this?"

"Don't worry about it. Money problems are a thing of the past. Come on, Kristin, stop being so negative. Aren't you happy?" He picked her up and swung her around like a doll.

"Yes, Jake," she lied to him. What else was she going to say—the truth? He didn't want to hear the truth.

He kissed her lips and smiled, placing her down on her feet. "I got carried away last night. I'm sorry I was rough with you." He kissed her cheek and handed her the car keys. "Well, go on inside and get dressed. We're gonna take Tommy for a drive." He grinned at her.

A little while later, they were pulling out of the driveway, Kristin behind the steering wheel and Tommy fastened in his car seat with plush toys for him to play with. Jake turned on the radio to his favorite alternative station and kicked his feet up on the dashboard.

Where did he get the money for a new car? She couldn't help recalling the phone conversation she'd had with Collin. She was sure whatever new string of financial luck he was having had to do with his newfound business relationship with Miguel and Robert.

"Jake, why a car? Why now?" she asked, turning down the volume on the radio.

"Damn it, Kristin! I just gave you great news, but you just have to find some way to throw it back in my face. Unbelievable!" he said, turning the volume up again and looking out the window.

Kristin continued to drive into town. "I'm sorry." He ignored her and mouthed the words to the song as the wind pushed his wavy hair back. Kristin looked in the rearview mirror at Tommy, who laughed every time they hit a small bump in the road.

They pulled into a diner thirty miles away from home. Jake made sure they didn't go to Joe's diner, worried that someone would spit in his food after the birthday drama. For an hour, they behaved like a normal family, munching on fries and eating hamburgers as Jake filled Kristin in on some new business that was headed his way.

"That's wonderful, babe." Kristin tried to sound supportive.

An elderly couple passed their booth and shook their heads when they saw the bruise on Kristin's cheek.

"Why don't you mind your damn business!" Jake screamed at them as the bell chimed when they walked out the door.

"Jake…" Kristin tried to calm him down, but there was no use. She could see the flame had already been ignited.

He threw two twenty-dollar bills on the table between their dirty dishes and stood up.

"Let's go." He picked up Tommy in his arms, who still held a French fry in his hand.

Jake looked down at Kristin's blouse, at a small ketchup stain. "Wow, you stained a perfectly good blouse. You must have a hole in your mouth." He laughed at her, pointing at it. He left the diner, leaving her behind as he headed toward their new car.

Kristin felt like a fool as other people watched him mock her. A single tear fell from the corner of her eye. She didn't know why she'd started to cry. Shouldn't she be used to the way he treated her by now? But it only hurt more and more each time he belittled her. Hiding her feelings wasn't exactly easy for her to do, especially when an audience was watching.

"What now?" he asked as he sat behind the wheel, knowing she was upset.

"Nothing." She got in on her side and sat down.

"Can't help it if you don't know how to eat. Put a napkin over your shirt next time. I mean, I don't know what else to tell you," he said, making her feel like even a bigger idiot.

∗∗∗

When they got home, there was a new, shiny, white 2010 Toyota Tundra parked in the driveway. His old, beat-up, white pickup truck was gone. *Another vehicle*, Kristin thought.

"That's surprise number two," Jake said. He hopped out and ran over to his new baby.

"How… what is this?"

"What do you mean? This is my new truck. That car is for you to take Tommy around to his doctor's appointments and do the grocery shopping with. This baby is all mine." He smiled, rubbing the hood of the truck with one hand as if he were waxing it.

"Jake?" Kristin called out to him, but Jake was captivated by the new truck. She had to call his name a second time just for him to hear her. "Jake!"

"What?" he said and walked over to her as she stood by the car.

"What is going on?" Kristin asked, concerned. "How is it that you are able to afford two brand new cars?"

"Kristin, just look at it as a string of good luck."

"A string of luck," she repeated, folding her arms underneath her chest.

"Yes," he said, opening the back door and unhooking Tommy out of his car seat. "A string of good luck." He put Tommy down on his feet and watched his little son run toward the house. Kristin ran after him before he got to the first step.

"Here, baby, hold Mommy's hand." Tommy stretched out his hand for Kristin, and they walked up the stairs. When they were all inside, she turned to Jake. "What does that mean exactly?"

"What? Do you still think I'm doing something illegal?" he asked.

"I don't know. This just seems awfully strange after we have been having money issues for the last year."

"Okay, then just be happy we are out of that mess. Seriously, do you think I would be that stupid to jeopardize the welfare of my family or my only son? Come on, you really don't know me then." Jake walked into the kitchen to grab a beer.

Kristin had no idea what to think. She just knew deep down inside something wasn't right. But she had a feeling whatever he was doing would soon be revealed to her.

Later that evening, a little past eleven-thirty, Tommy woke Kristin up from her sleep. He'd managed to climb out of his crib. With his tiny hands, he tugged on the covers that Kristin had wrapped herself in like a burrito. She had put the air conditioner on because it was humid during the night, but it was now ice-cold in the room.

Kristin rubbed the sleep from her eyes and turned on the bedside lamp. She took in her son, whose cheeks were flushed red.

"What's wrong, baby?" She reached down and picked up Tommy to sit him on the bed beside her. She turned to her left to see that Jake wasn't there. Placing her hand on Tommy's forehead, she could feel he was burning up.

"Jake! Jake!" she called out for him but got no response. She looked at the clock. Where the hell could he be at this time? Whenever she needed him, he was never around.

She reached into the drawer for her cell phone but remembered Jake had taken it away from her after the whole incident at the birthday party as punishment for disrespecting him.

"Shit!" She jumped out of bed, grabbing Tommy, and headed for the kitchen.

His face was flushed from fever, and he was crying and pulling on the lobe of his ear. Grabbing the phone off the wall, she paged his pediatrician. She waited about fifteen minutes before she called the emergency room.

The ER nurse asked her a few questions and told her it would be better to bring Tommy in so they could look at him. As soon as she hung up with the hospital, Kristin dialed Jake's cell, but all she got was voicemail.

"Unbelievable!" she screamed at the phone and slammed it down so hard she was sure she broke it. But she didn't care, she was too pissed. Tommy cried louder. After throwing on a pair of jeans and an old sweatshirt, she dressed Tommy quickly and began to search for the keys to the Camry.

"Damn you, Jake!" she shouted out of frustration when she found herself in the hallway with Tommy by her feet, who was still crying. "Hallway table!" she said, remembering Jake had placed them inside the drawer when they came home last night.

Kristin shoved the keys into her jeans pocket and grabbed Tommy and her purse. She felt uncomfortable not having her cell phone on her. What if they got into an accident? How would she be able to call for help? She couldn't think about that now, she told herself. Quickly, she opened the doors of the Camry, pressing the unlock button on the remote key in her hand. She placed Tommy in the car seat and buckled him in. Then she ran around to the other side of the car and got inside.

"Mamma," Tommy cried, holding on to his ear.

"It's okay, baby, we're going to the doctor," Kristin said to him hurriedly, reversing the car out of the driveway. Jake's truck was missing from where he usually parked it by the side of the house. But she wouldn't allow herself to wonder where he was at this time of night. Her priority now was to get Tommy to the hospital. She had heard crazy stories in the newspapers of children his age who had a high fever and their parents who neglected to have them seen by a physician. A few days later, the child would have died from some horrible undiagnosed infection. With those thoughts, Kristin pressed further down on the gas pedal.

She parked the car in the visitor parking lot and ran with Tommy in her arms into the emergency room.

After registering her son, Kristin was sent to triage. The nurse checked his temperature—104. Now, an hour later, Kristin was nervous as she played with Tommy on her lap, waiting for his name to be called. She looked around.

She thought at least after he was triaged, they wouldn't be waiting too much longer. There weren't that many people in the waiting area to begin with. But even though she expressed her concerns to the triage nurse, she had said it was probably just the common ear infection from the way he kept pulling at his ear.

After waiting a little while longer, a short, black nurse with closely cropped hair and dressed in blue scrubs walked into the room. All heads turned to look in her direction to wait for her to call out the next patient's name on a list she held in her hand.

"Tommy Summers?"

Kristin stood up and picked up Tommy in her arms. He held on to his favorite little race car. He hated sitting on the cold, thin paper that covered the patient table and feeling the end of the metal stethoscope on his bare chest, but when he had his little red race car in his hand, he seemed to calm down enough to get through a doctor's appointment without much difficulty.

"Follow me," the nurse said, leading Kristin through a shiny steel door. It locked behind them automatically.

Kristin followed the nurse down a long, gray and black hallway. She held Tommy in her arms tighter, kissing her son on the forehead. "It's going to be okay, baby. We're going to see the doctor now." At least he stopped crying. Kristin was thankful for that.

"I know you're worried." The nurse smiled at Kristin when they entered the room. A patient table stood in the center. The nurse gestured for her to put Tommy down on the table to sit and took a set of vitals, making notes on a piece of paper in his chart. "It's always scary when your child is sick. It makes you feel helpless. I understand. My son used to get sick all the time. Now he's a big, strapping, sixteen-year-old playing high school football. Who would have thought?" She chuckled, then placed her hand on Kristin's shoulder a bit more seriously. "I know how scary it can be being a first-time mom."

Tommy sat up on the table, playing with his toy car. Kristin looked at him, then looked back at the nurse. "How do you know I'm a first-time mom?" she asked.

"Because I've been doing this job for twenty years. I can spot them a mile away." The nurse smiled warmly and walked toward the opened door. "The doctor will be with you in a minute," she said, exiting the room into the hallway.

Before she could walk away, a young man's voice called out. "Rose!"

Kristin watched the friendly nurse stop dead in her tracks and turn on her heel to look in the opposite direction. A young doctor ran up to her with a chart in his hand and a stethoscope dangling around his neck. Two pens stuck out of his left breast pocket.

"David? What's wrong?" Rose asked.

Kristin got a better view of the doctor as he approached the nurse outside the room. Kristin tried not to watch them or listen in on their conversation, but she couldn't help but stare at the doctor as he shuffled through some papers. He must have sensed her staring at him, because he glanced over to her quickly then back down at the papers he held. He had green eyes, she noticed. They were beautiful green eyes, she thought.

"These labs—They need to be redone. We need to run some more tests on Mr. Ferguson," the green-eyed doctor stated, towering over the nurse. Kristin gathered he was probably around the same age as she was or maybe a year younger.

"Right away, Doctor," the nurse said, and he turned around, running off in the direction that he came from. "These young ones today are so thorough," Rose told Kristin when she noticed she had been listening.

"Hello, Doctor," Rose then greeted an older man in the hallway. He had salt-and-pepper hair and wore a white lab coat with a white pinstripe, button-down shirt underneath. "I took the boy's vitals; they were normal. Fever is a little high. It's recorded in the chart, next to him on the table," the nurse said to him.

"Thank you, Rose." The doctor walked into the room, closing the door behind him. "Hello, there," he said, moving over to Tommy, then looked over his shoulder at Kristin.

"Hi, I'm Dr. Wilkin." He smiled, looking at Tommy, who was still playing with his race car and making car noises. Kristin was thankful that he hadn't started crying again when the doctor walked into the room.

Tommy looked up at the old man and seemed a bit confused.

"You like cars? I like cars too," he said, picking up Tommy's chart and looking it over briefly.

Kristin stood nearby and watched as the doctor examined Tommy from head to toe. He checked his breathing, then his ears, nose, and throat.

"You've got a strong boy, Ms. Summers. A little ear infection, but nothing some antibiotics won't cure," he said, taking out his pad and writing a prescription. "No allergies to medications?" he questioned.

"No, Doctor," she said, then took the prescription from his chubby fingers.

"Good. I want you to call his pediatrician's office tomorrow and schedule a follow-up. But he should be fine once he completes the antibiotics." He smiled, giving Tommy a high five.

Kristin felt relieved as she drove away from the hospital with Tommy.

On her way home, she noticed Jake's new truck parked in the parking lot of the neighborhood bar. She pulled over to the curb to get a closer look and saw him walking out of the bar with a young brunette. He couldn't see her from the main road and was probably too wasted to care if he did. Kristin watched him from a few yards away. The only movement besides Tommy fidgeting in his car seat was her breathing. She could see them clearly now as they stood under the fluorescent yellow light to the right of the bar door. People walked in and out—people that she and Jake both knew in the community, but it didn't seem to bother him.

The skinny, short brunette was dressed in a purple tank top and short miniskirt with black heels. She tried to light up a cigarette with her lighter, but it didn't work. Kristin could see Jake had changed out of his work clothes and had on his favorite baseball T-shirt with black jeans. He took out a lighter from his back pocket and lit the cigarette for her. The young woman giggled and took a drag.

Kristin watched as her husband of eight years put his hands on the back of the brunette's neck, caressing it with his fingers. He took the cigarette from her grasp, took a drag, and threw it to the ground, mashing it with the bottom of his sneaker. He leaned in and kissed her passionately, and the young girl threw her arms around his neck.

Kristin put the car in drive and pulled away from the curb. She was surprised she had reacted so calmly, instead of getting out of the car or marching up to them in a heated rage. Maybe it was the fact that despite how hurt she felt, she couldn't really say she was all that surprised. She had suspected Jake had other women, but she had never seen him with one until tonight. The part of her that was somewhat in denial over his indiscretions the last eight years had died when she saw the two of them snuggled close together. Her heart and stomach felt hollow. Kristin sighed as she pulled into the late-night pharmacy and filled Tommy's prescription while he slept soundly in his car seat.

An hour later, Tommy was fast asleep in his crib, and Kristin lay awake, waiting for Jake to walk through the door. She had no idea if she would confront him about what she had seen tonight or act as if nothing had happened. But when he strolled in at four in the morning, stumbling into bed, she made her decision. The time for a confrontation would come eventually.

CHAPTER TWELVE

A week later, Miguel stopped by for an unexpected visit. Kristin was surprised, for it had been so long since she had seen any of Jake's business partners. She was going over letters and numbers with Tommy when there was a loud knock at the front door. Kristin stood up, dusting off her jeans, and walked over to answer it.

She opened the front door and saw Miguel standing in the sunlight behind the screen door. He was dressed in dark sunglasses, khaki pants, and a form-fitting blue button-down shirt.

"Yes?" Kristin asked with one hand resting on the doorknob, reluctant to let him inside.

"Where's your husband?" he demanded, standing with his hands in his pockets.

"He's around back."

Without saying another word, Miguel marched down the three steps of the porch with a sense of urgency and headed to the back of the house where Jake was installing a swing set in the yard for Tommy.

"A." Tommy picked up the letter block and showed it to Kristin, who had locked the door as soon as Miguel walked away.

"Good boy." Kristin patted Tommy on the head, but she wasn't really paying attention to him. Instead, she walked slowly into the kitchen, trying to be as quiet as possible as she approached the kitchen window that gave a perfect view of the backyard. The window was cracked halfway to let air circulate in the house. She stood at the corner of the counter, sneakily peeking from behind the kitchen cabinet to see what was going on.

"What's going on, Jake?" Miguel asked. Jake was on his knees, installing the foundation of the swing set. "You don't know how to return calls these days?"

Jake turned his head and shaded his eyes from the sun's glare. "No, just been busy, that's all." Jake turned back to look up at the kitchen window, and Kristin instinctively hid from view.

He turned back to look up at Miguel, and she sighed with relief. He hadn't noticed her. Tommy called for his mother from the living room. It wouldn't be long before he ran into the kitchen to look for her, so Kristin crept out of the room as quietly as she could to where she had left him with his blocks.

"Yes, baby. Here, make a house, okay?" Kristin demonstrated to him, stacking one letter block on top of the other. She was proud of her little boy. He was learning so fast and growing so quickly. She kissed his rosy cheeks and tickled his little round belly that poked through a yellow T-shirt. His ear infection was practically gone after being on the antibiotics for a week, and he was back to his bubbly self, full of joy and laughter.

Tommy started to stack the blocks one on top of the other, as she had shown him. Kristin slowly crept back into the kitchen, keeping herself hidden.

Both men were now arguing, she could hear.

"What happened to the shipment that was supposed to go out last week? They called from Amarillo and said they never received it!" Miguel demanded.

"It went out as far as I know. I let you use my business for close to a year to ship your materials. Sometimes these things happen. Maybe it was a new courier that did the pickup, and it's just taking a little longer than expected. What the hell is so special about this package anyway?"

Jake's question appeared to infuriate Miguel, and he grabbed Jake by the neck. "We had an arrangement, remember? No questions asked." As nervous as she was about what was going on between them, Kristin couldn't help but feel somewhat amused at how the shoe was finally on the other foot. "And it's *our* business. I gave you that package over a week ago. There shouldn't have been a problem. You know Jessica was down at O'Brien's the other night running her mouth about how you got a brand-new car for the wife and got yourself a nice truck. And how all she got was the piece of crap you used to drive?" He released Jake and pushed him away from him. Jake almost lost his balance.

That's where his old truck went! Her hand clenched against her thigh as she continued to listen by the open window.

"I didn't believe it until I saw it for myself just now in your driveway. I'm surprised with this new cash flow you got going, you would want to ruin a good thing. If that package doesn't get where it needs to be, then I'll have to come back here and do something ugly. You wouldn't want that now, would you, Jake?" Miguel picked up a long piece of metal from the pile of tools and materials Jake had laid out earlier and played with it in his hand. Jake backed away from him.

"Whoa, Miguel, let's not do anything stupid. Look, just give me some time, and I'll call the courier to find out what happened to the package. Must be a reasonable explanation. Just give me some time."

Miguel laughed at him and threw the metal part on the ground near the tools. "You've been saying that since the day I met you."

"Can you keep it down? My wife is inside," Jake said, seeming to get his confidence back.

Miguel walked slowly over to him, and Jake stood in front of him. They were speaking much softer, and Kristin had to really focus on what they were saying.

"If they don't receive that package in Amarillo by next Monday, your wife and mistress will be planning your funeral. Got me?" Miguel took off his sunglasses and glared hard at Jake. Then he turned around and glanced up at the kitchen window.

Kristin was sure as day that he had seen her just then. But if he had, he didn't mention it to Jake. Quickly, she joined Tommy in the living room, going over his letters again.

"Kristin!" Jake came into the house, yelling as soon as Miguel peeled out of the driveway.

She stood up and watched him walk past her into the kitchen, sweating like he had just come out of a sauna. "Yes?" Her eyes followed him as he walked over to the fridge, opened it, and grabbed a beer from the bottom shelf.

"Damn, woman," he mumbled under his breath, but Kristin heard him. He took a big gulp, chugging on the bottle as if he were drinking water.

"What did he want?" she asked, folding her arms as she leaned against the kitchen wall.

He turned around, looked out the window, then looked back at her, wiping his lips with the back of his free hand. He had perspired through his gray T-shirt. He looked like a hot mess. She couldn't help feeling somewhat sorry for him—she knew he was in some kind of trouble.

"Were you listening to me, just now?" he asked, seeming a little paranoid.

"Listening to what? I was going over the ABCs with Tommy."

He looked at her, half believing the lie, and finished off the beer before setting down the bottle on the breakfast table.

"I have to go out for a bit. I'll be back in a few hours. Just leave my dinner covered in the microwave." He walked past her toward the door. He bent over, gave Tommy a kiss on the forehead, then plucked his red baseball cap off the coatrack.

"Where are you going?" Kristin asked, knowing she should have just let him walk out without saying a word. But she had a feeling he was going to the brunette she had seen him with at the bar last week—Jessica was her name, she had just learned.

Putting his baseball cap on his head and tucking some hair that stuck out from under the rim, he looked at her and replied, a bit amused, "Since when do I have to tell you where I'm going?"

She walked over to him and looked him square in the face. "You're going to see her, aren't you?"

"Who the hell are you talking about?" He laughed.

"I saw you the other night with her in front of the bar."

"I don't know what you think you saw, but whoever you saw—that wasn't me."

"Oh, don't give me that! I saw your truck in the parking lot of O'Brien's. I had to take Tommy to the hospital, and you weren't here. He had an ear infection, but you were too busy with your head up that woman's ass to notice your son was even sick."

Jake backhanded Kristin across the face so hard she stumbled sideways into the foyer table.

"You see what the hell you made me do!" he yelled down at her. He looked over at Tommy, who seemed frightened, then fixed his hat. "Pick up Tommy before he starts crying. I'll be home when I get home. Don't you ever talk to me about my son like that again. Ever. I'm serious," Jake warned her and then charged out the front door steaming mad.

Kristin held her face in one hand as she watched Jake drive away from the house without looking back.

"Mama." Tommy seemed as if he were about to cry, but she picked him up and hugged him.

"It's okay, Tommy. Mommy's okay."

Kristin locked the door then turned back to Tommy, who was still looking at her.

"Daddy go bye-bye?" he asked her.

"Yes, Daddy go bye-bye. Mommy needs to do something. So, stay here and watch cartoons, baby. Okay?" Kristin handed Tommy his sippy cup and turned the television on, flipping to a cartoon channel.

She walked over to the window to see Jake's truck drive down the small hill of their home onto the main road.

Quickly, she walked into the bedroom. She didn't know how long he would be gone. What package was Miguel referring to? Now she was certain Jake was involved in something illegal. As she looked under the bed and searched his drawers for anything, she had a knot in her stomach. She wanted to know the truth, but she didn't. She couldn't help but remember the day that Miguel showed up alone and uninvited. *"I'm not a very good man. But then there are things you wouldn't like about your husband if you knew them."*

Remembering Miguel's warning compelled her to continue searching through Jake's things. She recalled seeing a strange black duffel bag in the back of Jake's closet two days ago when she took Tommy to the park. She had been looking for the missing pair to Tommy's black sneakers. Kristin turned around and eyed the closet before opening it. She turned on the small overhead bulb and searched underneath Jake's pants and shirts. Finally, her hands felt something all the way in the back to the left.

Pulling it out with both hands, she practically fell backward onto the floor because of the weight. There it was, the bag she had seen. She ran to check on Tommy, who hadn't moved from in front of the television. He saw her and smiled and pointed to the green dinosaur running across the screen. Kristin looked out the front window. No sign of Jake. Running back inside her bedroom, she threw herself to the ground and unzipped the black duffel bag. Inside there had to be over a hundred stacks of hundred-dollar bills. She stared in shock.

"Oh my God." She didn't want to continue to search the bag, but she knew she had to.

She separated the stacks with her hands and saw a package torn open with at least twelve clear Ziploc bags filled with a talc-like white powder. Kristin picked up one bag to examine it. It could only be one thing—and with the stacks of money inside, there was no denying it. *Is this what Miguel was looking for?*

Suddenly, there was a noise coming from the front of the house. She could feel a giant lump in her throat. It sounded like a car motor running outside. Quickly, she stuffed the powder-filled plastic bags back into the torn package and moved the stacks of money to cover it as she had found it. Zipping the bag closed, Kristin placed it back into the exact position of the closet.

"Kristin!" Someone rapped at the front door.

It was Tiffany. She hadn't seen her since Tommy's birthday party.

"Tiffany?" Kristin ran to the door and welcomed her friend inside with a hug.

"Where's Jake?" she whispered, looking behind Kristin to see if he might be in the kitchen. "I didn't see his truck in the driveway when I drove by before."

"He went into town, but I don't know how long he will be." Kristin grabbed the blocks off the floor and put them into the toy basket at the side of the couch.

"Look, I'm really sorry the way things went down at Tommy's party. I had to come by and check on you. You haven't answered any of my calls." Tiffany bent over and gave Tommy a quick hug. His eyes were sleepy.

"Jake took my cell phone away."

"Do you know where it is?" Tiffany asked her.

"I think he put it in the safe deposit box in his closet. But it's locked and he always has the key with him."

"Well, you have to get to it. Or I can go buy you a new one and reconnect it to my line. He won't even know you have one."

"That's not my biggest problem right now," Kristin said, picking up Tommy, who had fallen asleep.

She signaled for Tiffany to follow her as she laid Tommy down in his crib. She kissed his forehead and pulled his blanket over him.

Then, grabbing Tiffany by the hand, she led her into her bedroom, leaving the door cracked open enough so she could hear if Jake pulled up in the driveway. Tiffany looked at her friend, confused, as they now stood in Kristin's bedroom.

"What's up?"

"I found something, Tiff." Kristin opened Jake's closet door.

"Okay, the way you just said that doesn't sound like it was something good." Tiffany watched as Kristin got down on her hands and knees and pulled a black bag out from the back of the closet. Kristin laid the bag before them and signaled for Tiffany to join her on the floor. Tiffany knelt beside the bag.

"You want *me* to open it?" Tiffany asked, and Kristin nodded as her friend placed her hands on the zipper reluctantly. "Ouch! You really need to get some carpeting in here." Tiffany rubbed one of her knees and began to unzip the bag when Kristin urged her to hurry up. "Okay—okay, I'm opening it."

"There is no telling when Jake will be back," Kristin said, worried.

Tiffany opened the bag with one swift motion and dropped back into a sitting position in sheer amazement.

"Kristin, there has to be close to a million dollars in this bag." She picked up stacks of cash in her hand, looking at the bills closely in disbelief.

Kristin kept her eye on the hallway through the open bedroom door.

"Keep looking. Underneath it. Move the money to the side and see what's under it."

"Holy shit!" Tiffany exclaimed as she saw the plastic bag filled with powder in the torn package. "Wow, Kristin, you know what this is, right? There must be twelve kilos of cocaine here. What kind of people is Jake involved with?" She picked up one of the bags, then placed it back quickly as if it had bitten her. She covered it again with the stacks of money.

Kristin looked over at Tiffany with some surprise that she even knew what a kilo of cocaine looked like.

Tiffany zipped the bag closed and gave it to Kristin to place back into the closet. They left the room quickly and walked into the kitchen together.

Turning to Kristin, she said seriously, "You and Tommy have to leave *now*. There is no question about it. I don't care how many friends Jake has on the force; he's going to prison for that when he gets caught. And if they decide to call child services on you, they will take Tommy away for good. They'll think you knew about what he was doing all this time, for sure. I mean… you didn't know about this, Kristin—right?"

"Of course not. How could you think that? I mean, I had a feeling he was doing something illegal. Suddenly, he was buying new clothes—the cars. But I never thought for a second he would be involved with drugs. But when Miguel came over ranting about a missing package and—"

"Kristin, you can't think about that now. If Jake is being watched and this place gets raided, they will take Tommy away from you and you'll go to jail. Get your things packed tonight! Let me go home and I'll call Joe. He'll know what to do. We'll figure something out. As soon as Jake falls asleep, call me. I'll know more then." Tiffany held Kristin's hand tightly in her own.

"Okay."

"Kristin, you have to do this. No backing out now, you hear me? Think about Tommy's future. This is no longer about you now."

"I know that," Kristin replied. She knew her friend was only trying to help, but as long as she could remember, it had never been about her.

CHAPTER THIRTEEN

Kristin lay in bed, staring up at the ceiling fan watching the blades rotate. Tommy had been asleep for hours already. She turned her head to look at the alarm clock on the night table. Eleven thirty. Jake had staggered in an hour before and had passed out on their sofa after finishing off the last two beers from the fridge. Now she could hear him snoring away.

She had packed Tommy's bags, as well as her own, two hours before Jake had come home. One black tote and a medium-size red backpack now stood in the back of Tommy's closet, hidden from plain view. She had to pack light, but still take all the essentials like her identification, Tommy's birth certificate, and some money she had saved from what Jake would give her during the week to run errands. She was tempted to take one or two stacks of the money she had found in the duffel bag that stood in Jake's closet. However, the thought of it being associated with drugs made her rethink the idea.

Did she really have the nerve to go through with this? Tiffany had told her to call her when Jake fell asleep, so she could know what the next step was. But she hadn't moved from the bed since a quarter past nine. She was not only scared of what would happen to her if Jake knew of her plans, but also what could happen to Tommy.

Jake began to snore heavily. *It's now or never.* Slowly, Kristin rose from the bed wearing the same clothes she fell asleep in—black sweatpants and a gray tank top. She planted both feet on the floor. With her feet, she searched for the white Converse sneakers she had placed by the bed earlier and slipped them on. Quickly, she threw on the black button-down sweater she grabbed from her dresser drawer.

Listening by the half-open door, she waited to hear if Jake had stopped snoring, but he hadn't. Quietly, she checked on Tommy in his crib to make sure he was still asleep. She knew she had to move quickly. She looked down at his small, round, angelic face. Gently, she tapped his double chin with her finger. How she adored her little boy. He was fast asleep on his back in his white llama T-shirt and dark-blue jogging pants. She took his sneakers out of his drawer and gently placed them on top. She left him in the crib until she took out both bags she had packed earlier. Putting the red backpack over both her shoulders and throwing the black tote over her right, she raised Tommy from the crib and placed him to rest his cheek upon her shoulder. Holding him in one arm, she opened the bedroom door and listened by the doorway.

Move Kristin! Move now!

All she needed to do now was make it down the dark hallway and grab the car keys from the foyer table drawer, which Jake checked every night to make sure they were in there. If the keys were anywhere but in that drawer, he would physically remind her where they belonged. Kristin's heart raced a mile a minute as she tiptoed down the hallway to the kitchen to call Tiffany. She prayed Tommy wouldn't wake up as she laid him gently across the chairs at the kitchen island and picked up the phone. Cradling the receiver against her ear, she listened as the phone trilled. She had a pretty good view of Jake sprawled out on the sofa asleep, in his dirty blue jeans and a dusty white T-shirt. An empty beer bottle lay on the floor under his arm that hung over the side of the couch. There was a small puddle of beer on the floor. He must have fallen asleep drinking.

"Tiff, it's me," Kristin whispered into the mouthpiece when Tiffany answered.

"He's asleep?"

"Yes," Kristin confirmed, not taking her eyes off him. "Tell me what to do. Tommy and I are ready to go with our bags." Her heart was beating so fast she could feel her pulse in her throat.

"Did you get your cell phone?"

"No, I don't have time. Quick, where do I go?" Kristin needed Tiffany to speak quickly. She had to leave.

"Okay, I'm gonna meet you down by Buxton Street near the old abandoned farmhouse. We'll park your car there and both of you will get into mine. I'm leaving now, so it should take me no longer than fifteen minutes. By the time I get there, you will already have arrived. Park behind the farmhouse but keep your headlights on so I know it's you."

"I don't think I can do this, Tiffany... what if he wakes up?" Kristin asked, frightened, as Tommy started to fidget in the chairs. She reached out and patted his head as best she could with one hand, and he stilled.

"Yes, you can, Kristin. You need to do this—you don't have a choice. You are protecting your son. Now get your ass out of that house and drive fast. Don't look back. Just drive."

"Okay."

"Go," Tiffany ordered. Kristin carefully placed the receiver on the hook, trying not to make too much noise.

She scooped up the bags and then Tommy. The weight of both bags combined with Tommy in her arms and the fear inside her heart almost rendered her immobile. Hushing him, she headed towards the foyer table. As she pulled open the small, square drawer to retrieve the car keys, it became stuck from some papers inside it. Bending her knees, feeling the pressure of all the weight on her now, Kristin tried her best to keep Tommy as still as possible. He had started to wake now, so she quickly pulled his little red Hot Wheel car from the tote bag and gave it to him to play with. She pushed the papers down and pulled harder on the little silver knob of the drawer. Finally, the drawer moved forward enough for her to reach in and grab the car keys using the tips of her fingers.

Jake groaned from the couch, and his other arm that was resting on one of the cushions dropped suddenly to his side.

Kristin froze in terror with her hand closed tightly around the car keys. She could swear she stopped breathing as she waited silently to see if Jake would open his eyes. But he didn't. Her heart was pounding so hard in her chest, she thought she would surely have a heart attack. Tommy started to fidget more in her arms. She had to get out of the house now. There was no time to waste. Her eyes fixated on the front door before her. Only the bottom lock was on, she noticed. She estimated about three feet to the door, and the couch Jake was on was about a foot away on her right. Her eyes glanced over to Jake for any sign of movement, but there was nothing. He wasn't snoring as loudly as he was before.

Is he really sleeping?

Trying to make as little noise as possible, she made her way toward the door, glancing a few times over her shoulder to keep him in sight. But he lay perfectly still. Kristin placed her hand on the silver metallic deadbolt, turning it slowly. She took one final glance over her shoulder before turning the doorknob to leave the house.

Cold terror flowed throughout her veins when she realized Jake was no longer there.

Breathing heavily now, Kristin turned completely around, her eyes scanning the dark living room. It was as if he had completely vanished into thin air. She moved toward the center of the room, frantically turning her head to the right and left. Tommy readjusted his head on her shoulder with his eyes still closed. The only light in the room was the moonlight pouring in through the large windows behind her. She looked down the long hallway ahead of her and the entrance to the kitchen, but she could hardly see anything from where she was standing. She turned back to the door.

Tommy raised his head off her shoulder, looking behind her. "Daddy."

Kristin's knees shook as she froze in place. She turned around to face the hallway again.

Jake stared at her, nostrils flaring.

"What the hell are you doing, Kristin?" He flipped the light switch on.

Kristin couldn't answer him. She just stood there, holding her son in one arm and the keys in the other hand, blinking in the suddenly bright room

"I asked you a question. What the *hell* are you doing?"

"I-uh. I don't…" Kristin tried to find the words, but none came to her.

"You leaving me? Is this what this is? *You're leaving me*, Kristin?"

Jake's eyes were bloodshot from drinking all night, and she knew his temper was about to flare out of control. She moved back toward the couch with Tommy. Tommy looked at her and then at Jake, confused about what was going on.

"I think you better put him down," Jake said, running his fingers through his hair.

"Take it easy, I—"

"Put him down *now!*" he demanded.

"Okay, okay." Shoving the car keys into her back jeans pocket, she dropped the backpack and tote bag to the floor and walked over to the sofa with Tommy, doing her best not to give her back to Jake.

"Stay here, baby." Kristin placed Tommy on the couch with his head against one of the cushions.

"Two bags?" Jake picked up the red backpack and examined it, feeling its weight and thickness. He shook the bag fiercely. "Got enough clothes in there? I'd really like to know where you thought you were going tonight with *my* son?" He kicked over the black tote with his foot and started to walk toward her.

"Jake, please don't do anything stupid." Kristin raised her hand and began to move backward toward the kitchen.

"I wake up to find *my* wife with *my* son about to walk out on me. Yet, you're the one standing there telling *me* not to do anything stupid." He chuckled and continued to follow Kristin into the kitchen.

She could hear Tommy calling for her from the sofa as she continued backing away from Jake. The sink behind her forced her to stop. Without turning around, she placed both hands behind her into the kitchen sink and felt for something to defend herself with.

"Jake, please let me go to him. He's crying for me." She tried to distract him from what she was doing behind her back by placing the focus on Tommy. She hoped he would take the bait, but he didn't.

"You're looking for this?" Jake put his arm behind her waist and pulled out a long, serrated bread knife.

Kristin moved away from the sink immediately and toward the breakfast table, afraid.

"No—Jake, I wasn't," she answered, faltering.

"You want to kill me, Kristin?"

His eyes locked with hers, and he lunged at her with the knife. Kristin tried to jump out of his way, but he caught her by the hair. Grabbing her hair in his hand, he wrapped it around his wrist twice and pulled her close to him, holding the blade of the knife against her throat.

"No! No! Let me go, Jake!" She struggled against him, trying to pull away, but the blade nicked the skin of her throat and she stopped moving instantly. He was going to kill her this time, she was sure of it.

"Let you go?" He laughed again, turning her head to face him with one hand. She moaned in pain. "What was it that we said to each other on our wedding day? I think I remember the vows going something like, 'Till death do us part.' You know what that means, Kristin?" He glared at her as he shoved her back into the sharp edge of the kitchen counter. Kristin groaned in pain. "That means you're not leaving me until we are both buried six feet under the ground!"

Holding on to her hair, Jake banged Kristin's head into one of the kitchen cabinets and stomped on the back of her knee. Falling to the floor, she cried out in pain. She lay there for a minute with her head near the door of the laundry room and her legs next to the kitchen table, trying to catch her breath. Her eyes were closed as he raged over her head, pacing around the kitchen. A bloody tooth lay on the floor next to her chin; it was one of her own. Her head throbbed badly, and she could feel the skin near her left eyebrow burning. Feeling her forehead with her fingers, she realized she was bleeding.

"I can't believe you would try to leave. Don't I give you everything you need? A nice home? A brand-new car, but no, that's not enough for you! Not enough for the princess! Huh? Ungrateful—that's what you are!" He bent over her head, spitting the words at her with vileness. "Where were you going with my son! Who's meeting you? ANSWER ME!" he shouted at her, squatting down near her body that lay motionless on the floor.

"You're not going to answer me?" Seeing her body lying on the floor unresponsive, Jake gave her one hard kick to the ribs, still holding the knife in his hand. "Hello! Answer me!" He kicked her again as she turned on her side and attempted to slither away from him, but the pain was paralyzing. She just could not move.

"Stop it!" Kristin cried weakly, putting one hand up in her defense then dropping it to her side.

"You're crying for me to stop? YOU'RE THE ONE MAKING ME DO THIS TO YOU! DON'T YOU GET THAT? So, who were you going to meet? It was Tiffany, right?"

He went to kick her again, but this time Kristin grabbed his black boot and pulled on it with all her might, hoping by some chance he would fall to the floor. Jake wiggled his foot free and instead kicked her in the face. Kristin rolled over to her other side. She thought of just lying there and letting him beat her to death when, out of nowhere, she heard her Tommy's voice.

"Daddy, why you hurt Mama?" Tommy cried, standing behind Jake. He was still holding his Hot Wheel car, his face full of fear.

Kristin struggled to open her eyes. "Tommy, go back," she said, her voice weak, barely audible.

Her right eye was becoming more swollen as each second passed. It would completely close soon, but at least she could still see out of both for the time being.

"Get inside, Tommy!" Jake barked at him. Tommy started to cry for his mother.

Get up, Kristin! Get up, she fought with herself. She couldn't let him kill her in front of her son. That couldn't be Tommy's last memory of her.

Out of the corner of her eye, Kristin could see a long piece of wood next to the door of the laundry room as Jake yelled at Tommy to leave the room. It was the four-by-four Jake had left there from an old job he had done.

Tommy pulled on the hem of Jake's pant leg, but Jake continued to yell at him to get out of the kitchen. Kristin watched as Tommy stood by innocently, enduring his father's rage. With Jake's back to her, she started to slide closer to the laundry room door to reach for the rectangular block of wood. Tommy pulled again on Jake's pants, and Jake backhanded Tommy across his face, causing him to fall onto his back.

A fire ignited inside Kristin the moment she saw Tommy fall to the ground, his favorite little car slipping out of his hands. He lay there on the floor, hysterical. Enraged, Kristin managed to find the strength to wrap her hands around the block of wood as Jake yelled at Tommy for getting in his way. She could feel the adrenaline rising inside of her as she sprang to her feet and swung the four-by-four against the back of Jake's head. On impact, Jake fell to the floor unconscious. There was no way she would allow him to hurt her son. Not now and not ever. Kristin walked over to him slowly and looked at his face. His eyes were closed—he was out. She felt for a pulse, and felt it beating against her fingers. Dropping the wood to the ground, she picked Tommy up in her arms and kissed his tear-stained cheeks, which were reddened from the slap earlier.

"It's okay, baby. It's okay," she soothed him.

Tommy stared at his mother's bloody and bruised face, and his cries became even louder. Jake had slapped him so hard, his cheeks were fire red. She hugged him close to her.

"I'm so sorry, baby. Mommy is so sorry. That will never happen again, I promise you."

With each step forward, her thighs screamed out for her to stop, but she had to keep going. Her breathing became more difficult, her ribs broken for sure. Reaching the front door, she grabbed her backpack and tote with Tommy in her arms. Not knowing when Jake would come to, she had to move fast.

Hurriedly, fighting through the pain, she unlocked the doors of the car with the key remote. Kristin almost toppled over as she tried to get Tommy buckled into his car seat. She couldn't get one of the clips to snap into the holder between his legs and only had time to secure the seat belt straps across his chest. Running on fumes now, everything inside of her was begging for her to stop. But she had to keep going for Tommy—for herself. She threw open the driver's door and got in. Her fingers shook as she pressed the button to start the ignition. She backed out of the driveway, slamming her foot against the accelerator. She had to get to Tiffany. She needed to make it to that farmhouse before she passed out, which she was sure would be soon.

Tommy continued to cry in his car seat despite her efforts to calm him down. She started to sing one of his favorite cartoon songs.

"Everything is going to be okay." She smiled at him through the rear-view mirror, but he looked away and out the window at the rain that had begun to fall.

Kristin didn't know how much longer before her right eye would be completely closed. She could barely see the lines on the road, and switched the high beams on and off to help her.

"Mama, I scared."

"I know you are, baby. Just hold on. We're almost there." Kristin wished she could find his toy car. It worked wonders to calm him down. But in all the chaos and confusion, she couldn't remember which bag she had packed it in.

She was now coming up on the taillights of a blue Subaru in front of her that was riding his brakes. She honked at the driver. *Probably an old man*, she thought.

"What are you doing? Move!" she yelled and flashed her lights. She could feel her eye swelling and was scared she soon wouldn't be able to see. He was going way too slow. The car finally switched lanes to let her pass.

She knew by memory that they were about to meet the turn onto Buxton Road. Then Kristin noticed a blurry shape ahead of her. She blared her horn to alert the other driver she was coming toward them. But she couldn't tell if he was in her lane or heading in the opposite direction—her vision was diminishing and she could only see through the left eye. She couldn't slow down because the car behind her was following too closely. So, she continued down the road at sixty miles per hour. She was sure Tiffany was going to leave, thinking that she had chickened out.

Blinking her eyes again, the shape ahead of her was now becoming clearer. Kristin started to panic—the blurry shape was a stalled fourteen-wheeler stuck in the middle of the road. There were orange cones all around the truck. She hadn't seen them or the driver who had been waving his hat through his window to signal her to go around the truck. Kristin quickly slammed on the brakes in fear of hitting the truck ahead, but the car behind her slammed into her rear end, sending her flying into the side of the stalled fourteen-wheeler.

"Oh God!" she screamed as the car flipped over and skidded onto its roof down the road, veering off toward the trunk of a tall tree ahead of them.

Everything fell black.

***

Kristin woke up to the sounds of two unfamiliar male voices shouting back and forth at each other. Her face was burning, and there was broken glass all around her. Realizing what had happened, she called out for Tommy.

"WE HAVE TO GET HER OUT—THERE'S GASOLINE ALL OVER THIS ROAD!" a male voice yelled.

"Miss! Can you reach for your seat belt?" Kristin heard a man ask her. She tried to turn her head in his direction, but she could barely move. She moaned from the pain that was starting to overwhelm her.

As she squinted through her left eye, she could feel pieces of glass above her eyelashes. There were branches and leaves sticking through the broken windshield. It suddenly dawned on her that she was upside down, and there was a blurry outline of a man's head poking its way through the broken, jagged window.

"My... son. You have to get my son." Kristin strained to get the words out. An intense pain overcame her, starting from her chest to her abdomen. She tried to feel for the seat belt release with her fingers.

"You have a little boy with you?" the man asked and called out to his friend, "CARL! GET ON THE OTHER SIDE. THERE'S A KID IN THE BACK SEAT!"

"Come on, Miss, try to unhook the seat belt," he told Kristin again and threw his hands over her lap, trying to find the release button as well. "Carl, what's going on back there?"

"The seat belt is stuck—I don't think the kid is breathing," a male voice replied from behind her.

"No! No! No!" Kristin screamed out in a panic, more alert now.

"What's going on here?" An officer arrived on the scene. "Just got the call a few minutes ago." He got down on one knee on the other side of the car, being careful not to press his hand on the broken glass. "How many are in here?" he asked, peeking his head in.

"We got a kid in the back. The mother is up here with me."

The officer reached his head in further to take a look at the back seat. "Carl, is that you? Is that your truck out there?" Then he looked up at the front seat, where the good Samaritan worked feverishly to free Kristin. "Oh my God!"

"You know her?" James asked the officer.

"That's Jake Summers's wife. I'll go radio to get the ETA on that ambulance," he said and ran off.

"Get my son out! Leave me alone—get my boy out!" She swatted at the man's hands that were trying to free her. He found the buckle, unhooked the belt and moved it away from the midline of her body. Kristin dropped out of the seat, but she continued to push the man away. "You have to get my son out. Don't help me!"

"James, this thing is going to blow. I can't get the seat belt to open." The man tugged at Tommy's seatbelt, trying to unhook the two straps that secured his little body.

"Here, use my hunting knife." The officer reappeared, handing Carl a knife from his back pocket.

As Carl started to cut away at the straps, a sizzling noise prompted the officer beside him to turn back. A line of fire was heading towards them from the fourteen-wheeler straight to Kristin's car.

"You gotta move fast," the officer yelled at them.

"Come on, you son—" Carl tugged at the strap, cutting it. "Just a bit more."

"I have to get you out of here," the man in her window said. "Come on!"

"Not without my son!" Kristin protested firmly again, pushing his hands away as he gripped her by the shoulders.

"Got him!" Carl yelled out as Tommy fell out of his car seat and into his hands. The officer grabbed Tommy from him, running to safety. Carl followed right on his heels.

"Come on, now." James grabbed Kristin under her arms and yanked her out the car window by the shoulders. Getting a clearer image of him now that she was closer, she could see he was an older man, probably in his early sixties, with a gray beard and a baseball cap covering his square head.

"Did anyone else get hurt?" she asked.

"No, the driver made it out just in the nick of time. He's over there, giving a report to the other officer. Ambulance is on its way. Don't you worry."

Seeing the old man struggling, the truck driver ran over and draped Kristin's arm around his shoulder, and they proceeded to run away from the crash site. They ran toward an officer and Carl, who were already at the side of the road, hovering over Tommy. Just as they made it off the main road, a loud, fiery explosion rocked the area. Kristin looked behind her and saw her car still on its roof and the truck engulfed in flames. In the far distance, she could hear the sirens of a fire truck and ambulance heading toward them as the kind men laid her beside her son on the ground.

Kristin could feel herself getting cold. She turned her head to the left and could see a police officer hovering over Tommy's small body. It was the same officer who told her that day to work things out with Jake—Officer O'Neil. He counted out loud, repeatedly pressing down on Tommy's little chest with one hand over the other, while the other man Carl, gave rescue breaths

"Tommy!" She wailed loudly for her baby boy. She wanted to close her eyes, but she fought off the urge. He had to be okay. She stretched out her hand for him, but as close as she was to him, she was still too far. Tears flowed, blinding the remaining good eye she could open. This couldn't be happening. No, this wasn't happening.

His little face and white llama shirt were covered with broken glass. Blood stained his beautiful brown hair and trickled down his forehead.

"Come on, kid!" The officer pressed down harder with his hands over Tommy's chest. "One, one thousand, two, one thousand."

This can't be real. She tried to reach out for his little arm again. She felt so helpless.

"Tommy, wake up!" she cried, trying to move closer to him. One of the men stopped her.

"Don't move, ma'am. Help is on the way." James tried to comfort her as the other man continued to work on her son.

Kristin turned her head to look up at the dark sky. There was nothing but darkness around her. She started to hum Tommy's favorite song. This was where her life would end, she thought, on this dark night, on this dark road beside her son. The pain she was feeling would soon be over. At least she would be with her Tommy. She knew he was headed to the other side, and she would soon meet him there.

"Wait for me," she whispered, continuing to fix her gaze on the sky above her. She could barely hear the voices of the men around her. Everything was becoming blurry once again. Pain was starting to leave her; all she felt was cold. *Let go, Kristin. It's okay, just let go.*

"Stay with me, now. Don't you give up! Hold on!" the shadowy figure of the older man yelled at her, holding her hand. "Carl, where the hell is that ambulance?"

Kristin could hear the sirens. "Over here!" someone called out.

"The medics are here!" shouted another voice nearby.

"Tell them to hurry, man! She won't hold on much longer. Stay with me. Stay with me, sweetie." He squeezed her hand tighter in his.

Her eyes closed, then there was nothing. Lights out.

CHAPTER FOURTEEN

Dr. David Landry was sitting in the hospital's break room, looking at the empty plastic wrapper of a chocolate chip muffin he had just finished eating. Sipping coffee from a blue-and-white spiraled paper cup, he thought back to the events of the night before.

David had walked into his house after pulling a double shift at the hospital. He found his girlfriend, Allison, throwing some clothes into a brown leather suitcase that lay open on the bed they had shared for the last two years.

"What's up?" he asked, placing his backpack onto the white carpeted floor of their bedroom. He looked at the slender woman pulling clothes out of their closet. Without looking at him, she continued to throw them into the open suitcase, her long red hair hiding her face.

She glanced over her shoulder at him and said, "Look, David, this has been coming for a long time now." She turned back and placed the rest of the clothes on the bed into the suitcase and threw the flap over, zipping it closed.

David took a step toward her. "What are you talking about, Allison? What's been a long time coming?"

Allison sat on the edge of the bed, her hair flowing perfectly around her shoulders. She reached with one hand under the bed, feeling for the other pair to her black pumps and pulled it out from underneath the bed skirt.

"I'm not happy," she said calmly, slipping on her shoes.

"Really? This is news to me."

"We are just headed in different directions. You're more focused on your patients than having a life with me."

"Allison, this is my job. I'm out there saving *lives*. I'm a surgeon! You knew that when you met me."

"And what about when you're not at the hospital? You're down at that damn center helping *those* people out almost every day since Josh died."

"Don't bring Josh into this, don't do that. This is not about him and you know it."

"How long are you going to try to make it up to him? It wasn't your fault he died." She touched his cheek, but he pushed her hand away.

"I'm not trying to make anything up to him. I want to help."

"It's like I don't know who you are anymore. We don't talk. We live like roommates. No, I take that back. Because at least roommates see each other more than we do. There is no intimacy between us anymore. No connection. When you're not focused on your patients, you're always helping that pastor what's-his-face—with his million 'good causes,' ignoring me and what *I* need. Whatever you do is not going to bring him back. He's gone, David. Josh is gone," she said firmly.

"Don't you think I know that he's gone!" he fired back at her.

"There's no time for me in your life. And I want more. I *need* more." She shrugged at him. "I just don't think we are right for each other. I don't share your passion for medicine or this new calling you have to help the needy. I want different things. I'm not going to be a housewife, waiting for you to come home if and when you do decide to come home at all."

"That's nice, Allison. You couldn't have told me this before I put a ten-thousand-dollar ring on that finger. It was less than a month ago." He pointed at the beautiful princess cut diamond on her perfectly manicured finger.

"You want this ring, David? Is that what you're upset about—that you had to buy this ring for me? You know, I really don't even think you wanted to get engaged. I think you just saw it as the next step, a way to shut me up. You're always doing the right thing."

Taking his hand, she turned it over and placed the ring into it.

Staring down at the ring, David shook his head then shoved it deep into his pocket. "I don't believe this."

Allison stared at him with tears in her eyes, but he couldn't tell if they were genuine. "We just outgrew each other. I just don't love you anymore."

She grabbed the handle of the suitcase from the bed and placed it upright on its wheels.

"Have you met someone else? Is that what this is about?" He sat down on the bed now with his head hung down.

"Does it really matter?" she asked.

"Yeah, it matters."

"Your fiancée is telling you that she is unhappy. That she is leaving you.

I have a suitcase in my hand, and all you can do is ask if I'm sleeping with someone else? Don't you see? You were waiting for an out. So, take it. I'll get the rest of my things out of here by next Tuesday. Please don't be here." She kissed him on the cheek and said, "Goodbye, David."

Grabbing her leather jacket off the bedroom windowsill, she steered the brown Louis Vuitton suitcase out of the room and walked out of the condominium they had purchased together a year ago. David wondered why he just sat there and didn't run after her. But he felt no desire to. She was right. He knew their relationship was coming to an end. He had felt it for a long time. He just didn't think it would happen so soon. When his younger brother Joshua had died six months ago, things started to really take a turn for the worse.

He still remembered when Josh had phoned him to get a ride home late one night. Josh was an architect and had started to work pro bono on housing projects, drawing up building plans. That night in question, Josh had been working around the clock to finish the plans for the extension wing of the community center. His car was in the shop, and he really didn't want to wait for a bus after such a long day. But David hurried him off the phone, scolding him for interrupting his sleep. He told Josh he was nuts for not leaving earlier since it was close to midnight. It was his choice to be down there, David reasoned with himself when he hung up. He wasn't about to drive there when he had to be at work two hours later.

But that wasn't the only reason. David never drove into the inner-city developments outside of Parsons County. Maybe it was because he felt guilty for being better off financially than the people who lived there, or maybe he had become just as self-absorbed with his own life, the way Josh used to be, to even care about it. But his little brother understood, as he always did, when David told him he couldn't pick him up. A little disappointed, Josh told David he would take the bus. The next day, while Allison and David were both asleep in bed, they were awakened by two uniformed officers who showed up at their front door. Josh had been shot trying to stop three kids from beating up on a young boy. Josh had thrown himself in front of the boy as a shield when one of the attackers had pulled out a gun. The bullet pierced his carotid artery, and he bled out beside the young boy just before the police and ambulance arrived at the scene. Just like that, David's little brother was gone.

David was a surgeon and had saved many lives, but there was not a single thing he could do that night to bring back his baby brother. At his brother's funeral, David was surprised to see just how many friends Josh actually had. It was then that David realized he and Josh were not as close as they used to be.

Josh had once had a drinking problem that David tried to help him with. But after many failed attempts at rehab, David had finally given up on supporting him two years ago when Josh showed up intoxicated at their cousin's wedding. In the middle of the best man's speech, Josh had burst through the hall doors screaming, "DOES ANYONE WANT TO DAAANCE?" Many of the guests laughed, but the best man, the bride and groom—not to mention their parents— did not find it funny one bit. Instead, they felt humiliated as they always did when Josh showed up at a family function late and plastered as usual.

But then about a year ago, David had received a phone call from his little brother. He was so excited that he had quit drinking and was attending regular meetings, and had told David he felt as if "his chains were broken." He said he had stumbled upon a church when he was having a rough day and met a pastor who welcomed him with open arms—Pastor Greene. The pastor had done so much for him, counseled him and helped him work through some emotional issues at the root of his drinking and reckless lifestyle.

Josh was so enthusiastic about the transformation he was undergoing. David could hear him smiling through the phone as he rambled on about how much God had changed his life. David could even have sworn that at one point Josh was crying. He hadn't heard his brother cry since Josh had been a little boy. He told David that he wanted to do some good and had joined Pastor Greene on a community pro bono project. David was dumbfounded when Josh told him this. He couldn't believe that his spoiled little brother was not only sober, but finally doing something for others that didn't benefit himself. When Josh begged him to meet him for lunch one afternoon, David's curiosity got the better of him and he obliged.

On the day of their lunch date, as much as he could see a change in Josh, he couldn't help being wary of this new pastor who had suddenly entered his brother's life. He must have asked him three different ways if the pastor had taken or requested any extravagant donations for his church. Josh replied that Pastor Greene was a good man, and it was never about what others could do to help him but how he could be of service to others.

David regretted his attitude much later. Instead of listening to his brother, who was trying to share an intimate piece of his life with him, he'd criticized Josh's faith and called Pastor Greene a brainwasher who made Josh drink the Kool-Aid. But at no time did his brother get angry. Instead, he told David he had to get back to work and gave him a great bear hug, which David ended a bit abruptly, feeling awkward. How he wished he had allowed that hug to continue for as long as Josh wanted to.

David could still picture Josh waving goodbye to him before he turned down the block of the café where they had eaten lunch, then faded into the crowded street.

After Josh's death, David found himself sinking into a great depression. He started to think about his own life in retrospect. He may not have been as ready or open to a spiritual awakening, but he was ready for "more," just as Allison had stated before she walked out on him. He realized that all this time, he had been going through the motions. It was a never-ending cycle—home, work, home. Things had become so routine, and the depression had become so intense, that he found himself having to drink a shot of whiskey every night just to help him fall asleep. Even Allison had noted the change in him.

Several days after Josh died, Pastor Greene stopped by to ask if David would like to help out with the community project. He remembered that day quite vividly.

"I'm not an architect, I'm a doctor," David told the pastor.

"That's okay. It's all hands on deck, as I always say." Pastor Greene smiled as they stood outside in the hallway in front of David's door. David could see why Josh was so fond of him. The pastor had a welcoming smile and his voice was calming. He thought about inviting him into his house. But there was a part of him that also held him responsible for Josh's death. He reasoned if Josh had not been working on that project, he would never have been killed.

"I don't know… I'm very busy at work. You know I'm—"

"A surgeon, yes. Josh told me. He was very proud of you. Look, I know your brother believed in this project just as much as I did."

"Yeah, a lot of good it did him. Working on that project is what got him killed," David said, bracing against his door with one arm on the doorframe.

"No, David, he was murdered trying to do the one thing he loved to do—helping others. His death was not in vain. I'm sure it would mean a lot to him if you came on board to see that the work he invested so much time in wasn't for nothing."

David shook his head, running his fingers quickly through his hair. He stood up straighter and looked the pastor square in the face. "You know my brother used to preach to me about how God had done so much for him, changed his life. The same God that took it from him." David was aiming to see if he could strike a nerve. He carried so much grief inside, and he wanted the pastor to feel just a taste of that.

But the pastor placed his hand on David's shoulder. "David, I know you're grieving. I know you loved your brother very much. It was a terrible loss for all that knew him well. We all miss him. Think about it; just think about it. Call me when you're ready." The pastor patted him on the shoulder and gave him his business card, then left.

After that night, David took several days thinking over whether or not he even wanted to get involved at all with the community center. He felt he owed it to his brother to help finish the project, but he was more motivated by the guilt of not being there for him that fateful evening. So, reluctantly, he called up Pastor Greene, who was more than overjoyed for him to help out.

After several months of renovation, the new and improved community center was almost complete. But despite the generous donations from the local businesses to help with the cost of supplies, they were still forty thousand dollars short of meeting their goals. But David, in those several months, had now found a reason to wake up in the morning. He was still a dedicated surgeon, but now he had a purpose outside of medicine. It felt good to be part of something that his brother had believed in so strongly. Throughout that time, he and the pastor had grown quite close. As crazy as it seemed, anytime he was with the pastor, he could feel Josh was there with them, and he loved that.

Pastor Greene often invited David over for dinner at his house. At first, the invite came as a way of thanking David for all the hard labor he had put in at the center. But soon, it became an open invitation even when he wasn't working at the community center. David enjoyed all the funny stories that the pastor and his family shared with him. Pastor Greene had become just as fond of David as David was of him. He was like part of the family now. And David was just as grateful to him for the company. His parents were always away vacationing, and he hardly ever saw them, especially with the hours he worked at the hospital. He admired the pastor's family and how they treated each other with love and respect. He hoped that he would be able to have that one day—with a family of his own.

David could understand what Allison was talking about when she said she had felt the disconnect between them for months. He had changed, but he felt it was for the better. Now he thought twice before throwing away three hundred dollars on a three-course meal when it could be better spent on new materials for the center or helping indigent families who could barely afford to have one meal a day.

The jury was still out, however, on whether he believed in God or not. Pastor Greene reminded him a lot of his grandfather, who was always preaching about a loving, merciful father that looked down on him from heaven. But where was that mercy the night Josh died?

He had sensed Allison was getting frustrated with him helping out at the community center. When he told her his ideas for volunteering his services as a doctor down at the Riverbank clinic, she was somewhat supportive. But when he told her they needed to cut back their spending habits and go out once a month instead of every weekend, she grilled him so hard it felt as if she could sear the skin right off him with her glare. She had said she was accustomed to a certain lifestyle. Just because he felt the compelling urge to make a difference, it didn't mean she should have to suffer for it. He obviously couldn't fault her for being honest with him. She wanted more, and he just didn't feel the desire to give her that. So, when she left last night, he let her go. The only problem now was that with Allison gone, he would be home alone. Being alone was not something he was good at. Maybe that was the reason he had stayed with Allison as long as he had.

"David? David? Hey—are you all right?" Ned Daniels, the head of cardiothoracic surgery, stood by the open door of the break room in blue scrubs. He was David's mentor. A tall, slender middle-aged black man with no filter, he always said exactly what was on his mind. Whether a person wanted to hear what he had to say or not, that was a different story. David never saw him miss a day at work, and he was the most dedicated and brilliant surgeon David had ever met. But then Daniels really had no other life outside of work. With two failed marriages and his latest love interest taking a job in Arizona, the job felt more like his better half. Still, David aspired to be just as inspired as Daniels was about medicine.

For as long as he could remember, David always wanted to become a doctor. One Christmas morning, when he was about seven, he'd snuck out of his room to the family room where a six-foot Christmas tree stood in its center. Still believing in Santa Claus at the time, he was anxious to see how many gifts were left for him under the tree. He knew he should have waited until everyone opened their presents together as they did every Christmas morning, but he just couldn't contain his excitement. Grabbing one of the brightly colored Christmas gifts labeled for him, he'd ripped off the wrapping paper and revealed one of the items he had listed on his Christmas letter to Santa. It was a toy doctor set with a stethoscope and blood pressure cuff. He could still remember listening to his mother's heart with the cushiony black bell of the scope.

But what really pushed David into attending medical school many years later was when he lost his grandfather due to a misdiagnosis of pneumonia when it was really a pulmonary embolism. Ever since his grandfather's death, David had been on a mission to become the best general surgeon so no kid would ever have to lose his grandfather the way he lost his. However, Daniels constantly did his best to convince David that he belonged in cardiothoracic surgery.

David turned and looked over at Ned, who combed back his graying hair with one hand, seeming a bit anxious.

"What's up?"

"Got two coming in. From the description of the accident, it sounds like I could use your help."

Immediately, David rose from the table and pushed in his chair. Dressed also in blue scrubs, he ran down the long corridor after Ned. Near the emergency room doors, Daniels threw David a yellow gown that the medical team wore in trauma cases to protect themselves from being exposed to blood and other body fluids. David quickly pulled it on, as did Daniels, and tied the strings at his back.

"Gloves?" Daniels asked.

"In my pocket. Ready to go," David replied and waited outside with Ned for the ambulance to arrive.

David could feel the eeriness of the night as they waited by the emergency room doors. With sirens blaring, the ambulance pulled up. Ned yanked open the back doors of the ambulance while the driver and a paramedic jumped out of the rig, spitting out vitals to both doctors as they rushed the patient through the tall, white emergency room doors.

"Three-year-old male child involved in a two-car collision. Unresponsive when we arrived on the scene. A passerby stopped and was performing CPR when we arrived. He has a very weak pulse. Pulse fifty-five. BP seventy-two over fifty-two." As the paramedic continued to give Dr. Daniels the rest of the vitals, Tommy went into cardiac arrest.

"We need a crash cart, stat!" yelled Daniels as he wheeled the little boy into a trauma room with David. Three nurses and a resident came running to their side, one with a crash cart.

"David, go wait on the next incoming," Daniels yelled as he held the paddles of the charging defibrillator in his hands. "Clear!" he ordered, and everyone moved back from the bed.

David started to run toward the door as a nurse signaled the next ambulance had arrived. "Get me Morrison, now!" David yelled at one of the nurses as he hit a silver button on the wall that automatically opened the emergency room doors where the ambulances pulled up.

Within seconds, Morrison, a twenty-four-year-old intern, was by his side dressed in scrubs and a yellow gown.

"Gloves," David ordered as he put on his own pair of blue nitrile gloves.

"Yes, sir!" Morrison replied and assisted David in opening the back doors of the ambulance.

A young female paramedic immediately jumped out from the back, pulling the stretcher forward and unloading it with David's assistance. Morrison grabbed the front, and they headed through the emergency room doors.

"Car accident. Thirty-year-old female with trauma to the head and chest. Glass fragments around the eye. One eye is swollen shut."

"All of this happened in the accident?" Morrison asked, looking at the bruises by her ribs.

Dismissing Morrison, the female paramedic read off the vitals to David. "Pulse one-eighteen, BP eighty-six over fifty but not stable, respirations were at sixteen breaths per minute and shallow. Looks like she may have some fractured ribs. She's been slipping in and out of consciousness, asking for her son."

"He just arrived a few minutes ago." David wheeled Kristin into another trauma room with Morrison to examine her more thoroughly. "Okay, on three," he said to Morrison. With the help of the paramedics, they moved her off the ambulance stretcher onto a hospital bed.

Checking the airway first, David grabbed his stethoscope from around his neck and listened to Kristin's heart. Muffled heart sounds. Looking at Kristin's neck, he could see the jugular vein was distended. David and the intern rapidly inspected the rest of Kristin's body, removing fragments of glass from her skin. After another nurse finished inserting an IV line, she hooked Kristin up to the monitor so her vitals could be monitored continuously.

Another nurse connected a bag of fluid to Kristin's IV as David took shears from his pocket and cut Kristin's blood-stained tank top down the middle. He was immediately taken aback by the redness of her chest.

David watched for changes in her heart rhythm, as did Morrison. Kristin's heart rate was increasing while her blood pressure was dropping precipitously. With years of experience in the emergency room assessing patients after motor vehicle accidents, his instinct screamed that she had a rupture of the muscle tissue of her heart. *Cardiac tamponade*, David thought. A dangerous buildup of fluid around Kristin's heart was squeezing it and causing her pulse to increase and her blood pressure to plummet.

"Get her to the OR, stat!" David ordered. "Tell them to get the ultrasound up there, now! Prep for a pericardiocentesis. I have to get that fluid off her heart or we're going to lose her!" This patient was not about to die on his watch, he told himself.

"Morrison, run and get Daniels. Tell him to meet me up there!"

David knew this was out of his field. He had started off wanting to be a heart surgeon but changed to a specialty in general surgery, and he had only performed the procedure twice: once under the supervision of Daniels during his residency and once on a camping trip where a man had sustained a stab wound in a fight.

"Do we have a name?" David asked the paramedic, who had stayed to assist until they reached the OR.

"Kristin Summers. Her identification was found at the scene."

"Kristin?" he asked the paramedic, and she nodded. They turned the corridor and were now heading into the OR. The paramedic stayed outside while the young doctor and nurses rushed Kristin into the room.

"Kristin? Kristin, can you hear me?" David tried to get her to open her eyes and respond. But Kristin's eyes felt so heavy she couldn't open them.

"My baby," she said weakly and then blacked out again.

The anesthesiologist scrambled to place her oxygen mask, and a nurse hooked her up to a heart monitor as David prepared to do the pericardiocentesis. He raised his head and looked at the monitor as the technician assisted with the ultrasound.

Focus, David, he said to himself. Taking a deep breath, he knew there was no margin for error. He had to be careful not to puncture the lungs. He felt for the fifth intercostal space with one gloved finger at the sternum's left side and picked up the needle that the nurse had set on the tray in front of him. Carefully, he pushed the bevel of the needle under the skin and aspirated fluid from the pericardium.

Just then, Morrison entered the OR with Daniels after having scrubbed in.

"What's up, David?" Daniels said behind a white mask. "Talk to me." He stood beside David as he watched him withdraw the syringe filled with fluid.

"Cardiac tamponade. That's why I sent for you," David said, placing the needle on the tray. A scrub nurse removed it immediately.

"Did good." Daniels patted his shoulder. "BP rising and stable," Daniels said, watching the pulse rate decrease and the blood pressure start to slowly go up.

Then out of nowhere, Kristin's heart rate spiked.

"What the hell?" David's jaw dropped as he watched the monitor in disbelief.

"Must be a laceration in the myocardium. Make room. Nurse!" Daniels signaled that he was going to enter the chest cavity and to get the instruments ready. The anesthesiologist transitioned Kristin from moderate sedation into general anesthesia as the nurses prepped her for surgery. David stepped aside, allowing Daniels to take the lead. Everything was happening so fast, and the tension thickened as the team desperately fought to save Kristin's life.

"Blood pressure dropping fast, Doctor," one of the scrub nurses said to Daniels, keeping an eye on the monitor.

"Blood is filling up in here. More suction, David!" Daniels said, working frantically inside the chest cavity of the young woman on the table in front of them.

For some reason, David found himself quietly praying that God would spare her life. He had no idea why. But it was compelling, to say the least. The night would soon be over. The question was—would she make it?

CHAPTER FIFTEEN

David sat across from his mentor on the bench in the locker room. Ned Daniels was going over what had happened to the little boy in surgery as he got ready to leave for the day.

"We tried everything," Daniels said, slamming his locker door shut. "His body went into shock, and there were just too many internal injuries. Just couldn't get to the source of the bleeding in time. He bled out on the table... God knows what it would have been like if he had woken up. He was down for so long."

Daniels shook his head hard as if trying to erase the memory of performing CPR on the little boy after he arrested on the operating table. "We wouldn't be able to know what kind of neuro deficits he would have had."

"Damn...it was touch and go with her for a moment there as well." David sighed, imagining how awful the mother would feel when she learned that her boy had died.

"You've been hanging out a lot with that pastor down at the center. Right?"

"So?" David asked

"Well, do you consider yourself to be a God-fearing man?" Ned asked David as he stood up, grabbing his designer windbreaker from the bench. He threw his duffel bag over his shoulder.

David shook his head. "I don't know. When I see bad things like this happen to young kids, I just don't know."

"Well, then, ask your friend, the pastor, to say a prayer for that woman. Because when she wakes up and hears the news of her son, she's going to need it," Daniels added and left David alone to his thoughts.

David heard a voice call out from behind. "Dr. Landry!"

"Hey, Julia. How's it going?" he said, turning around and greeting the attending orthopedic surgeon. Her picture ID that hung low around her neck read *Julia Kramer, Orthopedics.*

"Do you have a moment? I had them run the extra scans you requested after surgery. I want to show you something."

"Sure." He followed the dark brunette in her long white lab coat. She led David into one of the hospital rooms.

Placing an x-ray on the lightbox for David to see, Julia began to speak about the image.

"This rib right here looks like it was broken before. Actually, there are a couple of them right here, from old fractures that healed. I also saw a few spots on the head CT," Dr. Kramer said.

"What do you mean?" David carefully looked over the images in his hand, also seeing what Dr. Kramer was referring to.

"What I'm saying is, I think this woman was being abused." She looked at David with a raised eyebrow.

"Thanks, Julia." David knew she was pushing toward recommending that he investigate further. He thought about doing so as he headed over to Kristin's room. He sensed that this was much more complex than a mere automobile accident.

Julia yelled out as David walked away, "She's going to be in that cast the next eight weeks for that tibia. The ribs should heal in about twelve. It's gonna be a while before she feels like herself again." David gave her a thumbs up from a few feet away to signal that he had heard her and then entered the elevator.

As the elevator doors closed, David pressed the button to the fourth floor—ICU. That was where Kristin would be after the life-saving surgery that had just taken place. He thought to himself that the emotional pain of losing her son would be far worse and may possibly hinder recovery. Maybe it was better to not make her aware of her son's death until she was out of the woods.

David made his rounds, checking on a few other patients who were in the same wing. Then he went in to see Kristin before ending his shift to go home. Sitting opposite her bed in the ICU, he noted her vitals on the patient monitor. He then scanned over the printout of her earlier EKG. He had ordered it due to the fluctuations with her heart rate documented by the night shift nurse.

Observing the rise and fall of her chest, her breathing seemed to be stable for now. From her respirations, he was encouraged that she could start weaning off the ventilator that was delivering oxygen into her lungs. He just needed to consult with the respiratory therapist first about decreasing the settings. Her face showed a purplish-blue discoloration from the lacerations she had suffered when the car windshield had shattered on impact.

Or was it really from the accident?

He stood up slowly, walking to her bedside. Placing one of his hands near the head of the bed and the other at the foot, he could not help but recall Dr. Kramer's suggestion of abuse. He would need to gather more information before jumping to conclusions. He'd learned from his past mistakes with making quick assumptions. He figured he would talk to family members to get a better idea of the story when they arrived.

"What happened, Kristin?" he sighed. Her eyes remained closed, but there was movement under her eyelids. He could tell when the eyelashes fluttered a bit. He wondered if it could have been in response to his voice.

Just then, Evelyn, a nurse from the station outside, walked in, catching him in mid-thought.

"Vitals seem to be improving, Doctor," the nurse said, observing Kristin's heart rate and oxygen saturation. "There's a woman by the nurses' station asking for her. She said she's a close friend of hers."

"Okay. I'll be right out," he said, and she left.

David took one more glance at the patient monitor, feeling a bit anxious from the sudden drop in her vitals earlier in the OR. As he approached the nurses' station, he found a very nervous blond woman standing beside a short chubby gentleman.

"This is the doctor, ma'am."

Tiffany looked over to Dr. Landry, placing one hand on his arm. "Doctor, please tell me the woman in that room is Kristin!" she said frantically. Tiffany had been a wreck the entire drive over to the hospital. She had seen the car accident with the police still at the scene on her way to the hospital with Joe. She felt riddled with guilt. It was she who had urged Kristin to leave Jake that night. Tiffany couldn't seem to grasp the reality of what was happening around her.

"Calm down, ma'am. What is your relation to the patient?" David questioned.

"I can't calm down. You don't understand; she was trying to leave—"

Joe put his arm around her back. "Tiffany, I'm upset too, but we have to answer the doctor's question."

"She's my best friend. Please," Tiffany managed to reply slowly.

"Why don't we go over to the waiting room where we have more privacy and can talk some more?" David suggested as he looked at all the nurses around them who had been staring at them.

"No, please. She is my best friend. Is this the woman who was brought in here? Her name is Kristin Summers. She has a little boy, Tommy. God, please tell me that they are okay." She covered her mouth with one hand.

"We did confirm with the paramedic and her driver's license that the patient driving the car was Kristin Summers—your friend. Her three-year-old child arrived at the hospital moments before she did. By law, I'm not allowed to disclose details, but they both sustained life-threatening injuries. The patient is in the ICU," David said as Tiffany clung to every word. He bent his head down and paused before continuing. "The little boy did not make it."

Tiffany felt as if a sword had pierced her side. "No, no, no. Oh God—Tommy. She won't survive this," she cried out, almost collapsing. Joe and David caught her, and David walked them over to the waiting area.

Tiffany sank back into one of the waiting room chairs as Joe took a seat beside her. With one hand, she covered her mouth to quiet her sobs as her body trembled with grief.

"What is your name, ma'am?" David rested his hand on her shoulder to give her some comfort as the man beside her threw his arm around her.

"Tiffany," she managed to say between sobs.

"Does she have any other family? A husband, next of kin you can contact?"

Joe sat forward and answered before Tiffany could reply. "No, we are her only family." Tiffany looked on, a bit confused, but then Joe signaled to her with his eyes not to reveal more.

"Are you sure there is no one else? You said she was trying to leave. What did you mean by that? Who was she trying to leave?" David asked Tiffany, following her gaze to Joe and then back to him.

Tiffany sat up straighter, now regaining her composure. "I'm sorry. I ramble on when I get very excited. She was driving to meet me tonight." Tiffany thought about the plans she had made for Kristin to meet her at Buxton Road by the old farmhouse, where the plan was to ditch the red Toyota in case Jake reported it missing. She was then going to drive them over the state line to her cousin's summer home, where Jake would never be able to hurt either of them again, until a more permanent plan was put in place.

Tiffany thought back to Tommy's smile and hugs at the birthday party and began to sob again. She was the one who made Kristin leave. Why did she push so hard? Kristin would never forgive her.

Looking over at Joe, she asked him, "What is she going to do? Oh my God, this is going to kill her." Tiffany grabbed hold of Joe's hand.

Just then, an officer showed up with a solemn look on his face.

"Doctor, can I speak with you for a moment?" the officer asked, excusing himself for interrupting their conversation

"Sure." David went to stand up, but Tiffany cut him off.

"Actually, officer, do you mind if I have a word with you?" Tiffany asked, wiping the tears away from her eyes.

"Ah, yes, ma'am," he replied as Tiffany led him a few feet away out of earshot. She turned him so that his back was facing David and Joe.

"Ma'am, I'm very sorry for your loss."

"Sorry? I'm sorry, you're apologizing for what exactly?" Tiffany looked back over and flashed David a fake smile. He was clearly curious about what exactly was going on.

"Ma'am?" the officer asked, confused.

"Officer O'Neil?" Tiffany read his badge. "Oh yeah, you're the one my friend spoke to down at the station with all of Jake's drinking buddies. You're the one who told her to go home to that maniac of a husband, who did nothing but beat her every day like she was his personal rag doll."

"Ma'am, you're understandably upset, but I have a job to do. I'm only trying to help."

"Let's play this out, shall we?"

"What do you mean?"

"Well, when she came to you for help? You did nothing. Now she is lying up in that hospital bed, and when she learns that her son is dead, God only knows what that will do to her. So, I want to know exactly how you are going to help her this time. Are you going to make a phone call to that son of a—"

The officer cut her off. "Ma'am, I understand you're upset."

"No, I don't think you know just how upset. So what are you gonna do? You gonna tell him that his wife is here, so that when she goes back to him this time, he'll be sure to kill her? Do you want that on your conscience, officer?"

"I don't understand what you are asking me to do. Are you asking me not to tell Mr. Summers that she is here?"

"I'm asking you, don't you think she has suffered enough? Couldn't you allow her to have some peace, especially now?" Tiffany pleaded with her eyes.

"Is everything okay here?" David interrupted, walking up behind them

"Ah, yes. We were just going over some questions I had about the accident."

"I see," David nodded. "Well, Officer, I'm sure you're going to be looking for a statement, but she won't be able to do any talking right now. She's on a vent until we can safely say she won't have need for one."

"It's all right. I'll come back to check in tomorrow." He bid farewell, and

Tiffany mouthed the words *Thank you* as he walked away.

"Doctor, can I please see her?"

"Of course. She's asleep right now. But you can go in and sit beside her. Talk to her. I have a feeling she'll be able to hear you." He smiled warmly at Tiffany and then led her to Kristin's bedside as Joe stayed behind.

Standing now in Kristin's room, David was able to speak more freely to Tiffany. "I don't think we should volunteer any information about her son just yet. She has been improving, but she isn't out of the woods. She is still on the ventilator there, which is helping give her lungs more oxygen, and she also just came out of a very complicated surgery a couple hours ago. For a moment there, I didn't know if she would make it. But she did. I think it would be wise for her not to know anything until she's in the clear."

Just the sight of Kristin, covered with bandages and an array of tubes and wires, caused Tiffany's breath to hitch on a choked sob. Tiffany touched the leg that was in a cast. She caressed Kristin's face with the back of her hand and tentatively touched the bandage that covered Kristin's head. The guilt pooling in her chest was almost suffocating. She looked at her dear friend, laid up in this bed because of her, and thought of Tommy being in a cold morgue. The thought of that beautiful little boy lying there was unbearable. She didn't know how she was going to break the news to her. She couldn't be the one.

She wiped away her tears. It couldn't be her that told her.

"Kristin, it's me, Tiffany. I'm here, baby girl. I'm so sorry." More tears flowed as she looked at her friend. She was covered from head to toe in bruises and her eyes were red and swollen. There was so much swelling, especially in her cheeks. If the doctor hadn't told her that it was Kristin lying in that bed, she would be unrecognizable.

Tiffany took a seat in the wooden chair beside her friend. "I'm going to stay right here, girl. I'm not going anywhere."

Tiffany sat in that uncomfortable, blue hospital chair all night, keeping an eye on Kristin as she slept. She would give anything to turn the clock back. Maybe there was something she could have done differently that would have resulted in a better outcome, instead of Kristin lying in this bed in front of her and Tommy's death. But it was too late now. All the what-ifs or what should have happened didn't matter right now. There was no time machine to go back in time, no matter how painful the reality was.

It was just too late.

CHAPTER SIXTEEN

Tommy... Tommy, Kristin thought as she opened her eyes slowly. The pain radiated in all directions, from her ribs to her neck, across her shoulders, down her legs. Her head felt as if a thousand heavy books were sitting on top of it. Kristin's vision was still a bit blurry. She didn't know what was going on or where she was as she looked around and saw a woman in a blue wooden chair opposite her bed. She could barely make out her face.

Her memory was somewhat foggy. But she remembered bits and pieces of what happened the night before. She remembered fighting with Jake in the house. Then Tommy's body hitting the floor when Jake smacked him across his face. She remembered dropping the four-by-four after she hit Jake on the head with it.

Oh my God, she thought. She could vaguely remember speeding down the road to meet up with Tiffany at the farmhouse. Then it hit her—the crash! Yes—she remembered—the truck in the middle of the road and then someone pulling her out of the car. Then the fire! Tommy was on the ground... and a man was trying to revive him!

Panic started to set in, and she felt an overwhelming tightness growing inside her chest. She felt like she was suffocating. There was something in her mouth. *I can't breathe*, she thought. She started to thrash around in the bed violently, tearing the pulse oximeter off her finger.

Tiffany raised her head from the windowsill, rubbing the sleep out of her eyes. She sprang to her feet and quickly pressed the call button to page the nurse. The monitor alarm was blinking. She tried to calm Kristin down, but Kristin clawed at the tube in her mouth and tried to rip off the electrode wires on her chest. She was having an anxiety attack, and her heart rate and blood pressure were climbing.

She thought she was going to die.

"Kristin—stop! You're okay. You're in the hospital. Nurse—Nurse!" Tiffany shouted for help, and within seconds a nurse ran into the room.

"Okay, Kristin. There, there. You're going to be alright." The nurse raised the head of the bed a little more and checked the tube's placement and the sensors monitoring her vitals. "We are going to help you. Try to stay calm."

In a flash, Dr. Landry was in the room. He looked over at the monitor display at Kristin's vitals. "What happened?" Her pulse had increased to 153, and her blood pressure was now 196/112.

"I don't know. One minute she was fine. The next, she was just trying to rip that thing out of her mouth." Tiffany pointed at Kristin's endotracheal tube. She started to pace back and forth.

Tommy. Where's my son? Kristin started to fight the nurse off her.

"Calm down, Kristin, we got you." The nurse did her best to stop her from moving around.

The doctor approached her bed. "Ms. Summers, I'm Dr. Landry. You are in Parsons County General. You were in an automobile accident. We are going to give you something to bring your heart rate down. Okay? Squeeze my hand if you can hear me." David turned to the nurse and said, "Nurse, push twenty milligrams of labetalol." The nurse complied right away and slowly pushed the requested units of the beta blocker into Kristin's IV. Kristin squeezed David's hand weakly and then dropped it to her side.

Tiffany, the nurse, and Dr. Landry watched the monitor as Kristin's heart rate started to come down and her blood pressure began to stabilize at a more normal level.

"Kristin, we are going to remove the tube from your throat. It will probably make you cough, and your throat is going to be sore." David explained the procedure to Kristin as she calmed. Kristin nodded her head slowly in understanding. "Are you ready?" David asked. Again, Kristin nodded. A respiratory therapist silenced the ventilator alarms, and David removed the endotracheal tube from Kristin's throat. She gagged, then coughed and winced.

"Where is my son? Where's Tommy?" Kristin asked in a raspy whisper. She scanned their faces one by one; they all seemed to avoid her eyes.

"Kristin—" Tiffany looked at her and then looked away. She didn't want to lie to her, but she also didn't want her friend to die. She couldn't lose her too.

"I want my son! Bring me—my son!" Kristin demanded. She felt a terrible feeling growing deep in the pit of her stomach. She had her suspicions as to what she felt, but she would not accept it.

"Kristin, relax." Tiffany held her hand.

"I don't want to relax," she said, grabbing hold of one of the sleeves of Tiffany's purple cardigan. "Tiff, where is Tommy?" But Tiffany would not answer. She just looked at Kristin with sad eyes.

"No," Kristin said. "You're lying. YOU'RE LYING!"

Again, Tiffany would not answer her friend. How could she tell her that her son was dead?

Dr. Landry, disheartened about being the bearer of bad news, responded, "I'm sorry, Ms. Summers. Your son did not survive the accident. He arrived at the hospital around the same time you did—he had massive internal injuries. We did everything we could but—⊠

"NO! BRING ME MY SON!" Kristin cried hoarsely out, cutting him off in mid-sentence.

"Ms. Summers—" the doctor tried to say, but Kristin refused to listen.

"NO! GET OUT! ALL OF YOU OUT—NOW!" She lashed out at the doctor, ignoring the soreness in her throat.

Tiffany tried to hug her friend, but Kristin pushed her arm away. "Kristin, please."

"No, Tommy's okay. He's got to be okay, right?" Kristin looked at Tiffany, who avoided her eyes. "Tell me he's lying, Tiff." But Tiffany wouldn't look at her. Kristin looked back at the young doctor who stood with his head down, understanding how difficult this news was to accept.

"Ms. Summers, I understand this is hard."

"Stop it! Don't tell me my son is dead. I refuse to believe you. You bring me my son! Now! I want my son!" Kristin yelled at the top of her lungs and then held her breath.

"Kristin?" Tiffany asked, a bit worried. Kristin had held her breath so long she started to turn blue.

"TOMMY!" she screamed out in anguish as she exhaled. "TOMMY!" she screamed again more loudly.

Tiffany grabbed her friend, who was fighting her, and hugged her tight, rocking them back and forth as she stained her sweater with endless tears.

David apologized and left the room, giving them their privacy. The nurse followed his lead. His heart felt heavier than it had since Josh had died.

"I want my son!" He could hear Kristin's loud wails down the hall as he headed toward the nurses' station and picked up a chart to review.

Moments later, Tiffany joined him. "Thank you, Doctor." She turned to the nurse. "Please call me if you need anything or if she needs anything." She handed the nurse behind the desk her phone number.

"She needs time to mourn. But I will keep you updated. For now, she needs some rest and some sleep." David did his best to offer some words of encouragement for Kristin's friend, but he knew nothing he said helped.

"But what happens when she wakes up? What happens, then?" Tiffany asked.

David really didn't have an answer for her. All he could do was stand there, shaking his head. "The only thing you can do right now is give her your love and support."

Tiffany thanked him again and made her way towards the waiting room to find Joe and head home.

"Good evening, Doctor. How is she doing?" said a voice behind David. David turned. "Officer O'Neil, right?"

"Yes, sir."

David walked over to him, holding on to the stethoscope around his neck. "I was wondering if I could speak with Ms. Summers for a few moments."

Curiously, David looked at the officer. He was hard to read, standing with a painted smile on his face. "I'll have to see if she is up for visitors. Is she in some kind of trouble?"

"No, no. Just wrapping up some paperwork regarding the accident."

David asked the officer to follow him around the corner and then told him to wait outside the room while he spoke to Kristin.

"Kristin, there is an officer outside to see you regarding the accident. I can stay if you would like me to, or I can tell him to come back if you're not up for this right now."

"Is it Officer O'Neil?" Kristin remembered his face as one of the people who worked on Tommy the night of the accident.

"Yes," David said, surprised she knew who the officer was.

"Send him in," she said grudgingly. He did, after all, try to save Tommy.

"Okay, I'll go get him," David said and signaled for the officer to enter the room. He looked at Kristin, who nodded that she was okay to see the officer alone. David excused himself but reminded Kristin of the call bell beside her if she needed assistance. Then he walked back by the nurses' station, looking back at the door of the room he had just left.

"Ms. Summers." O'Neil walked around the bed and stood by the empty blue chair beside Kristin.

"Sit down, Officer O'Neil."

"I'm sorry for disturbing you during a time like this."

"Oh, you mean Tommy," she said sarcastically.

"Look, Ms. Summers. I want to apologize. I feel really terrible about the way I acted that day back at the station."

"Ha ha. You feel terrible. Does it look like I care how you feel?" Kristin barked at the nervous officer who stood behind the chair, holding its back.

"Ms. Summers, I—"

"I get it, you feel remorseful and you want to help. So here is how you can help me. You can walk out that door and never tell my husband about what happened to Tommy or me. And when he comes to ask you for help to try to find me, you can tell him to go to hell!"

"Ms. Summers, please, I—"

"Did you get that, officer?"

Reluctantly, the officer bowed his head and nodded. "I assure you, if he finds out, it won't be from me."

"Please excuse me. I have to start planning my son's funeral."

The officer looked back at her once more, and then left the room in complete silence. As he passed David on the way to the elevators, he didn't utter a word.

David watched as the elevators closed and made his way back to her room. He stopped just outside her door, watching her as she lay there in the bed with her back to him, curled up in a fetal position, cradling the pillow tightly against her chest. She was probably imagining it was her Tommy, and just like Josh, he could do nothing to bring her little boy back.

He felt defeated as he walked away to continue his rounds.

CHAPTER SEVENTEEN

A week later, Kristin remained in the hospital. However, her vitals were stable enough to move her out of the ICU and into a private room, which David had arranged in light of the tragic loss she had just undergone. Joe had come by, informing Kristin that Jake had been by the diner looking for her and Tommy.

Well, at least Officer O'Neil gave me that.

She listened on as Joe told her he had warned Jake that he would report him to the police for abuse and harassment if he didn't stop. He told Kristin that no matter what she felt, she wasn't to reach out to Jake for anything, and despite what had happened to Tommy, going back to Jake would be signing her own death sentence. But Kristin could have cared less about what he was telling her. She wanted to just wither away.

To prevent Jake from finding out that Kristin was even there in the hospital, Joe worked with the hospital billing department on a payment plan to help cover her medical expenses. He told Tiffany he would mortgage out his diner before he allowed Jake the privilege of knowing where Kristin was. He thought of Kristin as the daughter he never had and would do everything he possibly could to make sure that "piece of garbage" never came near her again.

Dr. Landry met with the medical director of Parsons County General. Ned Daniels was also present at the meeting, and the three discussed the series of events that led up to the three-year-old boy's death from the time he arrived. With the approval of the medical board, the hospital waived all fees related to the surgical intervention of the little boy as a charitable contribution. Kristin was only billed for her post-op care. The board members were eager to help in light of her tragic loss.

David felt Daniels took the little boy's death on his watch harder than usual. Daniels had felt somewhat responsible even though David knew his mentor had done everything he possibly could to save the little boy's life. Because of that, David gathered that was why Daniels had mostly kept to himself in the days that followed. He did, however, stop by Kristin's room once during her hospital stay to offer his condolences. But Kristin, who was still grieving, did not want to hear anything from anyone and yelled at him to leave when he entered the room. Daniels never returned after that.

Dr. Landry couldn't help but feel that Kristin could have been a little further along in her recovery. He knew that any loss, especially the loss of a child, could very well be the factor to hinder or slow a patient's recovery progress. The mind was powerful and had great impact on a person's physical state. He knew that better than anyone, especially having dealt with the loss of his own brother.

On his orders, he kept Kristin for continued observation. He also ordered a psych consult to help with the grieving process and asked the hospital chaplain to visit with her. She was just nowhere near ready to go home. However, it didn't matter one way or another to Kristin where she was. Because of her lack of desire to eat, she was on the verge of being given a feeding tube. When Dr. Landry explained that if she didn't start eating, this would be an option they would strongly consider, Kristin began to eat in small amounts throughout the day. But she had to force herself to have a fruit cup or even a cup of Jell-O. She ignored everyone, including the nursing staff who came in to provide care and administer medications. She felt completely paralyzed from depression. Often, the nurses' aides would have to change her soiled bed sheets because she just did not want to get out of bed, even to walk a few feet to the bathroom. Most of the time, even when Dr. Landry checked on her during rounds, she just lay on her side, staring out the window. Life no longer had meaning. Her reason for living—Tommy—was gone.

Tiffany had shown up at the hospital every day at lunchtime to spend time with her. But Kristin never uttered a single word. It didn't stop Tiffany from coming to visit her dear friend. She knew this time was especially hard for Kristin, and she told herself being there for her would be enough, even if they didn't speak. During one of her visits, towards the end of the week, Tiffany tried to bring up funeral arrangements for Tommy's burial. She didn't think it right not to get Kristin's feedback or include her in those arrangements. But Kristin could not even bring herself to talk about it. Instead, she did what she had been accustomed to doing the last week in the hospital, ignore everyone around her and keep to herself. Tiffany was left with no other choice but to go ahead and make the plans for Tommy to be buried.

When the day came for Tommy's burial, Tiffany begged Kristin to attend with her after getting the doctor's approval to take her off grounds. But Kristin refused to listen or leave the bed. The idea of seeing his little casket being lowered into the ground was just too much for her to bear. She was still not ready to accept that her son had died. And she couldn't get how Tiffany was able to.

The funeral took place at Christ the King Baptist Church, which was Tiffany's parish. A few workers from the diner had gathered for the funeral and burial. Tommy's body was finally laid to rest.

***

One morning, Kristin woke up to find a breakfast tray in front of her with a bowl of oatmeal and a cup of milk. She glanced at the newspaper folded over to an article with a picture of Tommy in the middle of it. It was the same picture she had used for his third birthday cake. *Tiffany*, she thought, *she had no right! He's my son, not hers!* The article was entitled in bold letters, *Tragedy in Parsons County*. She opened the paper and read a couple of lines.

Angered that a report had been written without her consent, she flung the entire newspaper toward the open door of her room. Then she turned her head and looked out the window. It was sunny outside. Two birds were perched on a branch, and one bird had some trouble flying. It seemed as if its wing was broken from the way it fluttered. As it tried to flap its wings, it rose off its feet only to land right back down seconds later. The bird next to it flapped its wings and planted itself on the next tree branch a little higher up. The other bird with the broken wing tried to fly again but finally gave up.

I know how you feel, bird, Kristin said silently to herself.

There was a loud knock, snapping her out of her thoughts.

"Hello?" Tiffany peeked her head in and waited for an invitation. Not getting one, she walked into the room anyway, carrying the newspaper and setting it on a chair against the wall.

"Hey," Tiffany said again, approaching Kristin, who glanced over quickly then back out the window. She hung her little brown purse strap over the arm of the chair.

"Kristin, you can't keep doing this. They are keeping you on IV fluids just to keep you hydrated. You must start eating more or they will never send you home."

"Go home?" Kristin turned her head to face Tiffany for the first time since she had arrived in the hospital.

Tiffany seemed surprised that she'd finally answered her. She then gave

Kristin a half-smile and replied, "Yes, you can't stay here forever. You'll go home with me. You have to leave here sometime."

"Go home with you, Tiffany? So you can look at me with those pitiful eyes the way you're looking at me now. Tommy was my home and now he's dead! I have no home 'cause you buried him six feet under the ground without me there, remember?"

"*Kristin*, I begged you to come to the funeral. But you ignored me and refused to get up out of bed. We had to bury him."

"So now what? I'm a bad mother because I didn't want to see them put Tommy in the ground? Because I didn't want to see my baby boy have dirt thrown over his little coffin?" Kristin's voice quivered. "No, you're right. I didn't want to be there. And *YOU* went and told the newspaper what happened. Who gave you the right to do that? Tommy wasn't your son—HE'S MINE! And you want ME TO EAT!?"

Kristin picked up her bowl of oatmeal and threw it at Tiffany's head. Tiffany ducked just in time, and the little bowl flew over her head and against the back wall of the room, milk spraying everywhere. "I don't have a HOME to go home to!"

Tiffany picked up the bowl of oatmeal off the ground, cleaning up some of the mess with a towel she found in the room.

"I'm sorry, I was trying to help. Honestly, I was only trying to help."

Kristin stared back at her with hateful eyes. "WELL, DON'T! You made it worse! Seeing Tommy's picture in the newspaper this morning made it worse!"

"I'm sorry, I didn't want that."

"Just go. There's nothing to talk about. You're making my life out to be a three-ring circus for the whole world to see."

"Kristin, I was only trying to share your story so that other women in your situation would find the strength to leave before it's too late."

"'Cause I didn't, right?" Kristin spat out. "What about Jake? Did you even think about him for one second? Knowing when he sees this, he's going to come after me and blame me for Tommy."

"Jake? If he really wanted to find you, he would have come here by now. I honestly think he is scared to show his face around here after that night."

"How do you know that? Do you have some magic crystal ball that you can read what people are thinking? Too bad you couldn't use it to tell me that Tommy was going to die!"

"Kristin, I know what you're——"

"Don't! Don't you dare tell me you know what I'm going through! Losing a husband to cancer and having your three-year-old ripped out of your life is not the same thing! So don't pretend you know what I'm going through. Because you don't have a clue. You never had a son! You never spent every waking moment making sure he was okay, that he was fed, that he was safe. I will never hear his cry again. I will never get to see him smile or hear his laughter because he's gone—he's dead, Tiffany! He's dead! And you killed him!" Kristin spat the words at her like razors cutting flesh.

"Don't say that." Tiffany felt crippled by the accusation. She held on to the bedrails with both hands.

"I told you that night, it wasn't the right time. I knew he would wake up. But you insisted that I drive over to Buxton to meet you. And *this* is what happened!" Kristin pointed at her swollen right eye. "He even smacked up Tommy. But you told me I had to protect my son, and now he's gone." Kristin picked the rolled-up newspaper and plastic cup of water off her tray and threw them both against the window. The papers floated to the ground, and the water streaked the window as it trickled down.

"I'm gonna go. I'll be by tomorrow," Tiffany said softly. "You need to rest." She turned around and headed toward the chair behind her for her purse.

"No, don't come back here tomorrow or the next day. Or the day after that! You coming here and sitting in that chair every day is not helping me. It's just a reminder that I don't have a son anymore. And it kills me to look at you, knowing that you're the reason. I just want to be left alone." Kristin turned her gaze back to the window.

Tiffany turned around, choking back the tears. She picked up her purse and glanced back at Kristin. "You know, Tommy may not have been my son. But since the day he was born, I loved that little boy with all my heart and treated him like he was my own blood. He was my family too. I'm sorry you never saw that."

She turned around and exited the room. Kristin grabbed a pillow, hugged it tightly, and buried her face into it, screaming as loud as she could. She screamed until she could scream no more.

Oh, how her heart ached for him, to hear his sweet voice say *Mama* just one more time. How she wanted to go back in time and do things differently. She would have left Jake the night of Tommy's birthday party if she had known this would have happened. But she was too afraid that night of what Jake would do. The truth was she should have left Jake way before Tommy had been born. But now she had paid an incredible price for staying.

"You know, I like going to the batting cage when I get angry. But I'm sure punching the pillow would work just as fine," David Landry said, holding a printout of Kristin's EKG he had retrieved at the nurses' station.

Kristin raised her head to see Dr. Landry take a seat. He glanced over for any changes in her heart rhythm, but all seemed well.

David placed the folded printout inside Kristin's chart at the foot of the bed and crossed his legs.

"Was that a joke? Because it wasn't very funny,"

"I admit, I'm pretty bad at telling jokes. Ask the nurses, they'll tell you. My brother was the one who was good at telling jokes." He chuckled, then flipped through some other clinical notes in her chart.

"I really don't care. Can we just get on with this so you can leave, and I can go back—"

"To staring out that window? How's that been working out for you? Do you enjoy birdwatching?" David asked, glancing at the window and then back at her.

"You're right. You are bad." Kristin rolled her eyes and then placed the pillow behind her, lying down again.

"I try. So, you're eating less than half of your meals from what the nurses have been documenting." He flipped through the papers in her chart.

"I guess I don't have an appetite lately. Maybe it's due to the fact I just buried my son," Kristin said sarcastically.

"I heard you refused to attend the funeral or even meet with the psychologist in the hospital when he stopped by during the week," he said, sitting up straight and readjusting the stethoscope around his neck.

"I'm sorry, but I don't like telling my business to anyone but my close friend."

"It seems like you just chased away the *only* friend you have."

"You know, I don't need a lecture right now. Is that all?"

"That's all for now. If you don't start eating, I'm going to request that they put in a feeding tube. Inserting a nasogastric tube is often a difficult procedure for a patient. They gag repeatedly and their eyes water. It's very unpleasant."

Kristin rolled her eyes again at the doctor but felt somewhat intimidated by his threat. David rose from his seat and walked toward the door.

"Also, later today, you will join other *living* patients such as yourself in the east wing for a group session and recreational activities. It's non-optional."

"What do you mean group session? What are we supposed to do, sit in a circle, hold hands, and sing 'Kumbaya?' No, thank you. I don't want to go."

Ignoring Kristin's response, Dr. Landry said, "The transporter will come around six o'clock to take you. Try not to give him a hard time. Or else I will personally be escorting you myself. I have no plans for the evening."

Kristin threw a pillow at the door as he walked out. Who the heck did he think he was? Just because he wore an oversized white lab coat and had an MD, did that give him the right to order her around? As if she didn't have a mind of her own? If she didn't want to go, then she was not going. It was as simple as that.

CHAPTER EIGHTEEN

Around a quarter to six, Kristin heard a knock at the door of her room. She raised her head to see a tall black man with a bald head. He was probably in his mid-thirties, dressed in dark-green scrubs with short sleeves that showed off his biceps, which she was sure could have been the same size as Hercules'. He flashed her a big smile from behind a wheelchair that he had pushed into her room. Kristin laid her head back down and turned toward the window, hoping he would just take the hint and go away as others had done since she had been there. But no dice. He simply wheeled the chair to the right side of her bed and kicked the brake on.

"Hi. I'm Wilson. I'll be your transporter this evening." His voice had some bass to it. He waited for her to turn around, but she didn't. "So, are you going to give me a hard time? Or can we get this show on the road?"

"I'm not going." Kristin's eyes remained fixed on the window.

"Dr. Landry mentioned you might say that. Okay," he said, and Kristin could hear him sit down in the wheelchair at the side of her bed.

She turned her head, a bit annoyed. "Excuse me! What do you think you are doing?"

"Oh, I have to call the doctor. You see, he told me if you didn't comply or gave me any hassle, I was to call him so he could come down here and take you himself." He unlocked his cell phone and started to dial.

"Why is it so hard for you people to understand that I don't want to go?" she asked, more annoyed.

"Listen, I'm just doing my job," he said, covering the mouthpiece but still listening to the other line. "It's ringing. Hey, Dr. Landry, Wilson here...

124

oh, you're about to go into the OR soon… hmm… Well, I'm having a problem with…"

Kristin was now extremely frustrated. *This is just ridiculous*, she thought. *Absolutely ridiculous.* "Fine, I'll go! This is just stupid!" She threw her hands up in the air.

Wilson stood up from the wheelchair and smiled. "It's okay, Dr. Landry. We are leaving now," he said, ending the call and pushing his cell phone deep into his side pocket.

"Not going to stop him in the middle of some surgery to take me to some dumb group session." She sat up in her white hospital gown. Wilson lowered her bed and put down the side rail. Carefully, he lifted her up and placed her in the wheelchair, adjusting her casted leg onto one of the chair's elevated legs.

"Here, you might need this. It's kind of chilly in the hallway," he said, offering a hospital blanket.

"Thank you," Kristin murmured, reluctantly throwing it over her shoulder.

As Wilson wheeled her down the hallway toward the elevator, she realized he must have worked there a long time. Every person they had passed had greeted him with a smile, including patients. Some doctors even gave him a high five.

"Pretty popular here," Kristin observed.

"Yeah, well, I've been here over ten years. Kind of like my big family," Wilson said as he wheeled her toward the east wing of the hospital.

"What's in the east wing?"

"Psych department."

"Wait, what? I'm not crazy."

"Didn't say you were. Not everyone who participates in the group has a mental illness. Some patients just go to vent their frustrations. It gives them a chance to be heard because sometimes they don't have that at home. It helps them in their recovery process. I believe Dr. Landry is encouraging you to go because he really thinks you could benefit from it."

"I'm fine," Kristin replied, patting her knees, almost trying to convince herself.

Wilson stopped walking and turned the wheelchair around to face him, squatting down to look Kristin square in the eyes.

"Listen, I know it's none of my business. But I know you lost a son."

"You're right, it isn't any of your business." Kristin looked away from him.

He reached into his back pocket and took out a wrinkled photograph of a little boy. "This was my son, Marcus. I had picked him up from school one day because his mother couldn't leave work early. I remember being pissed that day because there was an important game on. I was in such a hurry to get home to catch the last quarter that I forgot to make sure he had his seat belt on. He never liked wearing them. We were almost home, only a block away, when some kid decided to use the street for a drag race. I never saw the other car coming. We crashed, and Marcus was thrown from the car. He died instantly."

"Why are you telling me this?" Kristin asked, a tear rolling down her cheek.

"You see this?" He pointed to a scar on the side of his forehead. "Every time I look in the mirror when I'm shaving or getting dressed, I am reminded of how I survived and he didn't. Every time. It still hurts—and that was ten years ago. You'll never forget, but if your son could see you now, would you want him to be proud of you or see you giving up?"

Kristin wiped her tears away as he turned her around and started to wheel her forward to their destination. "But you seem all together now. How did you get there?"

"Honestly, if I tell you, I don't think you'll be ready to hear it."

"No, please tell me. I want to get there."

"I promise we'll talk about it another time. Just not today. But it will get better in time. Everyone must go at their own pace. But trust me, you will." He patted one shoulder as they turned the corner and headed into a brightly lit room.

Just as Kristin had predicted, there were twelve people in the room sitting in a semicircle. However, what she didn't anticipate seeing was the different types of patients who were sitting there. There was a girl much younger than she was, who sat in a wheelchair like the one she was in, but both her legs were amputated just below her knees. Next to the young girl sat an older man who was badly burned on one side of his face. A couple of others had casts on some of their limbs and even one with a neck brace. There were also a few patients who were otherwise in similar physical condition she was in—but with no sign of life behind their eyes.

"Hey, Wilson, we were just about to begin," said a thin, long-legged woman with curly blonde hair and a pair of red-framed eyeglasses on her face.

"This is Ms. Kristin Summers," Wilson introduced her to the group leader, wheeling Kristin to a spot within the circle.

"Nice to meet you, Kristin. My name is Jane. Welcome to the group."

Kristin nodded and felt Wilson's hand pat her shoulder. "Well, I'll be back later to take you to your room."

"So, who would like to start off today?" Jane asked.

Kristin listened to the patients share their woes and troubled pasts after everyone introduced themselves to each other. The young girl who had no legs, Catherine, had been abused and molested by her stepfather since the age of five. Kristin could hardly stomach to hear the details of how he had raped her repeatedly while her mom worked late nights at the mall. He had burned her skin with the butt of his cigarettes whenever he got angry with her. At one point, she moved her hospital gown enough to show everyone the burns on her stomach. She went on to tell the group how one day she couldn't take it anymore and took matters into her own hands. While he was at work, she had searched for his silver Smith and Wesson that he always kept at home in the back of their coat closet. She knew he would try to come into her room for some "touchy-feely" fun while her mother was working, and this time, she would be ready for him. She waited under the covers with the loaded gun. Sure enough, he tried to get into bed with her—but before he could lay a hand on her, she aimed the gun at him. He wrestled with her, and the gun went off. When she saw the sight of blood, she ran away. She could still hear him moaning in pain as she ran out of the house, down her block, barefoot and in her nightgown. She had run to the nearest train station, but she had no idea where she was going to go. She'd just stood on the platform staring at the tracks below her. When the train came, she jumped in front of it. Both legs were crushed beyond salvaging and had to be amputated.

The older man, Alex, who had half his face burned, had come home to find his junkie wife had set fire to their home accidentally as she was shooting up in the kitchen. He found her high out of her mind on the curb. Their children, ages four and seven, were stuck upstairs in their bedroom as the house burned. He ran into the house to try and save them. But he couldn't get to them in time, and a firefighter found him trapped underneath a fiery beam that had fallen over him as he tried to climb the staircase to get to their room. That was how he got the burns on his face and hands.

"Kristin, would you like to share your story?" Jane asked her.

Kristin shook her head. She wasn't ready to speak about Tommy's death with strangers. If she could close her eyes, she could still see him on the floor in her living room playing with his cars.

"I think if we all have to go, she should too," said a dark-skinned Hispanic man. He'd had to have a steel rod placed in the back of his neck after his wife caught him cheating and ran him over with her car.

"Oh, be quiet, Carlos," Catherine said. "Everyone goes at their own pace."

"I'm just saying, it isn't fair that we have to bare our soul, and she gets to sit there quiet as a mouse," he mumbled under his breath, then didn't say another word.

"That's right, Catherine, this group is here for support and for us to show each other compassion with all that we have been through," Jane said. "I'd like to close the group with a prayer."

"Are you serious?" Kristin asked. God surely didn't hear her prayers and didn't save her son. So, in her eyes, there was no God.

"No one has to pray if they are not comfortable with it. Some of you who have been in this group a long time already know this prayer by heart—the serenity prayer."

Kristin stayed silent as most of the other patients in the group joined in with the prayer.

"Well, that concludes our session for tonight. Let's head over to the dining room where we will break bread together and enjoy a good meal."

"I'm not hungry," Kristin said as everyone dispersed from the group.

"Come on, Kristin. You can keep me company. You're not going to make me beg, right? Can't exactly get on my knees," Catherine joked as she wheeled herself to the room next door.

Where's Wilson? He'd said he would be here to take her back to her room. Kristin sat there until Catherine waved at her by the exit and gestured her to follow. Unwillingly, Kristin wheeled herself toward the exit and followed Catherine to a table where others sat and ate together.

"Every Wednesday, Jane orders dinner for the group so we don't have to eat the yucky hospital food. This Wednesday, it's pizza. She is an absolute angel. I love her." Catherine smiled, pulling her chair up to the table and taking one of the slices. "Girl, I know you can't possibly not like pizza. Everyone loves pizza."

Kristin stared at the slice for a second and picked it up to take a bite. It did look appetizing, but if she ate it, that meant she was rejoining the living population. How could she enjoy a slice of pizza while her son was lying in the dirt somewhere? She wanted to suffer. She didn't deserve to feel good or have her belly full.

"Now, if you're not going to eat that delicious slice, I'm going to." Wilson came up from behind her. "Hey, Catherine. How's it going?" He gave her a high five and turned his attention back to Kristin.

"I can't eat this," Kristin said.

He squatted beside her with one arm resting on the table. "Just because you eat that slice does not mean you love your son any less. Go on."

"I can't." She placed the slice back onto the paper plate.

"Hey, Roger, can you slide me that fork and knife over there?"

"Sure, Wilson," Roger replied and slid the utensils to his side of the table.

"Okay, let's do this," he said as he cut a piece of the slice off in front of

Kristin. "Today, you eat just this little piece, then tomorrow you eat a little more. But sweetie, you must take a step. Even if it's a baby step." He picked up a piece with the fork, placing it in front of Kristin's mouth.

She stared at the piece of pizza before her, like it was some type of pungent medicine she didn't want to drink.

"Baby steps," Wilson said again, and Kristin opened her mouth as he fed her the slice of pizza. "You see, that wasn't so hard. Okay, let's get you back to your room."

"Thank you."

"No problem. You and I are going to be pretty good friends."

CHAPTER NINETEEN

Kristin awoke in the middle of the night, hearing a young boy's voice in the hallway, outside her door. She rubbed her eyes and threw the covers off her. Again, she heard the faint voice of a young boy. She looked for the wheelchair, but it wasn't by her bed. What did Wilson do with it? Did he take it back while she slept? Why would he? She could see one crutch against the window. However, the other one was nowhere in sight

She inched her way to the edge of the bed and pulled its remote from the side rail to lower it. Stretching her hand out, she grabbed the base of the crutch with her fingertips, pulling it towards her. As she held the crutch under her right arm, she hobbled to the door of her room. She peeked out the door. The hallway was dark and quiet. Only a single light at the end, near the double elevators, flickered steadily. Kristin scanned the nurses' station, which stood empty a few feet to her right. There was no one in sight. *How strange.*

Just then, she heard the wails of a young boy again. She made her way out into the hallway, holding on to the rail against the wall and moving in the direction of the voice.

The boy's voice became much clearer as she moved down the dark halls of the hospital. It indeed was the sound of a little boy. He was laughing now, and it echoed throughout the hallway.

"Hello, is anyone there? Nurse?"

But no one responded. *Where did everyone go?* Kristin continued to totter with one crutch, feeling a bit out of breath. She almost fell backwards when a little boy with light-brown hair ran across her path into one of the hospital rooms down the hall, stopping her abruptly in her tracks. It was Tommy! She recognized him immediately.

"Tommy? Tommy?" she screamed, pulling herself along the rail. She could hear the laughter, louder now. It was his laughter.

Kristin entered the room she'd seen her son enter only moments before. She held on to the bed trays, the visitor chairs, anything she could use to help maneuver her to the center. As she looked around, she noticed it was the same room she had been in hours ago where she had the group session with Catherine. No one was around as far as she could tell. But there were still empty chairs formed in a semicircle as there had been before.

"Tommy?"

Scanning the room, she could see the back of a little boy's head in one of the chairs to the far right of the half-circle. She called out his name again. But he didn't turn around to face her. She moved slowly, holding on to the back of the chairs, until finally she was right behind him. Her heart was beating so fast, but she wasn't scared as she stood within arm's reach of him. But he didn't turn around. He just kept his head straight, staring ahead of him.

"Tommy, baby? What are you doing, sweetie?" Kristin asked him, but he gave no response. "Turn around for Mommy, please." She couldn't believe he was here. How she longed to look at him and hold him in her arms again.

She reached out to touch the back of his head. But before she could lay her fingers on a single hair, Tommy spun around in his chair and looked at her with an open gash on his head. Blood trickled down the side of his face. The front of his T-shirt was stained with his blood. His arms and little hands were covered with cuts and bruises. Kristin shrieked from the sight and fell to the ground immediately, the crutch falling behind her.

"Oh my God!"

He got up from his chair and, playing with her hair, she heard him say, "Mama loves Tommy?"

Kristin closed her eyes tight, shaking her head. She told herself, "This isn't real. This isn't real."

"Mama, don't leave me."

"No! This isn't real!" she shouted, trying to convince herself it was not happening.

Then she heard another voice. "Ms. Summers, it's okay. You were having a bad dream." Someone shook her gently.

Kristin opened her eyes again, but she was back in her hospital bed, inside her room. It was only a dream.

"Dr. Landry?" Kristin looked up and adjusted her bed into a sitting position.

"You were dreaming?" he asked, putting his stethoscope in his ears and listening to Kristin's heart and lungs.

"More like a nightmare. Isn't the nurse supposed to do this?" she asked him when he placed the blood pressure cuff on her arm and a pulse oximeter on her finger.

"I prefer to do my own assessments. I also like checking periodically on my own patients when I can," he replied. "So how did last night's group go? Wilson said you stayed for the entire session. That's good."

"Yeah, well, I didn't have a choice. Did I?" She watched him take the stethoscope out of his ears and wrap it around his neck.

"You always have a choice, Kristin. Your vitals are strong. I would say you should be released in a few days. Just need to work on eating more."

"So, now what? More group sessions and pizza parties 'til I go home?"

"Well, I would like you to continue with the group therapy sessions. I think it could only help speed up your recovery. But me, I never pass on free pizza." David flashed her a quick smile. "What are your plans for the day?"

"Besides sitting in this bed. Nothing," she responded a bit sarcastically.

"Hmm... well, I get off in about an hour. How about I swing by and keep you company?"

"And why would you do that?"

"Because I think you could use the company. How's your friend? Haven't seen her around the last few days?"

"I said some awfully mean things to her. I was angry, and I don't think she will be coming back. I know I wouldn't if I were her."

David looked at her as she bent her head down. She was fragile and so vulnerable. Why did he feel such an innate need to be there for her, to comfort her? He'd never felt this drawn to any of his patients in the past. He wanted to know more about her, especially the night of the accident. He knew there was more to the story than just the car crash. He knew there was much more beneath the surface than just a mother grieving the death of her son. But he didn't want to pressure her, because he also knew that if he did, it would be the fastest way for her to shut down.

"We all make mistakes and say things we don't mean out of anger. As they say, time heals all wounds."

"I hope you're right. She has always been a good friend to me." Kristin sighed, regretting how she treated Tiffany during their last encounter. She lowered her head.

"You should tell her that. I don't know if you know or not, but I placed a black tote bag to the side of your bed. The night you were admitted, a man who had helped you from the car wreck brought it in. I'll see you a little later," David said, removing his pager from his belt and looking at it quickly before leaving the room.

"My bag?" she said and leaned over the side of her bed. There it was—the bag she had taken with her and Tommy the night they left home. She placed it on her bed.

Rummaging through its contents, she found her wallet inside. There was also a clear plastic envelope that held Tommy's birth certificate, immunization records for the first three years, and a photograph of her holding him in the hospital an hour after he was born. Tiffany had taken the snapshot. The more she thought about what she had done to Tiffany, the worse she felt about it. She was truly sorry for having blamed her dear friend for Tommy's death. She didn't know why she'd said such horrible things. Tiffany had always been there for her, a good friend through it all.

How would things ever go back to the way they were? For starters, she would get up out of bed and get out of the gown she had lived in for the last two days.

After wrapping plastic over her casted leg, the nurse had suggested a bed bath. But Kristin insisted on taking a shower, and she refused to listen to the nurse's recommendations. *I need to feel like myself,* she thought, even if it was as small as having a shower.

The nurse helped her get into the shower and seated her on the shower chair with the cast sticking out of the curtain to keep it away from the water. Kristin stuck her head under the showerhead and closed her eyes as the cool water flowed over her scalp. It felt so refreshing against her skin.

As the water ran down her face, she could remember taking Tommy out in the rain in front of their house one summer evening. She had dressed him up in his little yellow raincoat and matching rain boots. He'd stretched his arms out, trying to catch the raindrops in his palms. She could see him jumping in the little puddles, even when she told him not to, because he loved the sound it made when it splashed. He would giggle, and his arms reached for her as he wobbled toward her, calling "Mama."

Time heals all wounds, she could hear Dr. Landry say. But this was a wound that would never heal.

Kristin's nurse assisted her into a fresh hospital gown after her shower. She couldn't help but yearn for Dr. Landry's company. He had made her feel safe and, somehow, comforted.

"I'll be back with your pain medication," said her regular night nurse.

"No, I don't need it."

"Okay." The nurse smiled and left.

Kristin, for the first time in weeks, felt better. There was still the pain that tugged at her heart. But for the moment, she felt she was going to be okay. She preoccupied herself watching talk shows and reading magazines.

She read some of the domestic violence articles in *Women's Journal.* There were personal stories that readers had shared to help other women who were going through similar experiences but were too afraid to leave their partner. She noticed at the end of each story, there were references to the National Domestic Violence Hotline and women's shelters. It made her wish she had reached out for help. Maybe if she had, Tommy would still be alive today.

As Kristin continued to read, she began to recall her own story of abuse.

Flash! Jake grabbing her by her hair and dragging her from the bed to the bathroom.

Flash! Kristin begging Jake not to rape her in his drunken state as she lay on their bedroom floor.

Flash! Jake shoving her into the kitchen cabinets and knocking Tommy off his feet with a hard slap to his face.

"Hellooo." Dr. Landry waved to get her attention. "You okay? I've been standing at the door calling your name for the last two minutes."

Kristin looked up to see a much more casual Dr. Landry. She smiled at him as he stood in a short-sleeve white polo shirt and blue jeans. He was a mix of preppy and casual, and she thought he looked handsome as ever. Suddenly, she realized she had seen him before. This was the same doctor she had seen in the hallway when she brought Tommy in to get his ear checked.

"Wow, isn't that a coincidence," she mumbled under her breath.

"I beg your pardon," David said, taking a seat in the chair.

"Nothing. I'm sorry I didn't hear you. I was reading some articles."

David leaned over from the chair and took a brief look at the magazine she had on her bed tray. "*Women's Journal.* Oh, oh."

"What?" She laughed, then caught herself and stopped, touching her mouth with her fingers as if she had just committed a terrible sin.

"Kristin, you're allowed to laugh. Why don't we go for a ride?"

"Where? I can't exactly leave the hospital."

"Who said we need to? Do you trust me?" the handsome doctor asked her.

She didn't know why, but she did. "Yes, I trust you."

"Good. Do you have a sweater because—?"

"These halls can get chilly, right?" Kristin smiled as she finished his sentence.

David chuckled. "I guess Wilson told you all about it, huh? He's always complaining to maintenance. But then if they turn down the air conditioning, it gets too hot. My opinion, I'd rather the cool air than being over-heated." He looked at her as she pulled her sweater out from behind her back. His gaze lingered more than he expected it to. Why did he feel so drawn to her?

He just couldn't understand it. He had never felt this way with Allison.

"What?" she asked, pushing her hands through the sleeves of the sweater and buttoning it up.

He helped her out of the bed and into the wheelchair that stood beside it, being careful not to jostle the cast on her foot. He smiled down at her as he released the brake. "It's just that you have a really beautiful smile. You should smile more often," he said and turned the wheelchair around to face the door.

"Thank you, Dr. Landry. If I didn't know any better, I'd say you were flirting with me."

David bent his head down to speak softly into her ear. "Shh. I'm David right now. Dr. Landry is off duty."

Kristin laughed at his sense of humor. It was refreshing to have a man who made her laugh for once, as opposed to a man who constantly beat her and made her cry. Even if he was just being friendly.

David wheeled her down the hallway to the elevator and then pressed the button to the sixth floor when they got in. As they exited, curiosity got the better of her.

"Where are we going?" Kristin asked as David wheeled her toward a security desk. "What floor are we on? I don't see any patients."

"We are on the observatory floor. The chief medical director had this put in for his wife before she passed about five years ago. She was diagnosed with pancreatic cancer, and since she loved stargazing, he spoke with the board to get approval to add this as an extension to the hospital." He pointed up to the glass dome above their heads. "The pediatric doctors arrange for the nurses on that floor to bring the children up here once a month for storytelling and stargazing when it's a clear night. The kids look forward to it. It gives them sort of an escape. So, they can focus on just being a kid, instead of constantly being reminded of how sick they are by being probed and poked by nurses and doctors all day long. Sometimes, the parents attend with their children. But aside from that, the floor is closed to the public and during the week is usually just frequented by medical personnel who need some time away from work to clear their heads."

David waved over at the tall security guard in uniform behind his desk. "Gerry, did you get my order?"

"Yes, Dr. Landry. Here you go—two cheeseburgers with fries and two vanilla milkshakes." The guard handed him two grease-stained white paper bags. David placed the bags on Kristin's legs.

"Hold this, please."

Kristin held them as he wheeled her to the center of the dome.

"What if I was a vegan?" Kristin asked with a grin.

"Are you?" He raised an eyebrow in disbelief. He dragged over what looked like a sunbathing chair that had a reclining back and helped her onto it.

Kristin held on to his arm as she adjusted herself on the chair. "No, I'm not."

"I guess then I'm lucky."

"Here you go." She handed him one of the two paper bags. But before he could grab it from her fingers, it slipped, spilling fries all over the floor. "God, I'm such an idiot! I'm so sorry," she exclaimed, feeling like such a klutz. Maybe Jake was right. She could never do anything right.

David leaned back, caught off guard by Kristin's overreaction and how she began berating herself. As she tried to get off the chair to bend down to pick up the fries, David immediately stopped her.

"Hey." He held her chin gingerly in his palm. "It's not a big deal. They're just fries. You'll just have to share yours. Right?" David grinned at her, making Kristin smile.

"I'm sorry." Kristin was surprised at how different he was from Jake. If it had been Jake, her head would have been facedown in the fries, eating them off the bare floor.

David looked at Kristin with concern. *Geez, what did he do to you?* He shook his head, knowing that either a husband or a lover from her past had to have traumatized her for her to react the way she did. She was like a little girl, afraid of being punished for spilling juice on her mother's white carpet.

Not wanting to make her feel any worse than she already did, he simply picked up the fries from the floor and threw them into the garbage basket.

He turned back to her and smiled. "Let's eat, 'cause I'm starving." He opened the wrapper of his cheeseburger, stealing one of her fries out of her bag as he kicked back on the reclining chair. "Mmm mmm… that's always been my weakness, French fries." He could see Kristin shaking her head out of the corner of his eye. "Don't look at me like that." He chuckled, and she laughed as well. "All I had was a health bar this morning." He stole another fry and took a sip of his vanilla milkshake.

This was much different, Kristin thought. Being with a man and not having to be mindful that he may erupt like a volcano at any moment. She could just relax, eat her burger, and enjoy the view… one of the views being Dr. Landry.

CHAPTER TWENTY

The next day, Kristin felt more empowered to do things by herself. Maybe it was the wonderful evening she had spent with Dr. Landry looking up at a starry sky the night before. He had told her to call him David. She didn't know if he was just being nice to a woman who had just lost a child or if he truly enjoyed her company as much as she enjoyed his. Whatever the motive may have been, she was thankful for the beautiful evening they had spent together. They conversed with one another about their childhood, where they went to school, and the common interests they shared, such as music. Kristin even told him her dream of becoming a nurse and that she was enrolled in a nursing program at one point but had dropped out not long after she married. She lied, however, about the reason she had left the program, telling him she had failed two important classes and would have to start from square one. Believing her, he encouraged her to go back to school when she had time to clear her head, if it was what she really wanted.

He inquired about the whereabouts of Jake. But she lied a second time, telling him he had left her and Tommy after she gave birth. Anything was better than telling him how she had allowed a man to beat her almost every day for eight years and then hurt her little boy. She was ashamed of herself, and she felt he would believe she was the real reason for Tommy's death. Maybe she was, but she couldn't bear for him to think of her in that way.

Late one evening, Kristin received a surprise visitor. She was sound asleep when he snuck in, standing beside her bed. She was the most beautiful thing he had laid eyes on, he thought to himself. Without thinking, he traced the outline of her face with one finger and down the nape of her neck.

The movement of someone against her bed woke her. She tried to scream when she saw his face illuminated by the moonlight that poured through the half-opened blinds of her window. He quickly placed his hand firmly against her mouth.

"Shhh," he whispered. "Don't want to alarm anyone, do we?"

Kristin nodded in agreement, and he pulled his hand away.

"Miguel—what do you want?" she asked, alarmed by his presence.

If Miguel had found her, then Jake must have as well.

"Oh, I think you know why I'm here." He smiled, taking a seat in the chair next to her. Now that he was a little closer, Kristin noticed he was dressed in scrubs similar to the ones Wilson had on earlier. That must have been how he got to her room unnoticed. Leaving the light off, not wanting to draw the attention of the medical staff, he spoke in a quiet but stern voice.

Miguel pressed, "You know exactly why I'm here."

"I don't know what you're talking about."

"Come on, Kristin. Don't play me for a fool. You found the bag with my money and my product. Then you high-tailed out of there." He revealed a 9mm tucked into the side of his pants.

Very frightened, she tried harder to convince him. "I'm telling you the truth. I don't know what you are talking about." But Miguel wasn't buying it.

"You know it's a real shame what happened to your son. But it must be even harder on you that you survived, and he didn't. I bet you lay awake nights wishing it had been you instead of him. Am I right?" he asked, egging her on.

She looked at him, her face red with anger. "Don't you dare talk to me about my son!"

Removing the 9mm from his waist, he raised the gun, giving her a much clearer view of it. "Now, now, quiet down."

Kristin put her hands up in defense. "I don't have it. Believe me, I don't want anything from you." She eyed her call bell hooked onto the bed rail, then focused her attention on him, not letting him know what she was planning.

Miguel pulled back the slide on top of the barrel of the gun and placed his finger on the trigger. "I really don't have time for games. Just tell me where the money is, and I'll leave you alone." He aimed the gun at her heart.

Kristin stared at him, becoming very aware of her own heartbeat. Her pulse raced

"Now, I'm going to ask you one last time, where is my money? Or I'm going to make sure that wish comes true."

"The last time I saw it, it was in the back of Jake's closet. Why don't you ask him?"

"You don't know, do you?" he asked, flipping the safety on and lowering the gun to his side.

"Know what?"

"Jake is dead. Apparently, he didn't do too well with your son's death. Did you know your little boy made it to the front page of the news? Such a shame. He was a really cute kid. I liked him." He smiled coldly.

"You're lying," she said.

"Yep, Jake sat right down at the kitchen table with the paper open to the page of your son's picture on it. Drank his last beer and blew his brains out all over your kitchen floor. That's what I heard, anyways."

Kristin grabbed her mouth with her hands. *"Oh God!"*

"God had nothing to do with it. Oh, we found the bag. But a hundred grand was missing. So, where's the rest of my money and where's my package?" He waved the loaded gun at her.

"I'm telling you the truth, Miguel; I don't know where it is."

"Okay, you know what? I'm going to be nice and give you a week to remember where it went. If I don't have that package and the rest of my money by the end of next week, I'll be coming back to make sure you get to see your son again. Don't let me down, Kristin," he said, and just like that, he was gone.

Jake—dead? She visualized him sitting at the breakfast table with a gun to his head. She put her hands to her eyes, crying. She never wanted him dead. It was too much death. Now both her son and husband were gone. She couldn't comprehend it.

But what on earth was Miguel talking about? She never took any money out of the duffel bag that she had found in Jake's closet. In fact, she had been careful to put everything back exactly where and how she found it. Maybe Jake had taken the money? But wouldn't he have run away if he had? The news of Tommy's death probably tore him apart so much that he felt he had nothing else. It was exactly how she felt. She knew that Jake had loved him just as much as she did, even if he wasn't able to show it.

Kristin wanted to call the police, but she was afraid. What if they arrested her for being somehow involved or protecting her husband, who she suspected was involved in drug trafficking? Her life would be over before she had a chance to start a new one. Then she would have to also explain to David why she had lied about her husband leaving her. She would have to tell him everything. No, she had to keep this quiet, at least for now. But what was she going to do? She couldn't stay in the hospital. Miguel would come back for her—and if she didn't have his money, she believed he would surely kill her. That was for certain.

CHAPTER TWENTY-ONE

"Good afternoon, everyone. Welcome to those who are returning and those who are joining us for the first time tonight. Before we get started today, I just want everyone to remember that whatever is said in this circle, stays *in* this circle," the counselor said. "There's a bond of trust here that we have built between all of us. We must respect that bond and do our best to not let it be broken."

This was Kristin's third session since she had arrived. She didn't want to do this but knew that this would be her last one. After today, she would sign herself out of the hospital and head someplace Miguel couldn't get to her. She had so much bottled up emotion inside of her. So much that she wanted to rid herself of. Heck, everyone here had something they needed to let go of.

"Can I go first?" Roger asked.

"Sure, Roger." Jane smiled, delighted about his enthusiasm to share. Roger had joined the circle a week ago, and Kristin was amazed at how much he had shared last week.

"I know everyone thinks I'm horrible for cheating on my wife. But I want you to know I loved her."

"Was that why you were poking the babysitter?" one of the men asked.

"You don't know what it was like. I tried to talk to her, asked her to go to counseling. But all she focused on was making partner at the firm she worked at. She was a lawyer and worked over fifty hours a week. Fifty hours! She even slept at the office some nights. My kids and I hardly ever saw her. I tried... I really tried. I'm not a bad man. I mean, I'm better than some out there. Some men really treat their wives bad. I—"

Some people booed him from the circle when Kristin finally spoke up in his defense. "He's right."

"What was that, Kristin? Do you have something to share with us today?" Jane asked.

"Oh, come on, man. It's a waste of time trying to get her to speak. Just let Roger finish up," said Alex, the man with the disfigured face.

Jane hushed him, then said, "Kristin, go on."

"I said he's right. There are other men out there that are worse than him. I know because I was married to one of them for a very long time."

"What do you mean?" Catherine asked, sitting in her wheelchair beside her, giving her full attention.

Noticing Kristin's sudden silence, Jane said, "It's okay, Kristin. You don't have to keep going if you don't want to."

Kristin nodded in agreement, feeling as if she couldn't say any more. She wanted to, but something inside her just wouldn't allow her. "Excuse me," she said and wheeled herself away from the group, heading back to her room.

"You see, I told you. It's a waste of our time, her being in this group," Roger told Jane, then shouted to Kristin, "If you're not going to talk, then don't bother coming to the next session."

"Roger, it's not up to you who joins this group," Jane reprimanded.

Kristin felt horrible, for she *was* wasting their time. Everyone in the group had shared so much of their own personal tragedies. Why couldn't she open up the way they were able to?

She continued to wheel herself down the hallway, her hands tired from turning the wheels, but still, she pressed on. She had to get to her room.

Suddenly, she bumped into someone's feet.

"Ouch, what are you trying to do? Run me over? It couldn't have been that bad," David joked as Kristin raised her head. She followed the hemline of his black pants until she looked into those dreamy green eyes.

"Hi." Without thinking, David leaned over and placed a kiss on her cheek.

"What was that for?" She touched her cheek, smiling up at him.

"I'm sorry, I didn't mean to—I don't know why I did that. I..." David stuttered, realizing how inappropriate it was for him to have kissed her.

"It's okay. I... liked it."

David returned the smile. "Is group finished already?"

"No, but... I... I can't... I'm not going back there."

"Okay? Can you tell me why?" David squatted down beside her wheelchair.

Kristin looked around, feeling the eyes of every nurse on the floor upon them. They both realized they had been standing in front of the nurses' station the whole time. Kristin could hear some of the nurses whispering amongst themselves as they stared at them.

"They're watching us," she whispered.

David rose to his feet and grabbed the handles of the wheelchair to push her down the hall. "So, let them look. You're helping my reputation by talking to me. You know, a beautiful woman talking to someone like me."

"Someone like you?" Kristin smirked.

"Yeah, you know the old fairy tale. The princess and the toad."

"I'm sure that wasn't the title of the fairy tale." Kristin giggled. She enjoyed how David made her laugh. Whenever he was around, she felt beautiful and special.

"Well, you know what I mean." He wheeled her into her room.

After pulling the sheets down, David picked her up in his arms. He could feel his heart flutter a bit when he laid her on the bed. Their eyes locked onto one another. Time seemed to stand still. He felt the sudden urge to kiss her. He hadn't felt that nervous around a woman since the day he asked Daisy Cotter to senior prom. What was it about her that made him come alive inside? It was like she turned a light on that had been out for so long. He knew she had to feel the intensity of their attraction. There was certainly a chemistry between them that he'd never experienced with anyone else.

Kristin felt as if he were going to kiss her, and she couldn't help hoping he would. She couldn't deny that within the time she had spent with him since their night in the observatory, she had developed strong feelings toward him. Even so, she feared the possibility that it might be one-sided.

On the other hand, she thought back to every act of kindness he had shown her since that dreadful night she arrived at Parsons County General. He would sneak her some extra pillows from the nearby rooms and even leave her some fries and a vanilla milkshake with a Post-it on the cup that said *Proceed carefully* with a smiley face. He would often stop by to check on her even after his shift was over, before heading home. Could she be reading too much into this? Was he just as caring and considerate with his other patients?

David yearned to kiss her lips. Despite how he felt, he had to remember that he was her doctor first. So, he placed her down upon the bed and pulled the white hospital blanket over her. She smiled at him, even though she felt somewhat disappointed. Still, she didn't let him see that. She was not about to let him know how she felt—not until she could be sure he felt the same way.

Just then, there was a soft rap at the door that interrupted their thoughts of one another. They looked over to see Dr. Daniels standing in the doorway only a few feet away. He looked at David and then over at Kristin, who stared back at him with surprised expressions.

"Are you here to see me?" David asked, then looked down at his pager to see if he had missed any alerts.

"No, Dr. Landry, I am not." He observed David disapprovingly, having caught him hovering over Kristin's bed just moments before. "I came to see Ms. Summers. I hear that you are leaving us."

David quickly turned his head back to Kristin, who seemed now to be a bit uncomfortable, avoiding his eyes. "Leaving?"

Dr. Daniels cleared his throat. He had never seen David become so emotionally attached to a patient in all the time he had worked with him at Parsons. Frankly, he was astonished that David would even consider crossing professional boundaries with Kristin. When David had asked to manage Kristin's treatment from the beginning, Daniels hadn't given it much thought. Technically, Kristin was his patient, but knowing David was an excellent doctor and surgeon, he allowed him to take over.

Daniels walked closer to Kristin's bed, observing the body language between the two of them.

"I was going to tell you. I think it would be better if I went home," Kristin told David, then looked over at Daniels. "I feel much stronger."

"That's good." He walked over to the bed, placing his hand on her shoulder. "That's the goal for our patients. Isn't it, David?" He waited for an acknowledgment.

But David seemed very annoyed, shoving both hands into the pockets of his lab coat.

Go home? Kristin wasn't ready to go home yet. She hadn't even opened up in her group sessions. Emotionally, he didn't feel she was well enough to leave the hospital on her own. She had no one at home to take care of her. As far as he knew, she still had not reconciled with the only friend she had. She was still grieving her son's death, and there was still so much inside of her that she needed to release. He felt with a little bit of time, he could be the one to make her see she could trust him and tell him what had really happened the night of the accident. He could be the one to tear down that wall she had put between them.

Or maybe the real reason he was so frustrated was that he wasn't ready for her to leave the hospital—or him.

"David, isn't that right?" Daniels asked again.

David raised his eyes to Daniels, knowing exactly what he was thinking. "Yes, that is our goal. But in my medical opinion, I don't believe she is ready."

"Well, in *my* medical opinion, I don't see any reason why she can't be discharged. She's shown quite an improvement within the last week. Her vitals have been stable, and she is eating well. She can continue with an out-patient psychologist for grief counseling. When would you like to go home, Ms. Summers?"

Kristin observed the discourse between the two men. It was almost as if they were father and son and not colleagues.

Before she could respond to Daniel's question, David inquired. "Who's going to be at home to look after you? You still have a cast on your leg, and it's going to be hard for you to move around on it."

Even though she knew David had a point, she couldn't stay. She wished she could make him understand, but she was afraid that he wouldn't.

"I have crutches. The occupational therapist did a great job teaching me how to get around. I'm resilient."

The truth was she did not want to return home. She didn't have a home to return to when she really thought about it. Tommy was gone, and home was non-existent. She could call Tiffany, but would she even take her call? She felt awful about how she left things with her, and she knew that she had to make things right between them. But right now, she had to focus on leaving before Miguel returned. She was afraid if he did, David would believe that somehow, she had been involved in the life that her husband had kept hidden from her for so long. With Tommy gone, Kristin had no idea how she could live past his death. But David had made her feel that there was a purpose for her life. That feeling was the only thing that made being alive conceivable.

"Kristin, I really think that you should rethink this. Maybe stay for a few more days or be transferred to our rehab facility."

She shook her head at him. "No, David, I'll be fine."

Seeing the frown that had replaced the smile he had earlier, Kristin placed her hand over his on the bedrail. Remembering Daniels was still standing there, she withdrew her hand quickly.

"Kristin, you should—" he tried to say, when Daniels stopped him.

"Dr. Landry, a moment, please?" Daniels signaled that he wanted to speak with him in private.

"One sec, Dr. Daniels," he replied, looking back at Kristin.

"*Now*, David," Daniels said more firmly.

David mouthed to Kristin he would be right back, then followed Daniels outside to the hallway.

"What's going on with you, David?" Daniels stood with his arms folded within earshot of the nurses who watched on from their station, even though they did their best not to reveal they were.

David shrugged. "I don't understand what you mean."

"Don't play coy. You know exactly what I mean. You've become emotionally involved with this patient. And I know that *you* know that is something that just can't happen here."

"I honestly don't know what you're talking about." David shifted his weight from one foot to another nervously. He did his best to avoid Daniels's harsh glare.

"Since this patient has arrived, you've spent more time with her than checking on your other patients. Did you even know that as of last Monday, your patient Reyes refused further treatment and signed a DNR?"

David stood tall. He didn't like being on the defense, but that was the position he felt he was in. "Of course I did."

Daniels stepped a bit closer to him and spoke harshly but in a low tone. "Is that so? Then can you tell me why you instructed *Morrison* to perform CPR when the patient coded? If the family found out, we could have been sued!"

David could not believe it. In all the years he had practiced medicine, checking the patient's chart for a DNR was not something he had ever overlooked. It was obvious now to him, no matter how he may have tried to inwardly deny it, that he was becoming emotionally involved with Kristin. And now his job was on the line

"I'm sorry. I… um…" He couldn't find the words. He was still shocked at the error he had made.

Still speaking quietly, Daniels continued to lecture him. "Get your head out of the clouds, David! And get yourself together! Or else you are going to cause this hospital a big lawsuit, not to mention possibly lose your license." Daniels poked him hard in the chest and stormed off down the hallway. David had never seen Ned so angry with him as he was at that moment. He knew he had let him down and probably would think twice about entrusting his future patients with him.

David returned to Kristin's room, feeling a bit foolish and uncertain. Daniels was right—he was slipping up in his work. Maybe the last two weeks he had spent getting to know Kristin and the connection he felt every time they were together had caused him to lose focus at work. But how could he be mad at that? He welcomed the idea of spending more time with her, but he just couldn't allow those feelings for her to ruin the career he had worked so hard to build.

"What happened? Is everything okay?" Kristin asked.

David pulled a chair up beside the bed and sat down. "Okay, seriously now, who do you have at home to take care of you?"

"It doesn't matter. It's time I went home."

"Where is home?" David asked, opening her chart and flipping through the pages.

Kristin kept silent. She didn't want him to know anything about her life back home. As soon as she told him, he would probably insist he took her there. What then? All the questions would begin. Questions that she was not ready to answer.

"You don't even have a next of kin listed on the emergency contact sheet. In fact, you don't list any family members at all. All I know about you is that your husband left you. But what about your parents. Where are they?"

"Both my parents died in a house fire when I was seven years old. I was raised by my mother's sister in Bayerville. My aunt never approved of my relationship with my husband. When I moved in with my husband, we lost touch. Then she passed away, and I never got to go to say goodbye."

"Kristin, I can help you." David leaned forward and took her hand in his.

She stopped him. "I'm holding up a hospital bed that could be used by someone who actually needs it. You even heard Dr. Daniels say I am doing much better. All that I have is a bad leg, and in two more weeks, this cast will be off. I can take care of myself and Tommy for—" She paused, realizing that it was only her life now she would be responsible for. She corrected herself and said, "I can take care of myself, David."

He looked at Kristin, knowing that her condition had significantly improved since the first night she was brought in by ambulance. He was astounded at the strength and determination she possessed. She reminded him a little of himself. Was that the reason he felt so attracted to her? He knew she could make it on her own. But the desperate need he felt inside to take care of her wouldn't leave him. He didn't want to lose her.

"I would like you to come live with me for a while."

Kristin was shocked at David's proposition. "What? But that's crazy! I can't do that. I can't put you out like that. You don't even know me, and you... you have a life outside of this hospital, outside of me."

"You are not *putting* me out. I *want* to do this, Kristin. And if you're worried about me hitting on you, you don't need to be." He nervously let go of her hand and avoided eye contact. He really wasn't sure, as the words came out of his mouth, if that was a promise he could really keep. It was getting more difficult for him to control his feelings for her the more he was around her.

"I don't have to worry, huh?" she teased.

David could feel the heat rush to his cheeks. Was this really happening? She was flirting with him. Again, she surprised him with her boldness. Up until now, he had not seen this side of her. He smiled. She was becoming more comfortable with him.

"No, you don't. I mean, not if you wouldn't want—what I mean is no."

He ran his hand through his brown hair and chuckled. David could not be certain about her feelings toward him, but for the moment, he felt they were amorous. He was okay with that. "I'll be able to take care of you, help you. And when I'm at the hospital, I'll have a nurse come in and check on you. Assist you with bathing, meals. We'll have you continue with outpatient grief counseling."

"I might have a cast on my leg, David. But I'm not in any way a cripple. I can bathe myself. My ribs are actually feeling better every day. I don't need any more group counseling sessions. I have had my fill of them."

"Kristin, I wasn't implying that you aren't fully capable. I'm just saying there will be help there if you need it."

She gave it some thought. It would be nice to start fresh. It would be a blessing not having to return to a house filled with memories of Tommy or the painful recollections of the abuse she had endured with Jake over the years.

She looked into David's eyes. "Are you sure you want to do this? You don't have to."

"A hundred percent sure. I would feel better knowing you are somewhere close by. A place where I could keep an eye on you, to make sure you were all right."

"Okay. But only 'til I can get back on my feet again. I don't plan on taking advantage of your kindness."

"Maybe I would enjoy you taking advantage of me." David smiled, feeling hopeful that their friendship might now have a chance to blossom into something more.

CHAPTER TWENTY-TWO

The next morning, Kristin woke up to sunlight beaming upon her face. Today was the first day of a new life—a life without Tommy. During her packing to leave Parsons General, she took out the photograph of her holding Tommy in the hospital that had been buried in her tote bag. As she looked at the wrinkled photograph, she closed her eyes and spoke to him. She promised him she would never forget him and never stop loving him.

Dr. Daniels stopped by to see Kristin off.

"Dr. Daniels, I never truly thanked you for what you did. It's because of you that I'm still breathing." Kristin limped toward him on her crutch and gave him a hug.

He wasn't comfortable getting compliments and dismissed it quickly by saying, "It's the job. Make sure you stay off your feet and get plenty of rest." He folded his arms, observing her. "How do you feel?"

"I feel okay. A little nervous, but I'm looking forward to leaving."

"It's normal to feel that way, and after what you have been through... Well, I have to be getting back to my patients. I just wanted to stop by and wish you well."

"Thank you, Doctor. I appreciate all that everyone has done for me since I have been here."

As Kristin continued to pack, her thoughts drifted to Tiffany. She still hadn't shown her face at the hospital since the day of their argument.

Kristin used the hospital phone to call the diner to speak to Joe to thank him for paying her medical expenses. He told her that Tiffany had also helped. She promised that as soon as she was able to pay them back, she would. But he told her not to worry about the money. He expressed how thankful he was that she was okay and how deeply sorry he was about Tommy. When she asked to speak to Tiffany, Joe told her that he hadn't seen Tiffany in the last few days, but that he would be sure to pass the message along when he did. As soon as she could walk around on both legs, Kristin would stop by to see her friend.

After signing her discharge papers, she waited for the orderly to escort her out of the building by wheelchair.

"Hello, Ms. Thing," greeted Wilson as he entered Kristin's room in his green scrubs.

"Wilson!" Kristin smiled and gave him a big hug.

"Are we ready to see the outside world? I see you already changed out of your hospital attire and are all dolled up." He helped her to the wheelchair, hanging her tote bag over the handles. "It's going to be a beautiful day."

"I feel so funny with this big cast on my leg and only one sneaker on."

"Hey, if it was me and I had a handsome doctor who was going to take care of me, I'd be milking it for everything it's worth. Ooh, Dr. Landry!" he teased her as he made a right past the nurses' station, heading toward the double elevators.

Kristin was shocked. Did everyone know that she would be living with David? "What? How do you know that?"

"Sweetie, please. This is gossip central… Ain't nothing secret around here." They got in the elevator and descended to the ground level of the hospital. "Dr. Landry is a really cool guy. Hear he has a nice place too. Anyway, you will soon find out. Between me and you, he broke up with his longtime girlfriend a month ago. But you did not hear that from me." Wilson winked at Kristin.

It had never dawned on Kristin to ask David whether he was single or not when he asked her to stay with him. But she was happy that Wilson filled her in on that little detail.

"Hey, Wilson." David slapped him a high five as Wilson pressed the brake on, and David took over the wheelchair.

"My work here is done." Wilson gave Kristin a farewell hug.

"So, are you ready to see your new home?" David asked her as he lifted her from the wheelchair and placed her on the leather passenger seat of his black Ford Edge.

David looked for a reaction from Kristin, but Kristin could not be read. He wondered what she was thinking. She was silent now.

"Not exactly the type of car you would expect a surgeon to be driving. Huh?" he asked as he started the engine and pulled off.

"I don't know what I expected, honestly." Kristin reached for her seat belt and clicked in.

"Well, I used to own a BMW X5. But I gave it up to cut back on the payments. It was expensive to maintain, and I found my money was better spent elsewhere."

"It's a very nice car. I guess I'm just feeling a little bit anxious."

David proceeded to drive away from the hospital and made a right onto the ramp for the highway. "Well, since you're going to be staying with me for a while, I thought we could stop by the mall and do some light shopping, get some clothes."

"That's fine. I have a little bit of cash on me."

David shook his head. "Nah, don't worry about it. It's on me."

"No, letting me stay with you is more than enough. I'm not going to let you buy me clothes too."

David was surprised at how independent she was. If it were Allison, she would have immediately asked him for his credit card.

"Consider it a loan. When you get a job, you can pay me back," he told her, exiting off the highway and pulling into a mall.

"How am I going to move around a mall with this big cast on my leg?" she asked him as he pulled into a parking spot and walked toward the back of the truck.

Moments later, the trunk popped open and David had brought her wheelchair around by her door.

"Your chariot awaits, princess," he said as he helped her out of the car into the chair.

Kristin never knew a man could be this gentle and sweet. David showed her patience as the women working at the store helped her try on many different clothes. He didn't seem at all irritated at the lengthy amount of time it took. Kristin wheeled herself over to a sofa David had been sitting on outside the dressing room. She giggled when she saw he had fallen asleep. As he lay there with his face against the arm of the chair, practically drooling from the side of his mouth, she wanted to kiss him terribly. He was such a beautiful man, so kind and pure of heart.

But David woke up in time to see the face of an angel staring down at him. What a beautiful face to wake up to, he thought to himself.

Sitting up straight, he asked, "All done?"

"Yep, all done."

David stood up and hung the shopping bags with her clothes on the handles of the wheelchair.

An hour later, they pulled into the complex of David's high-rise condominium. Kristin was walking into a new world. It was a way of living she wasn't at all used to seeing.

As he pulled up to the entrance of the building, a slender white male in his early twenties dressed in a red blazer, white shirt, and black pants immediately opened her door.

"Thank you, Earl. We just need to get the wheelchair out of the trunk."

"Good evening, miss," said Earl. "I got it, Mr. Landry," he said and went to the back of the truck to carry the wheelchair out.

Before she knew it, David was wheeling Kristin across the marble floors of the building's lobby.

Earl had taken the keys to his truck to park it, and another attendant by the name of Gregory followed them with her shopping bags.

Even the building's elevators look luxurious, Kristin thought as she looked at her reflection in the mirrored walls. The cuts and bruises on her face were practically gone, and the swelling of her left eye had receded. All that was left was a fading black and blue. She was starting to look like herself again, and soon the large cast around her leg would be gone.

When they reached the ninth floor, Gregory held the elevator door with his hand to stop it from closing. David wheeled Kristin out and headed down the red and gold carpeted floors of the hallway.

Entering David's condominium, Kristin had to bite her lip to keep from gasping at how spacious and lovely his condo was. David took the bags from Gregory and sent him on his way. Then, putting the bags off to the side, he gave Kristin a tour of the condominium. There were two bedrooms, a den, dining room, kitchen, a double-sink bathroom with Jacuzzi, a workout room, and an entertainment room with two leather sofas and a flat-screen television. Each room was double the size of the living room in the house she had shared with Jake—and beautifully decorated. The walls throughout his home were painted a creamy yellow, and each room was carefully yet comfortably decorated. There was a definite flow of positive energy throughout the house. It was a feeling she had never felt in her life—peace.

"You did the decorating?" Kristin asked, amazed at the beauty of it all.

"Actually, it was my girlfriend, Allison. She hired an interior decorator when we first moved in here," he said, feeling a tad uncomfortable that he had to even bring up her name.

"Oh." Kristin wheeled herself away from him and headed toward a wall filled with pictures from his youth and his various achievement awards.

"We were together for two years. But it's over now. She's not part of my life anymore," he said, but Kristin didn't turn around to acknowledge what he had said.

"You have lots of pictures," she stated, looking at photographs of David playing soccer, at football games, pictures of him in graduation gowns. He'd had quite an active childhood, she gathered.

"Are those your parents?" Kristin asked, looking at a picture of an older couple in a square silver frame.

"Yes, that's them," he replied. David chuckled and pointed at a picture of him and his brother posing with a big fish. "Boy, I remember when this picture was taken."

"Which one is you?"

"The one holding the fish. The other kid is my baby brother. I was ten years old at the time. Josh was about seven," he said, flashing back to that day. "It was very cold on the water. We must have been on Dad's little speedboat for hours, freezing our butts off. We caught nothing for the first three hours. Then finally, just as we were about to call it a day, Josh's line started to bite. Dad screamed at us, 'Pull up! Pull up!' So, I grabbed hold of Josh's pole because he wasn't strong enough and started to reel the line in."

David lowered his head, feeling a tear starting to form. "Dad made us take a picture together. I gave the fish to Josh to hold because he was the one who caught it. But he said to me, 'No, Dave, you hold it.' He told me, 'You can bring the picture into school and show Jamie Morgan'—this girl I had a crush on—'that you caught a big one.' So, he gave me the fish to hold and Dad snapped the picture. But then after the picture, Josh told Dad to throw it back in. My dad didn't want to at first, but Josh kept insisting, so we threw the fish back into the water." He rubbed his eyes, afraid Kristin might see the tear that rolled down his cheek.

"Sounds like you really loved your brother."

"I did," he said, his mind drifting off for a moment. He started to think back to the day of Josh's funeral and stopped himself quickly. "Let's eat dinner, shall we?"

"Sure, what are we eating?"

"You like seafood?"

"I love seafood, but I haven't had it in a long time. Not since I was a kid, anyway."

"What? That's tragic. Well, I've been known to make a mean shrimp scampi over linguine. So, go get changed and let's say in an hour we meet back here for dinner. After dinner, I'll show you the rest of the grounds."

"Okay."

David was about to ask her if she needed help, but she gave him a glare that said, *Don't you dare.* He smiled and watched her wheel herself toward the bedroom and disappear.

David took this opportunity to call his friend, Pastor Greene. It had been a while since he had been over for dinner, ever since Kristin had entered his life. He was still very involved in planning the summer barbecue fundraisers. He had invited all the head surgeons from Parsons General and hoped they would be motivated to donate to the city project after they heard Pastor Greene speak. Pastor Greene had sent him pictures of the progress of the center, which made David even more enthusiastic in seeing its completion.

David had texted the pastor about Kristin the night she arrived and when her son had died. The pastor supported his decision in his need to help her.

"So, she's here," David said as soon as the pastor answered his phone.

"Okay..." The pastor chuckled.

"I don't know—I mean... I don't know why I'm so nervous. She makes me nervous." David laughed.

"In a good way or bad way?" Pastor Greene asked.

"Oh, it's good. I just don't—"

"David, breathe. You're rambling, and you're usually not one to ramble. Anna-Mae usually has to pull your teeth to get you to talk at the dinner table."

"I can't explain it. I have never felt this way. She was my patient, for Christ's sake... I'm sorry."

"It's okay. She isn't your patient any longer. She was discharged, right? I know you like her. I just hope you didn't kidnap her from the hospital," the pastor joked. "It appears this woman has enamored you. You should bring her by the center this weekend."

"I think I will do that. I think it would be good for her."

"Move slowly and be patient with her, David. You are in a great position to help her because you know what it's like to lose someone you loved very much. But there is no loss like the loss of your own child. I wouldn't wish it on anyone."

***

Later that evening, over dinner, Kristin was happy to hear more stories of David's childhood and crazy college days. He was the first one in his family to have graduated from college. She learned that David's parents were retired and living in Michigan. She noticed it was also difficult for him to speak about his brother Josh, which she surely could relate to, having a past of her own that was hard to talk about.

David was very inquisitive about Jake and how he had been during their marriage. But Kristin kept her answers general, telling him that he wasn't a good husband to her or a good father. She still didn't feel comfortable enough to share the horror stories of the abuse she had suffered. David could sense her hesitation but decided to remain patient, remembering Pastor Greene's advice.

The grounds of the condominium complex were spectacular. The architecture and landscaping were quite graceful. Kristin had only seen such exquisite things in movies. There were two swimming pools that all the tenants could use, an indoor pool and one outside. There was also a movie theater within the complex that played some of the older movies that had been in the theater over a month. She was a long way from home.

The weekend had arrived, and David was excited to show her the neighborhood. Of course, if he was paged, he told Kristin he would need to bring her home and go into the hospital, which she understood completely. *He is a surgeon, after all.* His calling was to save lives. She wondered if nursing was her calling, and if not, when she would realize what it was.

"I want to show you something," he said as they drove around his neighborhood.

"Sure."

David pulled up to a small building currently under renovation. There was an extension being added, and it was in the early stages. At least thirty people were hammering away at the construction site. Others were scattered about, wearing paint-stained T-shirts and pants. They carried buckets of paint, rollers, and brushes. As Kristin looked up, she could see written in bold black letters on one of the glass doors the words River Bank Community Center. Men and women carried wooden beams in their hands to set on a space on the ground a few feet away. Others worked around them, installing floorboards.

David wheeled Kristin down a makeshift ramp that the workers had created to bring in wheelbarrows of supplies. They headed toward a tall, elderly black man who seemed to be supervising the workers.

"Hey, David!" The man extended his hand to shake David's. "Good to see you!" He gave David a wide smile and hugged him affectionately. His shirt was just as dusty as the others, but David didn't seem to mind.

David placed his hands on Kristin's shoulders. "This is Kristin."

"Hello, Kristin. How are you? So, you're the reason he hasn't been able to make it over to my house for dinner."

Kristin looked up at the man's tall, lanky body as he bent over and extended his hand. She loved his friendly and warm personality. Maybe that was why David was the way he was. He surrounded himself with people who were just like him. She took his hand and shook it. "Nice to meet you."

"Pastor Greene oversees the community's outreach programs for children. Right now, the goal is to complete the extension of the community center so that the children can have a new basketball court and space for more recreational activities for the elderly."

"Maybe when you're feeling better, you can come by and help us some time." He winked at Kristin then looked at David. "Thank you for that donation; I just got it yesterday in the mail. Your brother would have been so proud of you for the way you have helped to bring his dream to life." He patted David on the back.

"Yeah, well, we're still about forty thousand short."

"It's okay, we'll get there. Slowly but surely. God provides," the pastor responded with a wink.

David couldn't help noticing how Kristin's face quickly changed. It was the same face he'd had when Josh talked about God. Still, he hoped that she would welcome the opportunity to get to know the people he considered part of his family.

"David!" A rosy-cheeked elderly woman in her late fifties ran over to him with a smudge of white paint on her nose and a paintbrush in her hands. She was shorter than Kristin and had a small belly with wide hips and jet-black hair cut into a bob.

"Kristin, this is Anna-Mae. Anna-Mae is Pastor Greene's wife and an amazing cook."

"So, you're the reason we haven't seen him at dinner lately. She's so beautiful, David. You didn't tell us how lovely she was." Anna-Mae smiled at Kristin, wrapping one arm around Pastor Greene's waist.

"Thank you." Kristin blushed.

"Hope we see you at the barbecue in a few weeks," Anna-Mae said.

"Oh, I'll make sure she's there." David rested his hand on her shoulder.

Kristin felt suddenly uncomfortable. How could he know where she would be in a few weeks when she didn't even know? She was grateful to him for letting her stay with him, but to speak for her and assume she would still be there was just as arrogant as Jake was when he spoke for her and made decisions for her. One thing she would not go back to was being anyone's puppet. Losing Tommy had made her stronger in some ways, and that was one of them.

"David, can you help me bring these pails of paint over there?" Pastor Greene held up one pail by the silver handle. He turned toward Kristin, who he noticed was a bit on edge. "I promise I'll bring him right back to you."

"No, go on. I'm okay." She flashed a fake smile at him. She desperately needed space from David right now.

"Where do you want this?" David asked, picking up a pail as he followed Pastor Greene onto the site where the workers had started to line up the wooden beams of the roof.

The pastor placed the bucket down and gestured for David to do the same. "David, don't take this the wrong way. But ease up a bit."

"What do you mean? You mean back there? What, with Kristin?" he asked, knowing he might have gone a little further than he should have.

"Remember the conversation we had the other day about being patient… moving slowly?"

"Yes, of course I do."

Pastor Greene chuckled. "Well, back there—just now—that wasn't exactly moving slowly. Not only do you have her living with you, you're not allowing her to speak for herself. Let her breathe."

"I… didn't realize I did that."

"Look, anyone can see how taken you are with her. She's a beautiful woman, but there's a lot of pain behind her smile. And I suspect that pain was there long before her son died. It's funny how some people's pain is so transparent while others hide it so well." He raised his eyebrow, implying David was one that hid his own pain well. "How are you doing?"

"I'm good. Every day it gets a little easier," David said, flicking the earpiece of his sunglasses in one hand.

"Just tread slowly. There is a light in your eyes I haven't seen before. I believe she has something to do with that, and I wouldn't like to see it die out."

David looked over at him and smiled. "Thanks."

"You know I haven't given up on you. I still hope I'll get you to visit me at church one day—hear one of my sermons." He patted David on the shoulder.

David looked away from him and fixed his eyes on one of the construction workers hammering away at a nail.

"Yeah, well, maybe one day." He looked back at Kristin, who hadn't moved from the spot he had left her in. Anna-Mae was introducing her to her granddaughter, who was about the same age as her son, Tommy.

"My older son, Elijah, will be giving his first sermon in a month. You're part of the family now. It would mean a lot to Anna-Mae and me, and I know Elijah as well, if you could make it."

"Yeah, I'll think about it," David said, quickly dismissing the topic. "Better go check on Kristin."

"Think of her as a flower growing in the midst of some nasty weeds. If you trim away at the weeds too fast and give her too much water, her petals will wilt away." The pastor watched David hurry to Kristin's side.

"You okay?" he asked Kristin as he stood behind her now, watching Anna-Mae's granddaughter blowing bubbles.

"I'd like to leave if you don't mind," she said, staring at the little girl in front of her. She was remembering the summer before when she had taken Tommy to the bubble show in the city. Tommy's eyes widened with joy when the entertainer created a giant bubble around them as she held him in her arms. *Mamma, look at the giant bubble.*

"Of course, let's go." They drove home together in silence. David wanted to ask her what was wrong, but he could tell from Kristin's body language that she didn't want to talk—so he left it alone. *Exercise patience*, he told himself, even though sometimes it was difficult to do so. He was a problem solver. If he saw a problem, he would do the research and come up with ways to fix it. He could hear the pastor's voice in his ear saying, *Move slowly.*

Maybe it was so hard for him because his feelings for her were becoming that much stronger.

∗∗∗

Sometime in the middle of the night, Kristin awoke in a sweat. She heard someone in the kitchen. She got into her wheelchair, feeling regretful about the way she acted toward David. He was only trying to be good to her, and she was being ungrateful. No matter how she felt inside, it didn't give her the right to make someone feel as bad as she did about herself.

"David?" She looked at the dining table and noticed David hadn't cleared their dinner plates, which was a bit strange.

Then suddenly, she heard someone move again in the kitchen and the clanking of pots and pans. She froze and then called out again. "David? Is that you? I'm sorry about earlier," she said, wheeling herself into the center of the kitchen, but there was no response. She looked at all the pots and pans. Not one of them had been moved. Everything was exactly where it was supposed to be. No one was there.

She started to feel a bit uneasy. She knew she'd heard someone. "David, where are you?" Suddenly, someone grabbed her from behind and threw her from the wheelchair onto the floor.

"Where's my dinner?" Jake yelled, straddling her and holding her hands down on the floor.

Kristin screamed, kneeing him in the groin with her good leg, but she missed. Jake only laughed at her.

"Didn't I tell you to have it ready on the table when I get home? You're nothing, Kristin! Nothing without me!" His hands still pinned her down beneath him as she struggled to break free.

"Get off me! Get off me!" she screamed over and over.

"You will never be free of me! Never!" He grabbed her hair, wrapping it around his wrist and pulling her head off the ground to pummel her face.

"Stop! Please stop!" Kristin begged.

David ran into the room, flicking the light switch on. Rushing to the side of her bed, he shook her by the shoulders as Kristin fought off her invisible attacker.

"Get off me!" she screamed with her eyes closed tight.

"Kristin—Kristin! Open your eyes, Kristin!" He shook her shoulders harder, waking her out of her dream. She jerked upright in bed, shaking terribly and crying. She could barely catch her breath. It felt so real to her. She looked around the room. It was just the two of them.

David hugged her close to his chest. "It's okay, you had a bad dream. It's okay," he said, caressing her hair. He wished he knew what was haunting her. He wished he could make it stop. It was her third bad dream in a week. If only she would just trust him and tell him what was going on.

"He was here! Jake was here!" she screamed. Her words didn't make any sense to him.

David pressed her head tightly against his chest and caressed her hair. He wanted Kristin to feel safe and protected. He would stop at nothing until she felt that way. He rocked her gently in his arms.

Kristin did feel safe inside his arms. She wanted him to hold her like this forever. But would that be taken from her like Tommy was?

"Jake isn't here, Kristin. Did he hurt you? Is that what your dreams are about?" he asked, not letting her go.

Kristin refused to look up at him. She couldn't tell him. If she told him she had been married to a man who beat her for the last eight years—that she'd almost killed him that night and that was how she ended up on that road—he would leave her for sure. He would want nothing to do with her. He'd think she was crazy, for sure.

But David didn't ask again. He knew better this time. But finally, he had his answer. This was the thing she was running away from—Jake.

CHAPTER TWENTY-THREE

A few days had passed. Kristin hadn't said much ever since her visit with David to the community center. Since the night of that bad dream, he had tried different ways to get her to open up about her life before the accident. He spent one morning making her a big breakfast that she barely touched. He even left a gift box from Sophia's, a high-end boutique, on her bed. Inside was a white cardigan. But Kristin returned it to him by placing it on his bed while he was at work.

Through David's gestures and actions, it was becoming more evident that he was falling for her. But she didn't deserve him—or any man—to love her. Most of all, she didn't love herself. He was the nicest man she had ever met, and she knew he would be much better off with someone who wasn't damaged goods or came with so much baggage.

David was optimistic, even though he felt that day at the community center—for whatever reason—had set him back in trying to tear down those walls of hers. It wasn't like him to go out of his way to reach any woman the way he was trying to reach Kristin. But then Kristin was no ordinary woman. No matter how many times she would shut him down and refuse any kindness from him, he kept trying. In the back of his mind, he knew somewhere along the line he had fallen in love with her. How and when that exact moment was—he didn't know. But he knew if he confessed his feelings for her now, she would run. He didn't want to risk not ever seeing her again. His heart felt too strongly for her. He couldn't imagine not having her in his life. So, for the time being, he kept those feelings to himself.

Finally, at dinner one evening, he couldn't take the silence between them anymore and spoke up.

"Do you want to tell me what happened at the community center? Was it the little girl? I knew you weren't ready to go out. I shouldn't have pushed," he started.

"David, it's not your fault. It's mine," Kristin said, playing with her food with her fork.

"Yes, it was. I should have given you more time, and that little girl reminded you of—"

"It's not just the little girl, David—everything reminds me of Tommy. Everything and anything. I can't even pour myself a bowl of cereal without thinking of how I used to make him breakfast in the morning. He used to love when I put a little smiley face of whipped cream on his pancakes." Her voice started to shake, but she kept it together. *Don't cry, Kristin*, she told herself.

He walked over to her at the other end of the table, pulled out the chair closer to her, and sat down. "I want to help you, but you have to let me in. What happened that night?"

She needed to get off the topic. She didn't know when she would be able to tell him all the horrible details of that evening. So, she used a tactic that Jake often used with her when she questioned him about other women and picked a fight. "Why was the first person you introduced me to outside of the hospital a pastor? I mean, honestly, did you really think that was smart? A man of God is the last person I wanted to be around. I have no interest in getting to know anyone who believes in a God that would take an innocent little boy away from his mother," she said bitterly. She stabbed at the food on her plate.

"Look, I don't know if there is a God," David said. "And it wasn't like that—Pastor Greene is a friend of mine who helped me through a very difficult time when I lost my brother. My brother was killed trying to save someone from getting beat up by some punk kids."

"Exactly my point—where was God then?" she mumbled.

"Look, Pastor Greene knew my brother. They used to work together at the community center. I just wanted you to meet them. The family and I really became close after Josh died."

"Must be nice to be *sooo* perfect all the time. To be this perfect surgeon, the perfect brother—to live this wonderful life in this perfect house!" Kristin threw her dinner plate at the wall, and it shattered to pieces. She thought David would kick her out or yell at her. But he didn't say a word for a few moments. He just looked at her with sad eyes.

"Kristin, I know the pain you are going through. That feeling where you just want to shut down and tell life to go to hell." He placed his hand over hers. "I was there, just like you. Some days I still find myself struggling to make sense of Josh's death."

"You think you can relate to me?" Kristin slammed her fist against the table. David jumped back in his chair, startled. "Well, you can't—I know you think that losing your brother is the same as losing my son. But it isn't! There is an ache in my heart that runs so deep, I don't know if it will ever go away. It hurts me to my core, David. *To my core!*"

She grabbed her stomach where only three years ago, she could feel Tommy moving inside of her womb. That joy she felt when Tommy moved inside her belly was now replaced by an endless void that was taking over her. "I miss my son. I miss him every day. You have no idea how hard it is for me to live knowing that he's out there somewhere, buried in the ground, and I can't be with him. To know I can't hold him again. To know I can't ever hear his laugh again. It hurts even more because I could have stopped it from happening."

"How can you blame yourself for his death? There was no way you could have known what would have happened that night."

"That's just it. We shouldn't have been on that road that night. IT'S MY FAULT HE'S DEAD!"

"What are you talking about? Talk to me—let me in." He tried to grab her hand, but she pushed him away again.

"No! I know you're expecting me to open up to you so I can get over this and move on. But I don't want to move on! I don't want to move past my son!" She pushed herself away from the table in her wheelchair, wiping tears from her cheek. "Excuse me."

Kristin wheeled away from the table, mumbling, "I'm sorry for breaking your plate."

"Kristin, wait!" David called out for her to stop, but she continued to wheel herself across the room and into the bedroom.

David slammed his hand against the table. *What is wrong with you?* he scolded himself. Why did you keep pushing?

A few hours later, David found himself rapping on Pastor Greene's door in the middle of the night. "Robert, I need to talk to you." There was no time for formalities.

"David? What's wrong?" Pastor Greene said as he answered the door, drawing the belt around his robe.

"Robert, is everything okay?" Anna-Mae called down to her husband from upstairs.

"Yes, Anna-Mae. Go back to bed. I got the door," Pastor Greene replied.

"I'm sorry to wake you at this hour. I screwed up. I don't know what I'm doing. Why did I think I could be the one to help her?" David shoved his hand through his hair and shuffled his weight from one foot to another.

"Woah, David, take a breath. What happened?" Pastor Greene opened the door wider and invited David in.

David followed the pastor into the kitchen, where he poured himself a cup of milk and one for David.

"Milk?" David chuckled as he took a sip.

"Were you expecting something stronger?" the pastor asked as he quirked a brow. "Look, David, there is no handbook for this. There are no right steps in the grieving process. You should know that better than anyone. It took you months before you were even able to open up to me about the guilt you carried over Josh's death."

"I know." David set his glass down on the table. "I just wish she would talk to me. There is so much I know she wants to tell me but isn't saying. She's scared, I know that. She told me she wasn't supposed to be on that road that night. Lately, she's been having these nightmares. She woke up screaming the name of her husband—Jake, who supposedly left her after her son was born. But I don't know what to make of it. There is more that she isn't telling me."

"It's obvious. She has a past that she is running from."

"But I have a bad feeling that this Jake did something to her. Something horrible."

"Why do you think that? Did you try to ask her?"

"I did, but she always changes the subject or picks a fight." David was keen on Kristin's cleverness. "When she came in that night at the hospital, orthopedics took some x-rays, thinking she might have been abused. When she was in the hospital, a nurse asked her if she wanted to contact her husband, and she told her that he was long gone and wouldn't want to be bothered."

"Maybe she was abused. It's possible."

"But why not tell me? She has to know I care about her."

"David, knowing that you care isn't enough. She has to trust you. That comes with time."

CHAPTER TWENTY-FOUR

"Today is the day, my dear," David greeted Kristin as she wheeled herself to the kitchen table. He stood behind the stove, making pancakes for the two of them. "We'll head over to the hospital to see the orthopedist, have that cast removed, and you'll finally be able to say goodbye to that wheelchair."

"Whatever." Kristin couldn't care less. She lacked motivation to do anything, inside or outside of the wheelchair. She started to wheel herself toward the window to watch the kids play on the grounds that surrounded the condominium complex. She couldn't shake the flood of memories of Tommy that danced in her head.

David set the skillet back on the stove and placed a pancake on a plate he had set aside for her. "Kristin, pancakes are ready."

"I'm not hungry."

"Come on. I make some pretty good pancakes if I say so myself."

"I'm not hungry," Kristin said a second time.

David's cell phone started to ring on the kitchen table. Out of the corner of his eye, David could see that it was Daniels calling.

"It's the hospital. I have to take this in the study," David called out, but Kristin paid no attention. She just kept staring out the window.

"David speaking."

"David, I've been calling you all morning. Where the hell have you been?"

"I'm sorry, Ned. I had family business to take care of."

"You still have to check your emails. What's going on with you? This isn't like you. Andy wants you to consult on one of his patients."

"Okay, I'll be right there."

Kristin could hear bits and pieces of the conversation. He was messing up at work, and it was all because of her. It was a mistake her coming here. She already screwed up her life. She didn't want to be the reason he messed up his.

He came over to her. "Sorry, I have to meet with Daniels. They are asking for a surgical consult on a patient. I'm sorry, I really wanted to be with you when the cast came off. It shouldn't take too long, but here's the key to the condominium." He took a key off his key chain and slid it across the table to her.

Kristin picked the key off the table, nodding. She placed it in her sweatpants pocket.

"In case I can't bring you back home after your cast comes off, you can let yourself in. I'll have a car pick you up from the clinic and bring you back home, of course."

"It's okay. I understand," Kristin said, looking up at him with some disappointment. Even though she had acted coldly, part of her had been looking forward to having him accompany her for the cast removal.

"You know what? I can take you there now, and you can wait in the waiting room. And if I finish the consult in time, I'll join you at the appointment. Would you be okay with that?"

"Why not? Not like I have anything better to do with this day," she replied.

At the hospital, the orthopedist remarked at how wonderfully her leg had healed. There was some mild swelling still around the fracture site, but otherwise, she recommended Kristin attend physical therapy sessions three times a week for the next four weeks. She would follow up with her around the third week. Kristin couldn't have been happier to rid herself of the cast's extra weight.

David joined her at the appointment just as the doctor started to cut the cast open. Dr. Kramer's eyebrows raised when he joined them. But David didn't care what thoughts ran through her mind. He didn't have to explain his life to anyone. If he wanted to be there for Kristin, he would be—no matter what the hospital gossip was saying about him and a former patient.

After the removal of Kristin's cast, David told Kristin to meet him in the lobby after she received the physical therapy referral. He had to check on one of his patients who had just arrived in the ER. A few moments later, Kristin was making her way down the hospital halls to the main elevators on two feet now. As she turned the corner, she heard a familiar voice call out behind her.

"Wowee, good-looking!"

She looked over her shoulder and screamed with excitement. "Wilson!" She walked toward him with open arms and he accepted, gladly hugging her tightly.

"You are looking like a brand-new woman. Got your cast off, I see."

Wilson leaned against the wall, smiling down at Kristin.

"Yes, finally."

"Well, you look much better than when you left here. Could Dr. Landry have something to do with that?" Wilson flashed a wicked grin.

Kristin could feel her cheeks grow hot, and Wilson laughed again.

"Have you seen him?" Kristin asked.

"Yes, a few moments ago. He was in the lobby talking to Dr. Daniels. Just take this hallway down to radiology. Make a left and take the elevator to the lobby."

"Thank you, Wilson. Thank you for everything." She hugged him tightly and headed to meet David in the lobby.

$$***$$

"David, what are you thinking? If I had known this woman would have been so much trouble, I would have never allowed you to personally manage her treatment. I can't believe you have her living in your house."

"I'm a grown man, Ned."

"Behaving like a little schoolboy who has a crush. You have no idea where she came from or what happened that night. No one does. She gave a fake address to the billing department. Don't you think it a little suspect that her boss and best friend covered most of her hospital expenses? She is hiding something, David. You're going to get dragged into something that could risk your career. Do you really want to risk that?"

"I don't care where she came from. I care about her. I'm going to be there for her. I promised her."

"David—"

"Not another word about it. I have a lot of respect for you as my mentor, as a friend. But this is my personal life. Stay out of it. If you need me, you know how to reach me," David said and headed toward Kristin, who was standing a few feet away.

"How's the leg?" he asked Kristin, leading them out of the hospital onto the sidewalk.

"Great. It feels a little funny not having the cast on after being so used to it. But I'm happy I don't have to be wheeling myself around anymore. My arms have had a good workout the last few months," Kristin joked, trying to keep up with David's long strides as they headed toward the hospital parking lot. She paused, then asked, "So, what happened back there?"

"Nothing," David replied quickly.

Kristin reached for his hand. "David, was it about me? Is your job in jeopardy because of me? Tell me," Kristin asked him with soft eyes.

"Right after you tell me what really happened the night of the accident," David said sharply. He paused. "I'm sorry. I'm just a little frustrated with Daniels. Let's go home and relax. I think I'm gonna put in for some personal leave time. I have a right to it, and under the circumstances, I think it would be wise."

"What? I'm not gonna let you do that."

"No one 'lets' me do anything." He smiled. "I want to do it." David opened the car door for Kristin, and she hopped in.

Kristin was shocked at the lengths that David was going to just to help her. Now he was talking about taking personal leave—for her? She knew deep down inside she must have been the reason for the heated discussion between him and Daniels.

She glanced over at him. Why did a man like him even have any interest in her at all? She didn't think much of herself to look at. Was she a project for him, like the community center? Something to fix up and then discard like yesterday's news when he was done? She had to be careful to guard her heart from him. It would be so easy to fall for him if she didn't still feel so numb from having lost Tommy. It didn't matter how she felt about him anyway. No one like her ever ended up with a man like him.

She was nothing, just like Jake had told her many times. And it was better this way, she told herself. Better to be alone.

Because when you have nothing, there's nothing to lose.

***

"Have you lost your mind, David? You want to take leave after the discussion we just had," Daniels said.

"Yes, I'm entitled to it, I believe. Paid family leave. In the last three years, when have I taken a vacation? I live, breathe, and sweat Parsons County General."

"David, you and I both know it doesn't work like that. I hate to break it to you; Kristin is not your family."

"Okay, well then, as of today, I'm taking a personal medical leave. I went through an emotional trauma, which I don't care to disclose at this time. And I need some time to get my head together."

"Well, we finally agree on something," Daniels replied with sarcasm

"Or I'll quit. I can always find a job at another hospital. You know, St. Augustine's has been dangling the attending position, and they're willing to increase my salary significantly."

"Okay, let's not get crazy. First off, you know that money has never been a deciding factor for you. You told me that yourself when you came on board."

"Yeah, well, people change," David replied.

"Look…" Daniels took a deep sigh. "I can shift things around a bit here and give you your two-week vacation. I'll have Jackson cover your patients in your absence, and Morrison can help out. But not a day over, or else you will really have to consider taking that job at Augustine's. And David, I really hope this girl is worth it. For her sake and yours."

David still held the phone to his ear for a minute after Daniels had hung up.

What am I doing? I don't even really know her, he thought. *There is still so much she hasn't told me.*

But as soon as those thoughts came rushing over him, he caught a glimpse of her setting the table for dinner. His heart fluttered so fast he felt like it would come right out of his chest. He was so in love with her, and he didn't understand why.

Usually, it was the other way around. Female patients would have what he would call "Nightingale crushes" on him. He even had a few married ones among them. But never in all his years of medicine had he fallen for a patient the way he fell for her. Of course, he had encountered some very attractive ones. Still, he always made sure not to cross the professional boundaries, and he would warn interns of the same. But with Kristin, a strong magnetism drew him to her.

His mind drifted back to that night when she was lying on that table in the OR. She looked like an angel. An angel he worked hard into the next morning to save. Even though it made no sense to his colleagues or Daniels, it made sense to him to help her in every way he could.

David decided to make the next two weeks memorable for Kristin. He searched for ways to keep her mind off Tommy, even though he knew he would not be able to completely. He had learned from Pastor Greene there was a hot air balloon festival two towns over. So, the first day of his vacation, he took her to Avalon, a town fifty miles north of Parsons. He figured this could be a possible fail, but he felt it was worth the gamble.

Kristin was a little nervous. She had never left Parsons County before, and she didn't know what to expect. But when they pulled alongside the wide, open field, all her anxiety left her. There had to be close to five hundred brightly colored hot air balloons, some on the ground but most in the air. Kristin's jaw dropped as she took in the sight.

"Wow!" she exclaimed in amazement.

"Well, don't just sit there with your mouth open." David laughed as he turned the ignition off. "Let's go!"

David jumped out of the car in his Beatles T-shirt and blue jeans, sprinting onto the field ahead of her, and she followed. There was a nice cool afternoon breeze, and the sunlight beamed strongly upon their faces. He spread his arms wide and closed his eyes.

"Close your eyes, Kristin, take a good deep breath. Can you feel how crisp the air is out here?"

Kristin closed her eyes and definitely agreed with him. The air was indeed wonderfully fresh and cool, and she was glad she had worn a long-sleeved shirt with her blue jeans.

David took Kristin by the hand and led her through the crowd toward a purple, blue, and white checkered hot air balloon on the greenest grass she had ever seen.

"Wanna go for a ride, young lassie?" a tall man with a Scottish accent—probably in his late forties—asked Kristin.

"Sure... are these things safe?" Kristin asked, looking a little worried over the balloon and how it operated.

"Only one way to find out," the hot air balloon operator joked. "Hop on in. I've been doing this for twenty years. Not a single casualty." He chuckled heartily, but Kristin didn't find it amusing at all.

"Don't worry, we'll be okay. Trust me." David jumped into the basket and stretched out his hand for Kristin to climb in beside him—and without hesitating, which startled her a little, she did.

Before they knew it, they were flying high above the crowd below them. A few times the balloon jerked from left to right, sending Kristin stumbling into David's arms that were ready to catch her.

"I'm sorry."

"It's okay, I don't mind. You can fall into my arms anytime," David said and thought of how cheesy it sounded after the fact. He took a few pictures of her with his cell phone, and they took a selfie together.

The rest of the afternoon was filled with more pictures, a wine tasting, and visiting the little stands around them that sold souvenir T-shirts that promoted the Avalon Hot Air Balloon Festival. Just as they were about to leave, their noses led them to a burger stand with a huge white sign that read Avalon's Voted #1 Deep-Fried Hamburgers. The air was filled with the scent of grilled onions and peppers.

"Well, we can't leave Avalon without having Avalon's best deep-fried burgers."

"Deep-fried burger? I've never had one of those," Kristin said.

"Me neither, so let's try something new together. Shall we?" He offered her his arm, a little scared she wouldn't take it. But she smiled at him and wrapped her arm around his, and they strolled over to the burger stand.

Baby steps, he told himself.

Behind the stand stood a chubby old woman, probably in her early seventies, with her tall, skinny husband who was about the same age. She had her gray hair wrapped up in a high bun with a strand around the frame of her face. She wiped her greasy hands on her already stained white apron, then squirted a bit of gel hand sanitizer in her hand before she donned new vinyl gloves. She yelled the next order to her husband, who was now deep-frying a seasoned beefy burger and grilling some onions and peppers.

"Can I help you?" she asked them as they approached her stand.

"I was just telling my beautiful friend here that we couldn't leave without tasting Avalon's finest hamburgers… deep-fried, is that right?" David pointed to the stand above her head.

"Yessiree bob. For over ten years we've been doing this. The secret is the sauce." She smiled at them, sounding like a television commercial for a fast food joint.

"Well, I'll take two deep-fried cheeseburgers, please." He looked back at Kristin, who nodded in agreement.

"Would you like some grilled onions on it? Fifty cents extra, but they add to the flavor," the woman said with a wide smile.

"Absolutely. Kristin, onions okay?" David looked over at her again.

"Sure." Kristin smiled back at him.

"Frank, two cheeseburgers with onions!" she shouted back at her husband. After David had paid her, they moved to the right to pick up their order.

Moments later, they both stood next to some tables, eating their cheeseburgers.

David moved aside the ketchup and mustard bottles to make more room for their drinks. He took a peek underneath his bun after taking his first bite.

"This sauce is really that good! How's yours?" he asked Kristin, who was chewing on a piece, savoring every bite.

Just before Kristin could answer, a glob of sauce fell from the greasy cheeseburger all over the front of her T-shirt.

"Can't take you anywhere!" David joked, not knowing it would strike a sensitive nerve in her.

"I'm sorry, I'm such a slob. I always do this!" Kristin put her burger down, grimacing as she frantically wiped away at the corners of her mouth and sopped the oil from her T-shirt with a napkin.

"Hey, hey…" He wrapped up the rest of his burger in the foil and set it on the table in front of them. "What's wrong?" He looked at her with concern.

She looked down and frowned. She was always making a mess. She heard Jake's voice resonating in her ears. *You must have a hole in your mouth, such a slob.*

David shook his head. "Kristin, what did this Jake do to you?"

"I can't talk about it." She looked down at her feet.

"Okay, then there is only one thing to do," He said, picking up the mustard and ketchup bottles, one in each hand.

"You're not serious." Kristin laughed at his foolishness.

"Oh, I am dead serious," David said, making one of his funny, dorky faces.

"David, no!" Kristin giggled, trying to grab one of the squirt bottles from his hand.

But it was too late. David started to scribble with each squirt bottle all over his T-shirt, painting a big happy face out of ketchup and mustard. Laughing, Kristin pulled out the new cell phone David had set up for her and took some photos.

"What do you think? Is it me?" He placed his hands on his hips in a Superman stance as she snapped more pics of him.

They both laughed hysterically as they scanned through the pictures. "Don't think the Beatles would be too happy with the new colors I added to their name."

Kristin laughed even more as passersby shook their heads at them.

"Come on, let's go get some ice cream. I have been dying to try this new flavor at the parlor that opened up next to us."

"Sounds good."

David was happy to finally see that she was smiling more. He seemed to live for those smiles. They had been scarce, and he was overjoyed at the fact it was because of him. He was on the right track to making her fall in love with him. It had turned out to be a truly memorable day.

The days that followed were just as wonderful. David took her to an amusement park where she rode every roller coaster, not to mention the slingshot ride where he thought for sure he would pass out. They also took in a museum, an art gallery, and went to the drive-in to see an old comedy flick.

So, this was what it's like to finally enjoy life instead of watching others do it, she thought.

One early afternoon, Kristin decided to go to the supermarket in town. She wanted to thank David for being so kind and wonderful the past few months. In the many conversations they'd had, David had told her what a fan he was of New Orleans food. So she planned to make him a Cajun dinner from a recipe she had seen on *The Cooking Show*. She had spent many nights in bed when her cast was on watching *The Cooking Show* until she was finally knocked out from the pain meds. It was the only thing she could watch without being reminded of how Tommy was not with her any longer.

But she still talked to Tommy every day in her heart, telling him how much she loved him and missed him and how sorry she was for being responsible for his death. It was her way of keeping him alive somehow. One of the grief counselors from the hospital in outpatient therapy had recommended she do that to help in her grieving process, and as painful as it was, she did. She also wondered if there was anything in the news about Jake's death, but avoided the newspapers in case there was. That was one thing she didn't want to be reminded of.

As Kristin packed David's trunk full of groceries she had bought on the credit card he had given her, she heard the most beautiful singing coming from down the block. She shut the trunk and followed the music, humming along to the melody. The music led her to a small church called Christ the King. She recognized the hymn now as she stood in front of the steps that led up to the doors of the church. It was a hymn her mother used to sing to her before she put her to bed at night when she was a little girl.

Kristin walked up the steps and into the church. She took a seat in the back pews out of sight, watching a young black man sitting on a bench, thumbing away at the keys on a shiny piano with his long fingers. Pastor Greene sat off to the right in one of the front pews, tapping his foot and joining him in song.

"Yes, Jesus loves me. Yes, Jesus loves me. Yes, Jesus loves me—for the Bible tells me so," the young man sang. His voice was calming and smooth. Each note he hit sent chills up Kristin's spine and goosebumps down her arms.

A single tear rolled off Kristin's cheek as she remembered how her mother used to sing the very same song to her when she was a young girl. She could remember laying on her bed looking up at her mother, who would close her eyes as she lost herself in the hymn. Kristin had almost forgotten how beautiful her voice was. She buried her head in her hands. She had repressed the memories of her mother and father for so long so she wouldn't feel the pain of their deaths. None of it was fair, not her parents, not Tommy.

After the hymn was over, Pastor Greene walked over to the young man, smiling. They exchanged a few words, followed by some laughter. When the young man turned, he spotted Kristin and gestured to the pastor.

"Kristin, is that you?" she heard Pastor Greene say as he walked toward the back pews.

She lifted her head to see Pastor Greene standing there, worried.

"I'm sorry. I had heard the music, and I—" she began.

He put his hand up for her to stop and sat down in the pew directly in front of her. Leaning his arm on the back of the pew, he turned his body to face her.

"Come on now, we don't need a reason to enter His house. All are welcome here," he said affectionately.

"No, I really need to be going." She stood. "I have to get back and make dinner before David gets home from the gym."

"No, sit down. I'll buy back anything that spoils, I promise. The supermarket won't close for a few hours. We have some time."

"Honestly, Pastor Greene, I have to be going."

"Sit," he insisted, speaking in a fatherly tone, and Kristin did. "Is everything okay? Do you know that hymn? It's one of my favorites."

Kristin looked toward the front of the church as the choir practiced another hymn together. "My mother used to sing it to me as a child."

"Mothers are amazing creatures. They bring life into this world and have this unbelievable capacity to love their children unconditionally."

"Yeah, so tell me, preacher man, why did God take her away from me, then?" Kristin asked, annoyed.

"Sometimes, we may not understand God's plan for us or why He allows certain things to happen, but it doesn't mean that He has forsaken us when bad things happen."

"Was it also God's plan to take my only child after He gave him to me? Everything good I've ever had in my life *He* has taken away from me."

"Kristin, I know you are in terrible pain. No mother should ever have to bury her child. But it is not by coincidence you were led here tonight by the very same song that your mother sang to you as a child. At a time, when you happened to be right next door, as my son was singing it."

"So, what are you telling me, Pastor? That this is all part of His divine plan for my life? Me being in this church right now? That He loves me—unconditionally, the way my mother loved me?"

"I believe He does, Kristin."

"Well, isn't that something, 'cause I have never felt His love. All I have known is His suffering. How much more suffering do I have to endure before I know what His love feels like?" She threw her arms up at him.

"We all go through our own pain and suffering, Kristin. Just because God loves us doesn't mean that we will never experience suffering or pain in this life. But it does mean that by having faith in Him, when the storm does come, we will have been made stronger. Because in Christ, we are Overcomers. God loves you, Kristin, and I know you don't see that. But one day, His plan for your life will make sense to you."

"You don't know what you're talking about. I'm the reason that my son is not here today.

"It wasn't your fault."

"How do you know I wasn't a bad mother?"

"Because a bad mother wouldn't have cared to ask such a question. I don't know what it is that you're scared of, but I do know that David loves you. I love him like a son. He's a good man. And I know that even if you aren't willing to face it, you are in love with him too. But you will get in your own way and sabotage what could be the most beautiful gift God could ever give you—a second chance at love and life."

Kristin fought back her tears, although they were burning to get through. She stood up as if to leave.

Pastor Greene leaned over and grabbed her hand, offering some more insight. "Forgiving others is difficult. But forgiving yourself is even harder. You're never going to be able to fully experience God's love until you completely surrender to him." Pausing, he tilted his head to the side, taking her in. Then he leaned forward and began singing softly.

"Yes, Jesus loves you. Yes, Jesus loves you."

Kristin joined him quietly in song. "Yes, Jesus loves you."

Pastor Green sang the last line directly to her. "For the Bible tells us so." He paused a moment, then leaned in and spoke. "Kristin, you're gonna make it."

With those words, he stood, nodded his head to her and made his way back to the front of the church.

Kristin watched as he walked away down the aisle. The pastor's words stayed with her all the way home.

✳✳✳

Kristin hurried home to make the Cajun chicken and pasta dinner for David as she had originally planned.

"Smells good!" David called out enthusiastically as he walked into the kitchen with his gym bag. The aroma of Kristin's cooking smelled like heaven. He had only had his pre-workout energy drink before hitting the gym, and he was starving.

"Gonna hit the shower. I'll be out in a few." He smiled at her standing by the kitchen island, preparing the dinner rolls she had pulled out of the oven and arranging them on a serving dish.

Wiping her hands on her black apron, Kristin wondered if she should have mentioned her run-in with the pastor earlier. But she wasn't exactly sure how David would react knowing he had been part of their discussion. Jake had always gotten furious if he found out she discussed him with anyone. He called it being a private person, and said no one needed to know their business. Kristin knew, however, what he really meant was he didn't want anyone knowing he was an alcoholic or a wife beater.

As she gazed over at David, who was talking animatedly about a man who had been trying to pick up a girl at the gym using cheesy pickup lines, she knew there was no comparison. Jake and David were night and day. David was loving, funny, passionate. The only two things Jake was ever passionate about were his drinking and his workouts. Even so, she wasn't quite sure if it was the wisest thing to do to bring up her conversation with the pastor, especially at dinner.

"I can't believe you never made this before. This is really good, has a nice kick to it."

"David, I have something to tell you," Kristin said.

"What is it?" He wiped his mouth with the dinner napkin and sipped some more red wine.

"I ran into—"

His cell phone rang, and he gestured her to hold that thought.

"Hey, Daniels, two weeks isn't up." David chuckled over the phone. Then his smile vanished and turned into an expression she had never seen before. For the first time since they met, she couldn't read him.

"David, is everything okay?" she whispered.

"Okay, I'm coming. I'll be right there." He pushed himself away from the table and looked over at Kristin.

"Kristin, I have to run down to the hospital. I'll be back in a few."

"Is everything okay?"

"Yes, don't worry. I'll be right back. Promise." He kissed her forehead, grabbed his car keys, and hurried out the door.

Just great. She stared down at his barely half-eaten meal. Then she finished her dinner and cleaned up.

An hour later, David walked in. He told her that a friend was in the hospital and Daniels thought he might want to offer his medical opinion on the matter. But then he changed the subject rather abruptly, and there was a brief moment of awkward silence.

Kristin could sense he was avoiding her eyes. She stared at him, wondering what more there was to his story, but he moved past her hastily to heat up the plate of food he had left behind earlier. More silence ensued, and David broke it, suggesting that they go watch TV in the living room. She sat beside him, legs crossed, still waiting to make eye contact. But he kept his eyes glued to the television screen in front of him.

However, Kristin's focus remained fixed on him. It was the first time she felt he was keeping something from her. Just when she finally felt things were moving in a positive direction, there it was again, waving its ugly little hand—doubt!

CHAPTER TWENTY-FIVE

D avid was back at work two weeks later, although he wasn't working as often as he used to since he was trying to wrap things up down at the community center. He thought he would be met with some resistance by Daniels. But Daniels, knowing how important the community project had become, gave him a lot of leeway.

Meanwhile, Kristin was looking into doing some research on nursing schools nearby. She desired purpose for her life, and she felt this would give it to her. When she shared her thoughts with David, he was so excited for her and offered to help her in any way he could. Seeing how genuinely happy he was for her, Kristin shrugged off the reservations she still carried ever since the night he returned home from the late-night meeting with Daniels. *He went to check on a friend. That was all there was to it. He is not Jake,* she scolded herself.

One Friday afternoon, David was helping some volunteers from the congregation paint the walls of the new gym in the community center. Even though the center was nearly complete, there was still a bit of work remaining. And of course, there was the barbecue at the end of summer, which was now only a month away.

Pastor Greene walked over to him with two blue tickets in his hand.

"What's this?" David asked him as he set the roller brush in the tray of paint. He brushed the sweat off his forehead with the back of his hand.

"Two tickets to a concert this evening. I thought maybe you would like to take Kristin."

"Concert, huh? Where? What type of concert?" David asked, looking them over.

"Location is mi casa, and Elijah and his friends are throwing the concert. They have a cover band and do songs from the 80s and 90s."

"Your house?"

"Yeah, well, we have some acreage behind the house, and Anna-Mae found a way to put it to good use. Personally, I think she just wants to get together with her girls to throw a nice big gathering. But what better way to raise money for the center? Food and music! I think it will be a good thing. I hear Judge Reynolds is also supposed to come."

"The Judge, huh? Behold, I send you out like sheep amongst the wolves." David stood tall, mimicking his best preachy voice.

"I see there's some scripture left in you yet."

David let out a deep sigh. "Yeah, well, my granddad used to preach that stuff to me back when I was a boy. Guess some of it still stuck."

"Well, there's a reason for that, which you will find out in due time."

"So, you said there would be food?" David asked, changing the subject.

"Yep. Me and some of the church elders will be providing our culinary grill skills for the evening."

"There's no doubt you and Anna-Mae know how to cook. And I gather there will be some church songs in the mix."

"Well, Elijah is my son. Can I help it if he has good taste in music?" Pastor Greene joked.

"You know if I didn't know better, I'd say you were trying again." David turned around and started to clean up some paint with a small rag.

"Think of it more as an evening you get to spend with a lovely woman underneath the stars listening to some great music."

"I'll think about it. Better hit the showers and get this stink off of me, or Kristin won't want to be anywhere near me, let alone escort me to a concert." He flashed Pastor Greene a big smile, took the tickets he still held out, and threw his dirty, sweaty t-shirt over his shoulder.

"Couldn't agree with you more." Pastor Greene chuckled heartily as David headed to the locker room.

Around six o'clock that evening, he found Kristin sitting by the window, deep in thought. He was scared of her slipping back into a depression since his return to work and the time he was spending finishing things up at the center. Normally, she would have met him at the door.

He threw his bag of dirty clothes into the washing machine and then took out the tickets Pastor Greene had given him. Maybe this would be a good thing for both of them. They hadn't really seen each other too much the last week. Unlike Allison, who constantly nagged when he was away from home, Kristin didn't seem to resent the time he spent at the community center. Nonetheless, he missed the closeness they had started to build, and he didn't want that to slip away.

"Hey, you," Kristin said, looking over as he walked into the living room.

"Hey. Listen, would you mind escorting me to a concert tonight?" He squatted down beside her, showing her the tickets.

"To be honest, David, I'm really not up for a concert."

"Come on, remember the great time we had at that hot air balloon festival? This will be just as fun," David said with a smile.

Every time he smiled at her now, Kristin could feel her heart beat in her chest. She had fallen for him, but she kept silent about her feelings. She still didn't think she was good enough for him. *I killed my son. My husband is dead, my parents, my aunt.* Everywhere she went, she brought pain and death. Still, when he looked at her so adoringly, as he was doing now, she couldn't imagine leaving him. And no matter what he asked of her, she could not bring herself to say no.

"Okay, okay. I'll go with you." She gave him a half smile.

Kristin was surprised to see how many people had shown up at Pastor Greene's home for the concert. There were also some unmarked black Lincoln Town Cars with dark tints parked along the curb of the magnificent Victorian-style home. David had told her that the home had been in the family for many years, belonging to Pastor Greene's ancestors who served in the Civil War.

"Here you go. One popcorn and Coca-Cola," David said, clinking his glass bottle with hers.

He turned to face the stage that had been set up with drums, microphones, and an amplifier. The band was checking the equipment to make sure everything was working.

"This is insane." Kristin's eyes widened as she looked around at the people that were still pulling up in the driveway and crossing the front lawn heading to the back of the Greene house.

"It's a good thing. The ticket sales and refreshments should really help toward the remaining balance of the renovations down at the center."

"Well, with this crowd, they should be able to pay it all."

"I am so in love with your smile," David blurted out, allowing himself to be vulnerable with her for the first time. He wanted to kiss her so badly, and from the way she was mirroring his gestures, he thought she just might let him. He moved in closer to her, but then they were interrupted.

"Glad you guys made it out." Pastor Greene put his arms around their shoulders.

"Great turnout," Kristin said, greeting him with a kiss on the cheek.

"Yeah, Elijah is already up there warming up." He pointed at his son, who was leaning over a band member next to the keyboards.

"Wait, that's your son?" she asked, recognizing him as the young man who had been singing by the piano.

"You met Elijah before?" David asked, confused.

"No, I mean, I saw him at church that day."

"Church? Wait—when were you at church?"

"Okay, you two, I'm going to head over to the judge over there. See if he's feeling generous enough tonight to make a donation."

Kristin caught David, who still looked at her with some confusion. How was she going to tell him about the conversation she'd had with Pastor Greene that day in town?

Just then the music started, and they both turned their focus to the stage. The drummer started to beat on the drums and the crowd cheered.

Elijah grabbed the microphone and screamed, "IS EVERYONE READY FOR SOME MUSIC?" The crowd's cheers became even louder.

"Let me introduce you to the band. There's Nick on drums." Nick did a little solo, clashing on the cymbals. "Kevin on guitar." Kevin played a few riffs on the electronic guitar. "And I'm—Elijah. We are The Overcomers. Everyone make some noooise!" The crowd cheered again.

The band played a few cover songs from Aerosmith, Journey, and even Foreigner. David was surprised at just how good Elijah was, and he and Kristin sang along with the songs. During a short break, Elijah came off the stage and chatted with Kristin and David.

"My man." Elijah slapped hands with him in brotherly love. He turned to Kristin, smiling. "Nice to meet you, Kristin. You were at the church a week ago, right?"

"Yes, I was. You're very talented."

David again flashed her a confused look.

"Thank you."

"You are really good," David agreed.

"I have a song for you guys! It's a little newer than what we usually play, but you'll love it," Elijah yelled as he jumped back onto the stage.

David smiled at Kristin. "You know you're going to tell me about that later."

"Yes, I will," she laughed.

The music started and Elijah began to sing Sheryl Crow's "The First Cut is the Deepest," the gentle guitar slowly getting louder.

"Can I have this dance?" David offered his hand to Kristin. She looked around her as couples started to dance in front of the stage.

Kristin placed her hand in his nervously as he drew her in close to his body. Feeling self-conscious, knowing she never really learned how to dance, she avoided his eyes and looked around to see if anyone was watching them.

"Stop... you're with me," he said, sensing her insecurity. "I'm with you. That's all that matters." David pushed a strand of hair behind her ear and moved his cheek close to hers. Her hair smelled like coconut. He wished this moment could last forever.

"Are you smelling my hair?" She grinned at him.

"Yes, I'm glad to see that shampoo I bought on sale for five bucks was put to good use."

They both laughed. He was always saying something funny to make her feel at ease—the complete opposite of how Jake had made her feel for the last eight years.

Elijah sang the chorus into the microphone, giving David a thumbs-up.

"He was a fool... Jake or whoever it was that hurt you." David twirled Kristin around, but she didn't respond, her mind elsewhere.

She wanted to tell him right there and come out with it. She wanted to clear the air, but she was so afraid he would never look at her the way he was looking at her now, underneath the stars, dancing on the grass, with his arms around her.

David spun her around, and she giggled. Then, suddenly, her skin grew cold. *Was that Jake standing next to one of the drink stations?* Kristin came to an abrupt halt, and a woman dancing next to them bumped into her, spilling her drink down the side of Kristin's dress.

"Oh, my goodness! I'm so sorry. I didn't even see you there," the woman exclaimed.

"Are you okay?" David asked, noticing the look of worry on Kristin's face.

"Yes... I thought I saw... it's nothing." Kristin felt a tap on her shoulder and turned to find Anna-Mae at her side.

"Sweetheart, your dress is all wet." She took Kristin's hand and led her through the crowd on the lawn and into the house. "Let's get you into something dry."

"Thank you so much, Anna-Mae. It was really my fault." She gratefully accepted a dry change of clothes from the pastor's wife and, after quickly changing, headed back to the concert.

Just as she stepped outside, the song finished, and Elijah addressed the audience. "Okay, so like all good things, we must come to an end. You all don't have to go home, but you gotta get the heck outta here." He joked as the drummer did a rim shot—*ba-dum-bum.*

The sound of disappointment echoed throughout the crowd.

"Now wait one minute. Before we go, we have to share some good news. Thanks to the generous donations tonight, we have reached our goal of forty thousand dollars!" The crowd went wild, erupting in cheers and hugs. David picked Kristin up in his arms and spun her around so fast she felt dizzy when he placed her back on her feet.

Elijah continued. "My father—some of you all know him as Pastor Robert Greene—would also like to give a great thanks to our town judge, Judge Reynolds, for his extravagant, generous—*very* generous donation. Thank you. Give it up for Judge Reynolds!" Elijah started to clap, and the crowd joined in. The judge smiled and flexed his arm to show his support.

David couldn't remember being happier than he was at this moment. There was only one other thing that would transform this evening from fantastic into spectacular...

Kristin was glad he was happy. She knew this center meant a lot to him. After all the hard work and long hours he had put in, his brother's project was about to be successful.

"I want to tell you guys, you have been an awesome crowd tonight. DID YOU GUYS HAVE FUN?"

The crowd cheered again.

"Come on, I can't hear you. DID YOU GUYS HAVE A GOOD TIME TONIGHT?" Elijah screamed into the microphone. The response was almost deafening. "Good, good. Now the band and I must say goodnight. But not before one last song. And what kind of pastor's son would I be if I didn't give God some glory for this amazing night! So, we are going to end this night with a song by one of my favorite artists out there right now. His name is Jeremy Camp—and this guy knows what it means to be an overcomer. And tonight, that's what we have done. We overcame an obstacle that was in our path to finishing the center. It doesn't matter what color you are, what religion you do or don't follow. It's a feel-good song with a good beat to dance to. So, move to the beat and know you are blessed! Here it is— 'My Defender.'"

The guitarist started to play, and then the drummer picked up. Elijah started to sing again. Kristin moved her feet to the rhythm along with David, not caring at all what kind of song was playing. But they were not prepared for what happened next.

As Elijah sang, Kristin felt herself captured by the lyrics. It was like the gate that had been closed on all the memories she had of her mother had burst open, and they started to flood her mind. Memories danced in her head of going to church with her parents, of her dad saying prayers with her before bedtime, of her mother singing church hymns and her singing along to them. Emotions poured out of her like a fountain—she began to weep heavily. The tears kept coming, blinding her vision. She began to mourn the death of her parents, which she'd never allowed herself to do before.

Kristin's knees weakened, and she felt an overwhelming peace and love come over her. And then she knew—*He* was always there no matter how much she blamed Him for her parents' death, for Tommy's death, for the abuse she endured from Jake. God had never left her. But she wasn't able to feel it until now—she wasn't able to feel his love until she surrendered to Him. And when she did let go at that moment, she could feel all the anger inside—all the pain, all the hurt, all the unforgiveness she kept buried inside of her—release from her body. She fell to the ground, putting her hands up in praise.

When she lifted her head to the sky, she felt a drop of water on her face, then another, then another. And in the next moment, the heavens opened up and released a deluge. She prayed, *Father God, take this pain away from me. I surrender to You.* And she felt as if He did as the rain washed over her in a cleansing flood.

She looked up at David, who stood as if he was frozen in time. Paying no mind to the rain, David's mind had drifted off to memories of him and his brother when they were little boys. He remembered in particular how much his grandfather used to talk to him about God and how great He was. He always had a parable to tell.

Then he remembered the night Josh was ten and had taken very ill. He went to the hospital with a high fever and had to stay for a week. There was a point when his parents and David didn't think Josh would make it home. When Josh finally came home from the hospital, David gave him the Bible his grandfather had given to him, leaving a note in between the pages of his grandfather's favorite—Psalm 91.

Please, God, watch over my little brother. Don't let him get sick again. Love, David.

Three days later, his grandfather took sick and had to be admitted to the hospital. Within twenty-four hours, he died from an undiagnosed pulmonary embolism, and David never wanted to hear the word *God* again. When Josh tried to give the Bible back to him after he was better, David told him to keep it.

He never knew Josh had kept it all those years until Pastor Greene had given him a box of his brother's belongings after his death. In that box was the very same Bible David had placed beside him on the bed with the note he had written still marking the pages of Psalm 91.

David's heart was penetrated by the words as Elijah sang, and when he saw Kristin fall to the ground, he was scared. He didn't want to believe, but he remembered what Josh had told him once over breakfast when he started going to church. "David, God is the only one who can reach someone who is unreachable. He is the only one who can grab hold of a cold heart and make it love again."

At the time, Josh had been referring to himself. And now, as David saw the breakthrough in Kristin, his faith was restored. God had done in an instant what he had been trying to do for months. He knew that God was very real. He knew God did heal.

Kristin rose to her feet, letting out a deep sigh as the brief downpour ended just as quickly as it had begun. She felt free, renewed for the first time in years. She walked over to David and stood in front of him. "You're crying."

"I... No, that's just the rain," he protested.

"It's not the rain, David. You're crying."

"Yeah, well, you are too." He smiled, wiping a tear away. "Don't worry about me, I'll be fine."

"No, someone needs to worry about you," Kristin said. "Stop being so strong. You're with me; I'm with you."

David chuckled. "So, you're using my words against me now."

"I want to be there for you the way you have been there for me. You saved me from myself... David, I need to tell you something." This was it—the moment had come. "It's about the night of the accident."

"David, come here for a minute," the pastor called out from behind him, only a few feet away.

David signaled to him to give him a minute and then focused his eyes on Kristin. "Okay, tell me."

"It's okay. Go, he's waiting for you."

"I'll be right back, don't go anywhere. We *are* finishing this conversation," he said and turned to leave.

"Wait." She called out to him, and he turned back to face her. Throwing her arms around his waist, she pulled herself into him as he opened his arms to embrace her. She hugged him tightly.

"What was that for?" He tilted his head smiling.

"Just because."

"I'll take it. But I know you have something to tell me, and I'm not letting you off the hook." Then in his best Arnold Schwarzenegger impression, he made a funny face and told her, "I'll be back."

Kristin laughed at his silliness. As she watched him walk over to Pastor Greene and Judge Reynolds, Kristin decided that no matter what, this was the night she would tell him the truth. She would tell him that she loved him and tell him what she had been keeping from him for so long—about that night, about Jake, about everything.

"Handsome and funny, isn't he?" said a lady's voice beside her.

Kristin looked over her left shoulder at a tall, slender woman with long legs. Her long red hair was nicely blown out straight. She could have been a model, Kristin thought.

"I'm sorry, do I know you?"

"Sorry, how rude of me. I'm Allison Scott. You are?" Her voice was soft, yet strikingly confident. Allison offered to shake her hand.

"Allison. I'm Kristin," Kristin replied, realizing that standing in front of her was David's ex-fiancé.

"It seems as if you heard of me already." Allison smiled, but her eyes were mean.

"Allison, what are you doing here?" David asked, walking towards them, looking at Kristin and then back at Allison.

"David, darling." She aggressively threw her arms around his neck and planted a soft kiss on his lips.

Kristin's heart sank and she was infuriated, but she kept her emotions under control.

"What the heck are you doing?" David grabbed both of her hands from around his neck and gently pushed her off him.

Kristin felt too uncomfortable to look on. She couldn't bear to stand by and watch them, knowing how much history there was between them and how moments ago she thought she could be gazing into the eyes of her future. It was better if she left.

"Excuse me, I'm going to ask Pastor Greene to take me home. I'm sure you guys have some things you need to talk about." She tried to leave, but David stopped her.

"No, there's nothing to talk about. Not anymore." He looked back at Allison, who seemed slightly amused.

"That's not what I felt from you when you came to the hospital last week."

"What?" Kristin asked him. "She was the friend, the one Daniels needed your opinion on that night?"

"I was going to tell you but—"

"No, you don't need to say anything. I get it." Kristin started to storm away.

"Kristin, wait!" David tried to run after her, but Allison blocked his path. "What do you want? Why are you even here?"

"Well, I went by the hospital to look for you to thank you for your help that night."

"Allison, stop acting like a child. You fell off a spin bike in class and cut yourself. You just needed a few stitches. If I'd known that, I would have never come down there. You made it sound worse than it was. There was nothing to it, and there is nothing between us."

"If it was nothing, then why did you keep it from her?"

"I shouldn't have, and the blame is on me for that."

"Look, I just wanted to thank you."

"Stop the crap. You're here only because you found out about her. Sad thing is you don't even really care for me. The only reason you're here right now is because you see this as a competition. It's always been like that with you."

Allison put her hand up and tried to protest, but David stopped her. "But the thing that you don't get is there is no competition here. And even if there was, you'd lose by a landslide. We're done here." David pushed her out of his way a little harder this time.

He ran quickly to catch up with Kristin before she left.

"Kristin, Kristin! Hold up!" David called out to her, almost losing his balance.

But Kristin wouldn't turn around. She didn't want him to see how upset she was, because then he would know how much she cared about him. She couldn't leave herself open like that.

"Kristin! Wait, please." David caught up with her and stood in her path.

"It's okay, David. I know you guys have a history together."

"*Had* a history together. I don't want to be with Allison. You know that. Don't pretend for one second that you don't know I care about you. I know you feel it. Back there—dancing together—you felt it. I know you felt it."

"David, I…"

"No, don't say anything. Just this once don't—Say. A. Word." He drew her close to him and kissed her long and soft.

He had waited long enough to show her just how much he felt for her. Those days were over now. Kristin kissed him back, snuggling him even closer.

"I love you," David said to her, pulling himself away for a moment to look in her eyes when he said those words.

She bent her head down and said, "I love you too." He kissed her forehead.

Looking up at him now, Kristin confessed, "I do want to be happy. For so long, I felt I didn't deserve you—that I didn't deserve to be happy. But I want my happily ever after."

"What?"

"Something Pastor Greene said to me. I'll tell you about it another time."

"Okay." David chuckled.

"But there is something that I must tell you," Kristin said.

David's smile vanished, and his forehead creased with concern. Let's go home," he muttered.

***

He took her hand in his and never let go of it, knowing it had to be extremely difficult for her to finally tell him the events that took place the night of the accident. All the time he had invested, all the patience he had shown over the last few months had brought him to this moment. She finally trusted him enough to let him into the world she was trying so hard to keep him away from. He made up his mind that no matter what she said to him, no matter what she did, he wouldn't leave her. It was her past. Her future was with him now. No matter how atrocious it might be, what she was about to tell him would not stop him from staying with her. It couldn't stop him from loving her. Pastor Greene was right. It didn't matter how much he showed Kristin he cared. She had to trust him.

And throughout it all, the long talks about Tommy, the grief support meetings he took her to, they had finally reached a breaking point. They finally reached their breakthrough together, and they would tackle anything that stood in the way of their happiness—together.

Kristin, fidgeting nervously, looked into his eyes. He had professed his love for her only moments ago, but how strong was his love? Would he still love her after she told him what happened?

One of her legs could not stop shaking. David placed his free hand over it, nodding for her to begin. So, she did. Little by little, she began to divulge details of how she met Jake and how he had been charming at first, making her believe that he truly loved her.

At one point, he rose from the breakfast table. He stood over the sink gritting his teeth, pushing both hands down onto the countertop and doing his best not to smash something when she described how Jake had physically abused her throughout their marriage. But when Kristin revealed how Jake had repeatedly raped her on the cold, hard tiles of their bathroom floor or the numerous times he had broken her ribs, or broken her jaw, he had to leave the room to get some air. He returned, of course, apologetic and with teary, reddened eyes. David needed to hear everything and asked her to continue, so she did.

She confessed her plans to leave Jake when she found out she was pregnant with Tommy, but that she gave him a second chance when he had shown her the pamphlets from the AA meetings and said he was getting help. She explained she didn't want Tommy to have to grow up without both parents the way she had, and that was what made her stay.

At no time did David pass any judgment. He just sat there, comforting her, knowing how difficult this was for her to tell him. Then Kristin brought up Miguel and Robert and their shady business dealings with Jake—the unexpected visits and the drugs and money she found in the back of the closet. Lastly, she spoke of that night when things unexpectedly took a turn for the worse.

David sat back in his chair, nostrils flaring. He couldn't believe how any man could put their hands on a woman. He knew there was an underlying psychological component behind all of the abuse, but he wasn't thinking like a doctor. He was thinking like a man in love who would literally kill someone who even dared to harm a hair on her again.

"Tiffany told me they could take Tommy away from me. So, I had to take Tommy that night and leave. I didn't think I had any other choice. I was supposed to meet up with her behind the farmhouse off Buxton Road. I packed my bags and grabbed up Tommy from the crib. I could have sworn that Jake was asleep. I mean, I heard him—he was snoring, but I should have made sure. I was almost at the door, and Tommy, he called out to him. He said 'Daddy.'"

Kristin's lower lip quivered, tears shimmering in her eyes.

"I turned around and he was standing there... so angry." She began to sob uncontrollably.

It was enough. David's heart hurt too much seeing her break down like this. "It's okay, love, you don't have to continue." He raised his finger, placing it on Kristin's lips.

"No, I need to tell you everything. I need to get this out. It hurts too much to keep this inside anymore."

As painful as it was, she forced herself to continue, to recall what happened next.

"He shoved my head into the kitchen cabinets and started to kick me like he always does. Then Tommy... he came in crying. He wouldn't stop crying, and Jake... he got so angry and slapped him. When I saw him fall... he was crying so loud." Kristin placed her hands over her eyes, shuddering from the vivid image in her mind.

She rubbed the tears away roughly, then took a deep breath, trying to regain her composure. "I saw that long piece of wood lying there. I picked it up in my hands. I can still remember what it felt like—heavy. He had his back to me, screaming over Tommy's body, like it was his fault. So, I swung the four-by-four at his head and then his body hit the floor. I picked up Tommy and ran out of there. Got to the car and I floored it." Kristin paused before saying, "I swear I didn't see the truck ahead of us… it was raining so hard… and I couldn't see—my eyes were on fire… then Tommy was lying on the ground, and I couldn't help him. I couldn't breathe for him. He just lay there, and those guys were trying so hard to help him. But I knew… I knew he had left me. Someone was screaming over me, 'Hold on, hold on.'"

Kristin lowered her head, hugging herself as she rocked back and forth. David pulled her head into his shoulder, kissing the back of her head. "I looked over at Tommy—he wouldn't open his eyes."

David pulled her body closer to him. "It's okay now. I'm here now. You will never have to worry about me hurting you. I will never, ever lay a hand on you. I *promise* you. You are safe with me." He kissed her forehead and said again, "You hear me? You're safe with me."

"David, when I was in the hospital, one of Jake's friends—Miguel…" She took a deep breath, then continued, "He threatened me."

"Why didn't you say something before?" David asked her, staring into her brown eyes.

"I was too scared. I had told you that Jake left me. How was I supposed to tell you that his partner was threatening me because he thought I took his money? I didn't know what would happen if we reported him. The police would never believe that I didn't know what Jake was involved in. I didn't know if I would be arrested for assault. And I didn't want to lose you even as a friend."

"You could never lose me, Kristin. You acted in self-defense. Did you ever speak to Jake after that night?"

"No, but I'm sure he knew I was in the hospital. Miguel told me when he showed up that night that Jake had committed suicide. I don't know if it's true or not. All I know is when I left him, he wasn't moving. He fell face forward; he had a faint pulse, but I couldn't tell if he was breathing or not." Kristin's face went blank.

"Did this Miguel say anything else?"

"Yes. He told me that Jake saw Tommy's picture in the paper, and that was probably why he shot himself in the head. He was so smug. He told me if I didn't return his money, he was going to kill me. And I really believe him."

David held her chin. "Well, first of all, no one is going to touch you. I will make sure of that, and it's been over a month since you left the hospital. You haven't heard from him again. I'm sure he has many enemies, and maybe he met his match. No one is going to touch you," David repeated, staring deeply into her brown eyes. Then he stood up, rubbing his chin with one hand.

"What are you thinking?"

"You need to find out if what Miguel said about Jake is true. If he really committed suicide. Have you tried contacting Jake or the police?"

"No, I can't. Because what if he isn't dead? What if it's some sort of trap and he is alive, or the police make it seem that I was involved with the whole drug trafficking? I could go to jail for a long time. And I know that Miguel would kill me if he found me again."

"Those are a lot of what-ifs. First thing we need to do is find out whether your husband is still alive. Then, if money is going to make this man disappear from our lives, I'll find a way to get it together somehow. I'll refinance this condo if I have to."

"David, I honestly don't think it's about the money with him. I think he feeds off of instilling fear into people," Kristin reasoned

"You're right." David stood still, looking down at her. "If we gave him what he wanted, he would probably just find a way to extort more out of us. But like I said before, it's been weeks since you've heard anything from him. He doesn't know where you are. So, let's just pray this clown decided to leave you alone. If he does pop up, we'll be ready for him. But you really need to find out about Jake."

"I don't know, David. I just don't know." There was a deep-set frown on her face, and she shook her head in fear.

David placed one hand on the back of the empty chair he had been sitting in earlier. "Kristin, we can't start a new life together if your past is still haunting you. You also need to know for yourself—are you a widow or are you still married?"

Kristin hung her head low, knowing he was right. She had to find out.

"I also think that you should go visit Tiffany and reconcile. She was a good friend to you, and I know you miss her even if you don't want to admit it…"

"I really do." Kristin thought back to how many times Tiffany had been there for her and for Tommy. She had to make things right with her. While she was there, she could also find out if Tiffany knew something or had heard from Jake. David was right—Kristin needed to know if he was alive or not.

CHAPTER TWENTY-SIX

The next morning, David and Kristin worked out what steps they would take in finding out whether or not Jake was still alive. David had a friend at the hospital in administration that would help them at least find out whether anyone matching Jake's description had come in for attempted suicide. He also suggested that they contact the police department, and Kristin mentioned Officer Gavin. She told David how he had shown up at her house after their neighbors reported a domestic dispute. She told him he was very sympathetic to her and had said if she needed help to call him. David scribbled *Officer Gavin* on a notepad.

But Kristin also told David about the resistance that she received from the other officers down at the station when she inquired about filing a report against Jake. She told him they all loved Jake because he had done work for them on their homes. David shook his head and told her that they should focus on getting in touch with Officer Gavin as soon as possible. He also told her that Tiffany would be a good witness of Kristin's abuse in the event there were any legal proceedings brought against Kristin.

Kristin started to grow increasingly anxious, worrying whether the life she hoped to have with David could be derailed by all of this. But she knew the constant fear of the unknown was much worse than actually knowing.

A few hours later, they were in the car driving fifteen miles south to Tiffany's house.

As they turned down Forest Lane, Kristin could see the little blue house with the big bay windows standing quiet on the far-left corner. David pulled the car slowly into the driveway. Turning the ignition off, he took her hand in his and kissed the back of her palm.

"I'll be waiting right here, my love."

She had told David on the ride over that she wanted to talk to Tiffany alone. He was always so eager to help her in any way he could, and she loved him even more for that. But she had to start facing some battles on her own.

Kristin let out a deep sigh and hopped out of the car. From outside, she could see right through the white sheers into Tiffany's living room. Tiffany was moving about inside with a feather duster in one hand. As Kristin peered in from outside, part of her wanted to run back to the car and tell David to get her out of there. She was so embarrassed by the way she had acted. But she stood there, her feet planted firmly on the ground.

The July sun was being particularly unkind to her, and she could feel the sunbeams burning her bare shoulders. It also felt really good, though, to no longer have to worry about wearing short-sleeved tops like the one she wore today.

Kristin proceeded up the little stone path to the front door of the house and rang the doorbell. After several minutes, Tiffany finally answered the door.

"Kristin?"

"I'm sorry. I should have called first, but I didn't think you would agree to see me if I did. I needed to come here in person."

Tiffany looked over Kristin's shoulder at the parked car in her driveway. David waved hello and she nodded, then turned her eyes on Kristin. "Please come in."

As Kristin walked in, it felt as if she were walking back in time. She strode down the hallway lined with photographs of Tiffany and her late husband, which led into the living room, and took a seat on her cushiony brown sofa. On the table in front of her, she could see some late notices on the mortgage and other bills. Tiffany must have been reviewing her mail shortly before she had arrived.

"Tiff…" Kristin started.

"Kristin, please. Let's just put the past behind us."

"I'm so embarrassed by the way I treated you," Kristin explained, observing her friend, who looked very tired. Kristin gestured for her to sit beside her. It almost felt like old times, sitting on the couch with her again.

"You were grieving; I understood. I left you alone so that you could have the time to grieve. But I never thought so much time would pass between us. I'm surprised you caught me at home. Usually, I'm always at work—pulling doubles every other night just to make ends meet."

"I didn't know you were having such a hard time. Why didn't you come to me?"

"You had enough on your plate. You look good. When did you get out?"

"Been a couple of months now."

"Jake came over here a few times looking for you after our little spat in the hospital."

'Tiff, you've seen Jake? He's alive?" Kristin tensed, grabbing hold of Tiffany's shoulders so suddenly she startled her.

"Well, yes, as far as I know, he is. It was about a few days after you were admitted."

Kristin paced around the room with one hand covering her mouth, trying to understand.

"Why did he come here? What did he want?"

"He thought you and Tommy were here. He didn't know about the accident. Maybe the officer never told him. Anyways, he demanded to know where you two were. But I wouldn't tell him." Tiffany stood up and walked over to Kristin, who stood with her back facing the bay windows. "But I don't get it—why are you asking about Jake? I thought for sure you would want nothing more to do with him after Tommy's death."

"When I was still in the hospital, Miguel showed up. He threatened me. He thinks I took the money we found in Jake's closet."

"What? How…" Tiffany sprang up from the sofa.

"I don't honestly know. He must have snuck in. Maybe he knew someone that worked there? But he got in and made his way to my room dressed in green scrubs. He was talking crazy, saying that I better get his money—he had a gun." Kristin turned towards the window with arms folded. She gazed onto the street through the white sheers, speaking softly now. "He told me Jake was dead. That he shot himself and his business partner found him with his head over a newspaper clipping of Tommy's death."

Stunned, Tiffany sank down into the sofa, her mouth agape.

"Oh no… what did I do? What did I do?"

"What is it, Tiffany?"

"I did something terrible."

"What is it? What did you do?" Kristin probed for an answer.

"I know where some of that money went… because I took it," Tiffany confessed with shameful eyes.

Kristin's eyebrows knitted together. "What do you mean you took it?"

***

David made a call to Parsons Police Headquarters and asked to speak with Officer Gavin. After a brief hold, the officer picked up the line. David introduced himself, explaining the reason for him calling. From the details that David disclosed about Kristin, the officer knew right away who David was referring to. He had heard not too long ago about the Summers's boy, Tommy, being killed in an automobile accident and that the mother had barely survived. He couldn't deny that Kristin had popped into his mind from time to time ever since the day he showed up to the Summers's house on that domestic disturbance call. He had written her off after their last conversation when she had refused his help to connect her with a counselor.

Then, when Gavin had tried to visit the hospital to offer his help again, O'Neil had somehow found out where he was headed and told him that she was to be left alone. Gavin didn't push, knowing she had just lost her boy, and that if O'Neil said he would handle it, that meant he would. As grim as the thought was, that little boy's death may have saved her life.

Gavin was happy to learn from David that she was no longer with her abusive husband. But what Officer Gavin couldn't wrap his head around was what had prompted Kristin to reach out to him now. And why would a doctor from Parsons General be calling him to arrange a meeting? He figured he would get his answers soon enough. He was just pleased to know that Kristin was still alive.

He hung up the phone after David had given him a place and time to meet. A bit of anxiety washed over him, unsure of what he was walking into. So, he took out his revolver from the drawer and placed it in his holster.

"Hey, Gavin, you good, man?" asked Peterson. He had been watching Gavin's face during the phone call.

"Yeah, I'm good," he responded as he headed for the door, wishing everyone a good evening.

***

"Wait a minute, how much money are we talking, Tiffany? How much money did Jake give you?"

"A hundred thousand dollars."

Kristin's jaw went slack, and her eyes widened. "But why? This doesn't make any sense. Why would Jake give all that money to you?"

"I went by his office one day when he was at work. I was afraid that the hospital would make you leave once they realized you had no insurance or financial means to cover your stay there. Joe had no idea of my plans to meet with Jake. And trust me, Kristin, I didn't want to tell Jake where you were, but I had no choice. I figured he would find some way to give me the money to cover you at the hospital and…"

"And what?" Kristin stood over Tiffany, who looked up with those please-don't-hate-me eyes.

"I told him about Tommy. I gave him the newspaper article, and he slammed it down on his desk. He blamed me for everything, for you leaving him. He looked like a hot mess, like he hadn't slept in weeks. I told him that he was to blame for all of it, even Tommy's death and that he should pay for the funeral and your hospital bills. He just glared at me real hard but said nothing. He left the room and then returned with a blue bag in his hand. He opened it in front of me. There were stacks upon stacks of one-hundred-dollar bills. Then he spoke. He demanded that I take it and not ask any questions. So, I took it and paid the hospital and used what I needed for the funeral. I tried reaching out to him a few days later to tell him where the funeral was going to be held because I felt if you couldn't be there, he should have been. He was still Tommy's father. I texted him the address, but he never responded, and he never showed up either at the funeral. Two weeks ago, I drove by your house. There was a For Sale sign in your driveway. But his truck—it wasn't there." Everything that Tiffany had unveiled danced around in Kristin's head. But she couldn't be angry at her. She did what she'd always done from day one—she acted like a good friend.

"There's one other thing, Kristin."

"There's more?" Kristin responded incredulously.

"That day when I was in his office, as I was leaving with the bag of money, two men walked in. They wore plain clothes and practically hurried me out of the office before one of them shut the door behind me. I was curious, so I headed to the back of the building and saw Jake's office window cracked halfway open. I kept out of sight, but I could hear the three of them talking. They introduced themselves to Jake as DEA agents."

"What did they say?" Kristin sat upright now.

"One of them I couldn't hear 'cause he was speaking very low. There were still men on the site working. But the other one… I heard him mention that guy Miguel. But they called him Miguel Rojas. I was trying to listen for more, but Jake came over and slammed the window shut. He didn't see me, but I guess he didn't want anyone outside hearing their conversation. I ran to my car and left. I didn't want anyone seeing me snoop around there."

"It's okay. I understand."

"Jake was in a dark place, though, Kristin. It's possible that he did what Miguel said. I've never seen anyone look so dark. But I haven't heard anything about him in town."

"Okay."

"I'm sorry I told him about the hospital—about Tommy. I'm sorry I took the money. Please forgive me, Kristin."

"For what, Tiffany? You have done nothing to be forgiven for. I love you for what you have done and what you have tried to do for me and Tommy. I was horrible to you, and you didn't deserve that. If anyone should be asking for forgiveness, it should be me asking you to forgive me."

She hugged Tiffany tightly and they cried, holding each other. There were tears of joy, tears of pain, tears for the time they lost, and tears for Tommy.

"So, what now?"

"I have to find Jake and get Miguel's money back to him so he can leave all of us alone."

"Okay. I'm with you. But first, tell me. What's the deal with Dr. Landry?"

Kristin smiled at her friend and proudly professed, "I'm in love with him, and he loves me. I mean, he really loves me."

"Good. You deserve it, Kristin. I have a confession—I saw the two of you together in Avalon at the Hot Air Balloon Festival. George goes to it every year, and he invited me to go with him. I wanted to say hello, but I was afraid you were still angry with me. You were standing next to those stand-up eating tables. He was with you and you guys were eating deep-fried cheeseburgers." She chuckled.

"You were there?"

"I was there." Tiffany nodded. "I saw the smile he put on your face. In the past few years I have known you, the only time I've ever seen you smile like that was when you played with Tommy. So, I decided to just stay away and give you your space. I hoped one day you and I would be able to mend our friendship."

Kristin threw her arms around her dear friend. "He really does make me happy." Her eyes glistened as she continued to speak about David. "He's affectionate and loving. Always gentle with me and he has this dorky sense of humor." She let out a small laugh, smiling from ear to ear.

"I saw that with the ketchup squeeze bottle." Tiffany laughed along with her. "I'm so happy for you. You truly deserve it."

They talked a bit more about the past few months and how Kristin realized how much she wanted a do-over at life. She invited Tiffany to Pastor Green's barbecue in two days to celebrate the reopening of the newly renovated community center.

"It's going to be held at Redman's Field Park down the hill from Christ the King Baptist Church. David has been working so hard on this project and it's finally complete. It's going to be a great time with lots of food. And, oh my goodness, you have to meet Pastor Greene! He such a great man. He really helped me take a good look at myself. He made me realize that I needed to forgive myself in order to free myself of all this guilt I have been carrying around since Tommy's death. He helped me realize that I want to be loved and that I'm worthy and deserving of someone's love."

"Pastor Robert Greene from Christ the King Baptist?"

"Yes! You know him?"

"Kristin, he was the pastor that did Tommy's funeral. Tommy is buried in the cemetery behind that church."

"What?" Kristin's eyes swam with tears. Why didn't he tell her when he saw her that day at church? All that time she had sat there, being somewhat disrespectful to him, not knowing that he was the one who presided over Tommy's funeral.

"I went to several churches, but no one was able to do the funeral on the short notice I had given them. And it cost money to keep Tommy's body in the funeral home. Plus, there were other expenses like the tombstone. When I went back to that church—because that was where I was married—I asked to speak to the pastor. And the secretary had me meet with Pastor Greene. I told him the story of how you and Tommy were in a terrible car accident and how I needed a funeral and burial for him. He told me he would do both, funeral and burial service, for free. That whatever I was going to pay him for his pastoral services to just put toward buying the plot and coffin. He also said if I had it in my heart to give, I could make a donation to the church as much or as little as I wanted to. But there was no pressure to do so. So, I did just that. I bought the most beautiful coffin for Tommy and paid for the plot and got him this beautiful tombstone. Whatever was left of Jake's money I put toward your medical expenses."

"This whole time… he never told me he did that for me." Kristin figured whatever the pastor's reasons for keeping that from her had to be good ones. "I never even knew you went to church, Tiff."

"That's because when Adam died, I lost the motivation to go. Haven't been to that church in years. But as long as I have known you, you never expressed you had any desire to go."

"Well, things change. I feel like I'm changing."

Kristin realized then how all their lives—Tiffany, David, Pastor Greene, and hers—had intersected at one point. Could this be part of God's plan, like Pastor Greene would say?

Tiffany promised Kristin she would meet her at the barbecue tomorrow and that she was really looking forward to seeing Pastor Greene again.

When Kristin returned to the car, she noticed David had fallen asleep waiting for her. She leaned over to the driver's side and kissed his lips tenderly.

He woke, stretching his arms above his head and his legs out underneath the steering wheel. His eyes were still groggy as the corner of his lips turned upward into a small smile. "That's a very nice way to wake up. I love you too." He sat up and gave her a proper kiss. "So, I spoke to Officer Gavin. He said he would meet us at the diner."

"Now?" Kristin looked at her watch. It was almost five o'clock.

David glanced down at the time on his cell phone. He quickly started the engine. "Oh man, I didn't realize I fell asleep for so long. He's probably already there thinking we stood him up." David reversed out of Tiffany's driveway and headed down Forest Lane again.

On the way to the diner, Kristin filled David in on the conversation she had with Tiffany. He was partially relieved to hear that Jake was alive, which meant Kristin was in the clear for any criminal proceedings that might have been brought against her.

That was if Jake didn't press charges—and given that if he did, the people in town would know about his drinking and abusive nature, David felt he'd have nothing to gain by doing so. Kristin also explained how Jake had given Tiffany some of Miguel's money to pay off the medical bills and Tommy's funeral expenses. Still, David was confident that things would be okay. He told her that wasn't her or Tiffany's problem—it was Jake's. He also added that she would need to reiterate everything she said to Officer Gavin to gain some legal insight on the matter.

Hand in hand, Kristin and David walked into the diner together. A strong whiff of nostalgia hit her as she scanned the diner, surveying customers being waited on. She could picture herself scribbling down orders, running back and forth between the tables and kitchen, or listening to one of Joe's tall tales.

"I don't see any officers in here." David searched the room, for a moment remembering the last encounter he'd had with an officer, the devastating morning he learned about Josh's murder.

"I see him." Kristin smiled, and David snapped back to the present.

Officer Gavin noticed Kristin almost immediately. He rose from his seat halfway, gesturing them to come to his booth at the back of the diner.

Kristin led David by the hand behind her as they approached the officer. There were two cups on the table; one had a coffee ring underneath it and the other sat half full.

"I was waiting until I finished my second cup, and then I was going to leave."

"I'm sorry, time slipped away from us," David apologized, scooting all the way to the end of the booth across from Officer Gavin, making room for Kristin.

"Kristin." Officer Gavin nodded. He was out of uniform.

197

"Thank you for taking the time to meet with us, Officer Gavin."

"Well, the sound of desperation in Dr. Landry's voice was quite puzzling. I never thought anything worried you guys." Gavin flashed David a half-smile.

"I don't think I came off as desperate," David said defensively. "Worried a little, maybe," he hedged.

"David, please," Kristin said, hinting for him to stay quiet.

"I'm just saying…" David started to say in his defense when he saw Kristin becoming a little frazzled. Knowing she must have been anxious about the meeting, he retreated. "Okay. Okay." David played with the ends of a sugar packet.

"So, what's up? I figured that whatever I was about to hear from you, it would be better to talk here than down at the station with all the other members of Jake's fan club," Gavin said.

Kristin gave him a nod of appreciation and, for the second time, relayed the events of the night of the accident.

It was so hard to read what Gavin was thinking. He showed no signs of emotion, even though David flinched a few times when he once again heard Kristin describe Jake's behavior that night. Officer Gavin absorbed every bit of information Kristin shared like a sponge. Kristin reasoned that his cool, calm demeanor was probably because he had heard this battered wife story a thousand times. The only time Kristin saw a raised eyebrow was when she mentioned Miguel and how he had threatened her at the hospital.

"Miguel?" Recognition dawned on his face. "Does Miguel's last name happen to be Rojas?"

David glanced over to Kristin, anticipating her reaction.

"Yes, that's right. Miguel Rojas." She nodded.

Gavin turned his eyes on David. "Well, first off, Dr. Landry, you guys really need to do something about the security at your hospital. Talk to your site manager, because that is just ridiculous that he was able to get to Kristin the way he did." Looking back over at Kristin, he continued, "Miguel Rojas is a very dangerous criminal. He preys on the desperate seeking financial relief. He makes these 'deals' with businesses promising a nice compensation if they allow him to use their shipping courier to ship his packages under the owner's name. The comp he offers is so alluring that these owners who are close to having their business go bankrupt don't care what the packages are. They just take the money—no questions asked. You won't believe how many of these men he has screwed over. It's really sad because some of these men are just trying to stay afloat… We've been trying to lock this guy up for a long time now. I'm quite surprised that your husband would do any type of business with him."

"Jake had a lot of debts," Kristin mumbled under her breath, but Gavin didn't hear her.

"He isn't exactly someone you can trust. Your husband must have had some bad debts he was trying to get rid of. Each time we get that son of a gun before a judge on racketeering charges—like drug trafficking, extortion—his case gets thrown out."

"What, why?" Kristin questioned. David placed his hand on her shoulder.

"He has this weasel of a defense attorney that floods the DA's office with all these motions, and before we know it, Miguel is back on the street again. I'm sure he's paid off some high-ranking people. Money has a way of altering people's morals. Your husband got mixed up with the wrong people, and unfortunately, you got caught in the middle of it."

Kristin couldn't help but pity Jake. She knew his motivation for getting wrapped up with Miguel was split between his ego and hoping to have a successful business. He was always seeking approval from the ghost of his father. She realized right then that Jake was battling his own psychological abuse that he'd suffered as a child.

"Kristin?" David tapped her shoulder gently.

"I'm sorry. I just remembered one other thing. I forgot to mention this to you." She glanced over at David and then back at the officer, who watched her curiously.

"Tiffany had gone by Jake's office without me knowing, while I was still recovering in the hospital, to ask him to help her out with Tommy's bills. She said as she was leaving, two DEA agents showed up."

Officer Gavin spoke up, "I can only assume they were trying to cut a deal with your husband. Being that he was working closely with Miguel, he could be facing some serious charges himself. However, their goal was probably to get to Miguel just as ours has been. Look, I'm not going to sugar-coat anything for you, but I'm also not going to lecture you on how you should have filed a report against him the day I came to your house. That moment has come and gone. But there would have been a history of abuse on file, in the case he did report you for assault."

"Officer," Kristin said, "Miguel told me he had heard Jake committed suicide. Do you know if there were any suicides reported around that time...? I mean, soon after Tommy died?"

Kristin's eyes started to tear up. David placed his arm around her shoulder, comforting her.

Gavin realized how all of this was upsetting for her, and offered her some hope.

"I don't know offhand, but I will check. I don't remember hearing of any, but that may not have made it to my desk. In any case, if he hasn't committed suicide, some time has passed, and if your husband wanted to report you for assault, he would have done so already. Besides, he has bigger fish to fry with these agents on his tail. I'm truly sorry about your son."

"Thank you," Kristin replied, and placed her hand on top of David's.

"Miguel is the issue right now. So, if he calls you, shows up again, you let me know." He reached into his back pocket and opened a bulky, brown leather wallet. Pulling his business card out, he handed it to Kristin.

"Wait a minute, shouldn't she file a restraining order against this man? You said he was dangerous," David countered.

"You could do that. But that would mean giving him the knowledge of where you live, where you shop for groceries. Because how else would he know where to stay away from?"

"I don't want to do that." Kristin shook her head with a deep frown.

"But you would have it on paper, if he tried to do something to you," David reasoned.

"Look, it's been a long time since you've heard from him. Maybe your husband has settled his debt with him, and you'll never have to worry about him again."

Kristin highly doubted that. Where would Jake get that kind of money from?

"Don't hesitate to call me if anything comes up."

"That's it? We just sit around and wait for this guy to show up?" David's eyebrows pulled together in question.

"Right now, there's nothing you can do. I'm going to head back to the office and see if anyone knows where he's been hanging around lately. If I find him, I'll be sure to give him a warning to stay away from you. I'll also see if anyone has heard from Jake." He stood next to the table and took his cell phone out of his pocket. "Let me get your number. I'll be in touch if I hear anything."

David and Kristin drove back to the condo in silence. Later that evening, David found it hard to fall asleep. His mind raced with thoughts of Miguel hurting Kristin. He hoped Gavin was right, and that Miguel had been paid off. Because he honestly didn't know what he would do if anything happened to her.

✳✳✳

Early Sunday morning, Kristin woke David from the little bit of sleep he managed to get. They had to make a stop at the supermarket on their way over to the barbecue to gather some refreshments. Pastor Greene would preach at the early morning service as usual, and the barbecue would be held afterwards at the nearby park.

It was nearly one in the afternoon when David and Kristin finally made it to the park, with shopping bags full of frozen hamburgers, drinks, and family-size bags of chips.

Tiffany had also arrived around the same time with George, who she introduced as her boyfriend. Kristin was happy to see that her friend had found some happiness of her own. David introduced himself to George, and the four of them headed towards the center of the park.

Lemonade refreshment stands and picnic benches had already been set up. Hamburgers and hot dogs were on the grills with people lined up, empty plates in hand, eagerly waiting for some good old-fashioned barbecue and Mrs. Greene's famous potato salad that Kristin heard others raving about as she walked by.

The children of the youth group were scattered about, happily asking for donations for the local charity with little tin cans in their hands. There were also complimentary face painting booths set up for the children, which were already getting business from the families that arrived. On the other side, they had potato sack races and pie throws. David tried to go behind the grill to help Pastor Greene and Mrs. Greene with distributing plates of food, but Pastor Greene wouldn't hear of it. He told David that this was his day off, and to go eat and enjoy the barbecue with Kristin.

"Who's up for a potato sack race?" David asked, tickling Kristin under her arms.

"Oh, you're dead meat!" Kristin playfully threatened and ran off to get in line.

The four of them raced against each other in teams and then individually. Kristin and David won the couple's race, but David beat all of them when they competed individually. For the first time, Kristin allowed herself to finally enjoy all that was happening around her. There was no more guilt behind her laughter or her smiles. She had rejoined the land of the living as David would put it, and it felt exhilarating. When she closed her eyes, she could picture her parents, her aunt, and Tommy smiling down at her from heaven.

After the race was over, David grabbed a couple of burgers and Anna-Mae's potato salad for him and Kristin. George had also done the same for him and Tiffany.

"Yum, this is really good," Kristin said around a forkful of potato salad. "Are you having a good time?" she asked, looking sideways at Tiffany as they waited for the men to return with some colas.

"The best. I actually said hello to Pastor Greene while you were doing the one-on-one race with George."

"Oh, what did he say?"

"Nothing, he was just happy to see me here. He told me that I had to get back to church, as any pastor would do." Tiffany smiled.

"Well, maybe one day I'll go with you," Kristin offered.

"I'd like that."

Elijah took the microphone and asked everyone to focus their attention on the stage. George and David returned with the drinks and handed them to the girls.

"My father and I just want to thank everyone here who worked hard on the remodeling of the community center. All the time and love that was put into rebuilding and renovations is greatly appreciated. We now have a new basketball court with a state-of-the-art scoreboard, new exercise equipment, and a new heated swimming pool. Not to mention the new arts and crafts studio and bingo section for our seniors." A few of the elders around danced in jubilation as others at the barbecue cheered.

"I would like to give special thanks to Josh, who had this vision a year ago and teamed up with my father to sketch out plans for the renovations. Josh, I know you can't be here with us today, but I know you are smiling that big, wide smile of yours as we gather to celebrate. And I know right now that Josh is especially proud of his big brother, David." Elijah pointed David out in the crowd, whose eyes were starting to swell with joyful tears. "David, man, you saw this thing through. You committed yourself to your brother's dream, invested so many hours of hard labor when you weren't being a surgeon at work. No matter how busy you were, you dedicated the time, and you made available so many resources for us to use throughout this whole project. You're a blessing and an example of greatness to all of us. Today, you have helped everyone see here what great things we can accomplish when we work together."

Kristin wrapped her arms around David's neck, planting a big kiss on his cheek. Elijah moved to the end of the stage and played Lee Ann Womack's "I Hope You Dance" as slides of the community center renovation started to play over the large projector screen. The words *For Josh* flashed across the screen in big white script letters. The first few pictures were of Josh leaning over a drawing table pointing out the building plans to Pastor Greene. They were followed by slides of Josh loading blocks of wood into the back of a van with other workers, Josh and Elijah at fundraisers for the center, and a few more of Josh playing basketball with the kids at the center on the old basketball court.

David couldn't have been prouder of his brother at that moment. It was the first time he had seen any of those pictures, and he realized how much Josh had changed in the latter part of his life before his untimely death. Kristin rubbed his back, knowing how difficult it was for him to see Josh's pictures after all this time. She could see the resemblance between the two brothers.

The pictures changed over to images of David and Pastor Greene working alongside other men painting the gym and installing the basketball net, then finally the newly renovated community center with the new elder wing and swimming pool.

When the song ended, Elijah returned to the microphone, thanked everyone for coming and started to clear the stage. Kristin saw his band start to come on the stage and set up.

"Looks like they're setting up to sing again," Kristin told David.

"Seems that way. They're pretty good, don't you think? Why don't we get a little closer?"

"Sure," Kristin waved for Tiffany and George to follow her. But Tiffany gestured for her to go on with David as she stayed back with George.

Kristin shrugged her shoulders, not understanding why Tiffany wouldn't follow her. As David led her closer to the stage, she noticed that the crowd of people in front of it had dispersed. Now, she and David stood in the middle of the huge semicircle people had formed around them. Pastor Greene and Mrs. Greene turned their heads to the stage to see what was going on. David took Kristin by the hand again and winked at Elijah.

Elijah took the microphone off the stand and handed it to David.

"David, what are you doing?" Kristin giggled nervously, scanning the crowd of people around them who now made them the center of their attention.

David tapped the microphone two times and then spoke into it. "Kristin, this last year has been an eye-opener for me, from losing Josh to meeting Pastor Greene. But the biggest eye-opener for me was when you came along. I don't know when it was or how. All I know is I'm in love with you. I have never been able to tell anyone that. I guess because I've always had a hard time expressing it. But from the moment you walked into my life, it's had more meaning now than it ever did without you in it. I promise you—I will never hurt you. I promise to always be honest and true to you. I promise most of all to love you until I take my last breath on this earth."

"David?" Kristin's eyes grew big and round.

"Will you marry me?" David got down on one knee, taking out a diamond engagement ring from his back pocket. The heart-shaped diamond glistened in the afternoon sun.

"Yes, YES! I'LL MARRY YOU!" Kristin exclaimed, and he placed the ring on her finger. He stood up and she threw her arms around his neck, almost knocking the microphone out of his hand. Holding her now with one hand, he used the other to hand the microphone off to someone in the crowd and spun her around in his arms gleefully. Setting her down on her feet, he took her gently by the chin, kissing her softly and passionately.

"I love you." He looked into her beautiful honey eyes and kissed her again. "I know things are up in the air with Jake missing, and you not even knowing if he is alive, but I'll wait as long as it takes to make you my Mrs. Landry. I'll be right here," he whispered into her ear. Then he kissed her once more.

The crowd cheered and the band started to play. People began to dance, and others went back to grabbing second plates of food.

"Tiff, you knew?" Kristin looked over at Tiffany and George, who headed toward them.

"Well, kind of." She glanced over at David. "Sorry, I overheard you talking to Elijah when we first got here."

"It's okay." David chuckled, and George shook his hand as he congratulated him. The men decided to get more drinks, allowing the girls some time to talk between themselves.

Kristin turned around to see that Pastor Greene was heading over to them.

"Hello, hello. Congratulations are in order, I see." He hugged Kristin.

"Thank you, Pastor Greene… listen, I want to thank you for doing what you did for my son. I know you were the one that did his funeral and burial service."

He tilted his head, eyeing Tiffany, realizing that she was the one who had told Kristin. Then he looked back at Kristin with soft eyes. "I was waiting for the right time to tell you. I wanted to tell you that day you stopped by, but you were still so full of anger, and I didn't know how you would react."

"I understand," Kristin nodded.

"Well, got to get back to the grill and Mrs. Greene. I see David is over by the refreshment stand. Gonna head over there to congratulate him too. Remember, Kristin, you deserve your happiness and your prince." He winked and waved goodbye to Tiffany.

"Kristin, I have to get going. I'm working the late shift. Someone called out sick, and I just got the text."

"Oh, Tiff, really? I wish you could stay."

"I do too. But I have to pay the bills. I'll call you later tonight, okay? I'm so happy for you. David seems like a wonderful man. I'm happy for you both." She hugged her dear friend tightly and made her way over to George just as he and David were returning with cola cans in their hands.

"Come on, hon. Nina called out, and I have to cover her shift," she said to George. He congratulated Kristin and David again, and then they both left.

"Too bad they couldn't stay longer," David said, and Kristin nodded in agreement.

Someone from one of the booths nearby came over and asked for David's help. One of the legs of the table had given way, and their lemonade stand had suddenly collapsed. David told Kristin it wouldn't take too long, and he would be right back.

Kristin wandered off to a corner and leaned up against a tree away from the crowd, taking in the fresh air and scenery. Everything was falling into place. She looked up at the sky, only wishing Tommy were here to celebrate with her. She knew he would have liked David. She knew David would have liked him too. She wanted to savor every moment of this day. People waved from afar and smiled at her in congratulations. This would now be her life, and they would all be part of it. She took in a deep breath and sighed.

"Seems like you're fitting in just fine, for having a husband and a kid die on you only a few months ago," said an all too familiar voice.

Kristin spun around on her heel.

Miguel towered a foot above her. She was about to scream for David, but Miguel tightened his lips and shook his head. Kristin followed Miguel's left hand as he pulled up his shirt, revealing a gun tucked in his waistband. Kristin quickly glanced over to David, who was still helping the old man at the lemonade stand.

"Shh… we don't want to make a scene. Just come with me—quietly— and no one gets hurt." He leered at her.

Kristin stepped back a bit. "I'm NOT going anywhere with you. Who the hell do you think you are—threatening me?"

Miguel bent his head over her shoulder, draping one arm around her neck.

"You will, or else your new fiancé over there will get a bullet to his head. You already lost two people that you loved. Do *you* really want to be the reason you lose a third?"

Kristin could see that the pastor had been watching them, and she locked eyes with him. He excused himself from the group of men he was talking to and started to make his way over to them. Her eyes fell again on David, who still had his back turned to her. Kristin couldn't live with herself if anything were to happen to anyone else because of her. This was her mess, and she had to take care of it. So reluctantly, she complied with Miguel's demands.

"Remember, don't do anything stupid. I just want to talk." Miguel walked closely behind her, his hand on the small of Kristin's back under the strap of her white sundress.

He led her away quickly, away from the park and up the hill in the direction of the church.

***

David noticed that Kristin was not where he had left her. He scanned the perimeter and then walked around, asking if anyone had seen her, still carrying the lemonades he had brought for them. As his eyes continued to search the crowd, he became aware that Pastor Greene was also missing. An uncomfortable feeling started growing deep in the pit of his stomach. He did his best to try to brush it off.

She's okay, he told himself. *She has to be!*

David felt a tap on his shoulder and turned to see Pastor Greene. He was bent over in a tripod position, with his hands on his legs, trying to catch his breath.

"Pastor Greene, are you okay?" David asked, still holding the cups of lemonade in his hands.

Breathing heavily, the older man said, "David, I've been looking for you. There was a man here with Kristin a few minutes ago. She looked very uncomfortable. I tried to catch up with them, but when they saw me heading toward them, they sped off up the hill toward the church."

David's heart sank as sweat started to break out over his eyebrows. *There it was*—the reason for the uncomfortable feeling. It had to be either Miguel or Jake, but he was betting on Miguel. He had found her, but David didn't understand how.

David dropped the cups of lemonade to the ground and reached into his wallet for Officer Gavin's card. He shoved it at Pastor Greene. "Call this number right now and tell Officer Gavin to meet me at the church. Tell him that Miguel has Kristin."

Pastor Greene took out his cell phone, dialed the number, and yelled out to David, who had already started running through the park, "Wait! Who's Miguel?" But David was long gone.

Kristin—danger! Those two words were all that David needed to send him running up the hill toward the church to find her. He just hoped it wasn't too late.

***

"I want to make sure we are not interrupted," Miguel announced. Kristin tried to shrug his hand away, but Miguel would not budge until they reached the cemetery behind the church. The cemetery that, according to Tiffany, was where her son was buried. Kristin had planned to visit it, but not this way.

She felt her heart racing. What if he had led her here just so he could kill her? And he'd get away with it too, she thought. There was not a single person on the church grounds. Everyone was at the barbecue. And she knew she was taking a chance coming here alone with him, knowing he was fully capable of ending her life at any moment.

But she didn't want anyone else paying for her mistakes. She felt this was the right thing to do, even if she ended up losing her life over it.

Kristin looked Miguel straight in the eye, doing her best to show him no fear, even though she could feel her knees buckling underneath her. Yet, she continued to glare at him with fire in her eyes, both heels firmly pressed into the earth beneath her.

"What do you want?" Her nostrils flared.

"You know what I want," he replied with a slight grin.

"I told you that night. I do not have your money. I don't know where it is. So, if that's all there is, I need to get back…" Kristin tried to play cool, but her voice gave away the uncontrollable feeling of shakiness she felt inside.

But before Kristin could move past him, Miguel whipped the 9mm from his waist and pointed the head of the black barrel toward her heart.

"Who do you think I am? You tell me you don't have my money, and I'm just going to believe you. Jake always said you were too naïve. Do you *really* think because we are standing in broad daylight, behind this church, that I won't pull this trigger? Baby, I'm a businessman. You screw with my business? Then I screw you." He leaned to the side, looking behind Kristin, noticing something that made him laugh. "It's quite ironic that you happen to be standing in front of your son's tombstone." He moved in closer.

Kristin spun around and could see Tommy's tombstone was indeed behind her. As she read the epitaph, she could feel her cheeks wet from her tears. *Here lies our beautiful little angel. Gone too soon, our Tommy, Forever you will always be in our hearts.*

She looked back at Miguel, more enraged than ever. He was just as to blame for her son's death as Jake was. Miguel moved closer to her, the barrel of the gun only inches away from her chest.

✳✳✳

David finally caught up and ran through the big wooden doors of the church. It was so silent. The only thing he could hear was the squeaking of the hardwood floors, which he tried to minimize with every step he took. He looked at the empty pews, seeing no one. Just as he was about to turn around and leave, the faint sound of voices emerging from the back of the church stopped him dead in his tracks. Carefully, he made his way down the aisle, heading to a closed door behind the pastor's pulpit.

***

Kristin was doing her best to keep Miguel calm. He was growing increasingly impatient with her, waving the gun at her while she stood silent about his money. Not taking her eyes off the gun, she tried to appeal to his sense of reason. This couldn't be happening. Not now. Not when she had finally got to a place where she felt she wanted to live. And not when she finally had the love of a good and decent man.

"Miguel, someone will realize I'm gone, and they will call the police. I'm sure my fiancé has already done that. You can't just shoot me here without someone seeing you. Just please put the gun down. We can find another way to get your money. Okay?"

"See, the problem with you Americans, you think that everything has a price tag. That anything and everyone can be bought. But back home, if someone steals from you, it is a sign of great disrespect. And the only way to get back your respect is by sending a clear message to others that there are consequences when you disrespect Miguel. Today, I'm going to send that clear message that you do not screw with my business, and it's going to start with me killing you." Not taking his eyes off of her, he pulled back on the slide and released a round into the chamber.

Kristin could feel panic set in. There was a tightness growing inside her chest. Miguel stood there before her, his eyes so black and filled with hatred as he tightened his grip on the gun. It was almost as if he was in a trance. Kristin put her hands up, pleading for him to stop. *Think of something! Say something! Anything!*

"Wait—you said that Jake committed suicide. That means I own the deed to Jake's house. You can have it. You sell that house—the money's all yours." Kristin searched for any response that signaled Miguel was even listening to her. But she found nothing behind those eyes.

"I think that's going to be pretty hard to do." Kristin turned in the direction of another familiar voice. *But it couldn't be.* She watched as the gun moved off her and now pointed to someone standing behind her.

"Jake?" Kristin was dumbfounded. She felt as if she was about to faint as she looked into the eyes of what should have been her dead husband. "It *was* you that night."

"Miguel, put the gun down," Jake walked calmly over to them. He had no weapon on him that Kristin could see, but even with Miguel's gun pointing at him, he continued to move toward him.

He was alive and well with not so much as even a scratch on him. Kristin continued to look him over from head to toe. His appearance was more rugged now. He had grown a goatee since the last time she saw him, and his once wavy hair was now a short fade.

Kristin's eyes went back to Miguel, who was just as stunned to see Jake as she was. "It's impossible—you can't be alive. Robert told me you were dead—that he found you in your house—that there was blood everywhere." He lowered the gun to his side and clicked the safety on.

Was she dreaming, Kristin asked herself? No, it felt too real. For months, she had contemplated what she would do or say if she ever got the chance to see Jake again. But all she could do was stand there in utter disbelief.

"Robert saw what I wanted him to see. I knew he would run back and tell you," he said, then looked back to get a good look at Kristin, who stood behind him in shock.

"What? You were involved in all of this?" Kristin asked almost in a whisper.

Jake touched her shoulder. "Kristin, I might be a lot of things. But a drug dealer was never one of them." He turned back to face Miguel. "So, guess who paid me a visit at work, when I was with a client a few weeks ago?"

Miguel shrugged his broad shoulders with a half-smirk, not showing any great concern.

"Federal agents. That's right, DEA agents." Jake laughed to himself. "Because of you, I have been under surveillance for a while now. You've been using my business as a front to traffic drugs all over the South. The day you came by the house threatening me over that package, I knew something was up. And when the DEA approached me, I was more than happy to help them nail you."

"So what?" Miguel shrugged his shoulders

"SO WHAT? You put my family in danger! YOU SON OF A—" Jake charged at him, grabbing him around the collar.

Then he felt the nudge of Miguel's gun against his chest.

✳✳✳

David, in the pastor's office now, could hear the voices more clearly. He peered out the large double windows that stood in front of him. Two men on the church grounds were arguing with one another, and Kristin was caught in the middle of their crossfire. David's eyes widened when he saw the sun's reflection hitting the end of Miguel's gun, which was pointed at the other man. Slowly, David raised the window, trying to not draw attention to himself. Sizing up the frame, he was sure he could make it. He picked up the chair from the pastor's desk and gently placed it near the sill. He knew the real danger that was present. But he could not just sit back and watch while Kristin's life was hanging in the balance.

Jake raised his hands, backing up, and moved in front of Kristin to shield her.

"This is between me and you, Miguel. Let her go. You know she has nothing to do with this."

"Do I? Hmm. Well, I'm thinking she does. You shouldn't have stolen from me, Jake."

"You left the bag of cash in the back of my truck when you borrowed it, you idiot. When the DEA showed up the first time, they told me I had to work with them or else I could be facing some serious prison time, and I wasn't about to lose my family over that." He looked over his shoulder at Kristin and was now speaking to her. "So, when I saw the bag there in my truck, I hid it in the back of my closet. I was going to hand the bag over a few days later to the DEA to show them I was not a part of this. But then that night happened—Tommy died."

He turned back to face Miguel, whose glare became even more intense. "So, yeah. I took some of your money to help pay for my son's funeral. I felt it was payment due for all the scrutiny you put me under. And every day after that, I worked with the DEA so they could get to you and the rest of your people. They knew you would eventually show up at my house looking for that bag, so they placed a tracker in it. It's just a matter of time before they show up here. So, why don't you just leave and save yourself?"

"But he saw you. He said you were dead!" Miguel barked angrily, still not believing that Jake was alive.

"He only saw what I wanted you two to believe. It was all staged... Pig's blood." Jake grinned at Miguel. Kristin listened on, stunned at what was unfolding before her.

Miguel, feeling even more humiliated that he fell for Jake's staged death, lifted the gun, ready to pull the trigger, and pointed it at Jake.

"Well, this time, there won't be any staging. Today you will be reunited with your son. I promise you that."

"Miguel, please don't do this," Kristin pleaded.

"Even now, she defends you? Even now she tries to save you?" Miguel asked incredulously. "Tell her how you took money from me to help pay off the bank when you took out a loan against that house of yours because your business was going under. You weren't asking any questions about how you were getting your cut then. You didn't care about where the money came from."

"That doesn't matter now. So, if you're going to shoot me, go on, 'cause you're finished anyway. It's done." Jake stepped forward, showing more courage than Kristin ever witnessed in the time they had been married.

"Oh, it's done. Is that right? Well, then I guess you won't mind seeing me kill the one person you loved more than yourself." Miguel stepped out to the right, turning the 9mm back at Kristin, and pulled the trigger. Jake grabbed Kristin and threw them both to the ground just as the gun went off.

"NO!" Kristin yelled. At that moment, David jumped out the window two feet above them, taking Miguel down to the ground with him and knocking the gun out of his hands. They both exchanged punches. David caught Miguel's right hook to the side of his face and responded with an uppercut to Miguel's ribs. Catching him off guard, David then delivered one hard punch to Miguel's jaw, knocking him out cold.

Blood trickled down the side of Jake's dark-blue t-shirt, and Kristin realized he had been hit. She pulled his half limp body into her arms, shaking him hard to keep him awake. Her white sundress was soaked with his blood.

Pastor Greene, Elijah, and some other men the pastor had rounded up stormed the church grounds suddenly. They assisted in keeping Miguel on the ground until the cops arrived, while David ran over to Kristin's side to examine Jake. Police cars were flying across the park up a path that led up the hill to the church

Soon the sounds of sirens surrounded the church. Officer Gavin was the first officer to respond to the scene. He immediately cuffed Miguel, hauled him up off the ground and took him away. Police swarmed the grounds, and moments later, Kristin noticed federal agents arriving just as Jake had predicted they would.

David, his hands stained with Jake's blood, traced his finger to where the bullet had entered him but saw no exit wound.

"We have to get him to the hospital, Kristin. The bullet is still in there. It's probably lodged inside his lung." David took note of Jake's respirations, which were fast and shallow. He ran off toward a cop car to find out how much longer before the ambulance arrived.

Jake grabbed on to Kristin's hand, knowing he had very little time left.

Kristin covered the wound with her other free hand, so much blood seeping between her fingers. As she held him sideways in her arms, she felt something hard against her back. Looking behind her, she realized she had been leaning against Tommy's tombstone. He had made it known that he was with them, even now.

"That's our boy." Jake pointed weakly behind her at his son's name on the tombstone. He managed to take something out of his jeans pocket and placed it in Kristin's hand. Kristin looked down to see what he had given her. It was the little red toy car that Tommy had dropped in the house the night they fled.

"I was bringing it for him. I remembered how much he loved it," he said, his voice shaky. He lay in Kristin's arms, his blood staining the grass around them.

"Hold on, Jake."

"Kristin—Kristin. I'm sorry. Please… forgive me," Jake managed to say in between breaths. He was weeping now. "I'm cold, Kris. I'm cold." Kristin could see the life behind his green eyes was slipping away second by second.

"Shh… don't talk. Just hold on, Jake. The ambulance is on its way. Just hold on." She shook his body hard to keep him from closing his eyes as he lay in her arms, his head on her lap. She caressed his hair with her blood-stained fingertips

Jake's grip began to loosen on her hand a little at a time.

"No, Jake, hold on!"

"I—love you. Always love you." His eyes pleaded for forgiveness as he looked into her amber gaze one last time.

She cried out, "I forgive you, Jake. I forgive you!"

Suddenly, his hand dropped at his side and his eyes rolled back in his head. Just like that—Jake was gone.

✳✳✳

The ambulance came and the medics began to work on Jake, but David knew it was a lost cause. Kristin and David stood by Pastor Greene and Elijah as the paramedics whisked Jake's body into the ambulance, still trying to resuscitate him. The doors closed and the rig pulled away. The ominous lack of lights and sirens told David everything he needed to know.

Holding Kristin close to him with one hand around her waist, David kissed her forehead and said, "It's over."

CHAPTER TWENTY-SEVEN

A week had passed since Jake's funeral. Collin had shown up to pay his respects, as well as many of the officers who had known him. Kristin was grateful to God for giving her the strength to forgive Jake in that moment, allowing him to die in peace. She also knew it freed her from the power he'd had over her all those years.

She made sure that Jake's body was laid to rest beside Tommy. In the end, he was still his father and loved him.

Since Kristin never made it to Tommy's funeral, she had Tommy's tombstone replaced with a new one.

"It's beautiful," David said, looking at the new epitaph on the bronze headstone: *Here lies the beloved son of Kristin and Jake Summers, a beautiful angel who will forever be in our hearts and surely missed. Until we meet again.*

Kristin reached in her purse and took out the little red car that Jake had given her before his last breath.

All of a sudden, David and Kristin could hear music coming from behind them. A woman was singing, and then they heard Elijah's voice.

"Hey, I need to do something," David said.

"What is it?" Kristin turned and asked him.

"I have to be somewhere. I'd like you to come with me. But you have to promise to have an open mind."

"I trust you. Wherever you want to go, I'll follow you."

David smiled at her and kissed her lips. "Well, we aren't going very far. Come on."

Leaving the cemetery, holding hands, they walked around to the front of the church where Pastor Greene stood on the steps in his best Sunday suit, welcoming people in through the big wooden doors.

David held Kristin's hand in his and took a deep breath. "It's Elijah's first sermon as a minister."

"Then we should be there to support him." Kristin winked at him.

Pastor Greene caught sight of David and Kristin standing at the bottom of the steps. His smile got wider.

"You came!" He made his way down the steps to greet them.

David smiled at him, Kristin still holding his hand.

"Well, I thought *that day* could be today."

Pastor Greene smiled back at him and placed his arms around them. "Come on, let's go hear my son deliver the Word."

***

Six months later, Pastor Greene had married David and Kristin. It was a beautiful beach wedding—small and intimate as they had agreed on. Tiffany was the maid of honor, of course. David's colleagues and a few members of the congregation attended. Dr. Daniels was there as well, and Kristin finally met David's parents, who had returned from their summer in Europe. She was nervous about meeting them for the first time, but they were very happy that their son had finally found a woman who loved him for the person he was and not someone she thought she could mold him to be. Kristin was overjoyed to finally have two people in her life she could call Mom and Dad, even if she had adopted them through marriage. She had found the peaceful life she had only dreamed of with David by her side. She used to think she did not deserve happiness. But every day, David reminded her how much she did.

After a long, beautiful reception, Kristin and David stayed the night in the five-star hotel where the reception had been held, as did many of the guests who attended to avoid having to drive home after a long night of celebration. The Bridal Suite was lavishly decorated with every convenience, including a fully stocked fridge, California king-size bed with Egyptian cotton sheets, and plush pillows. The bathroom had a double sink with a shower and a whirlpool bath. A bottle of champagne on ice with two wine glasses was set to the side of the bed on the nightstand, with a bowl of chocolate-covered strawberries.

Kristin was extremely nervous. She knew that this was the night she would finally give herself to David. She could sense David felt the same way when he went into the bathroom a second time to brush his teeth, forgetting that he had done so only an hour before.

"I thought I was nervous," Kristin laughed, sitting on the bed in a long white negligee as David emerged from the bathroom walking toward her.

A million thoughts danced through Kristin's mind. She wanted their first time to be special. She prayed to be completely comfortable, allowing herself to be taken by him. The last time she had, it was forced as usual with Jake. She stared at his bare chest, broad shoulders, his skin more bronze now than when she had first met him because of the summer sun.

"You look absolutely amazing." David smiled at her as he took a seat beside her on the bed. He traced her soft, milky shoulders with his fingers. He kissed her neck and she arched it backward, allowing him to lay her body down on to the bed.

More kisses and caresses followed, as he cherished her body from head to toe, neither wanting this night to end. With every kiss and gentle touch, Kristin felt as if he was trying to take away all the years of pain she had endured before him. She fought away the flashes of Jake forcing himself on her the last time she had been with him. She pushed it as far as she could to the back of her mind, telling herself she was making love to the man she loved—her husband.

After, they fell on top of each other, their skin covered in glistening beads of sweat. He kissed her nose as he cradled her in his arms. Body against body, their hearts had finally found the rhythm. They were together; they were complete.

"Was it the way you imagined it to be?" Kristin asked, kissing his chest as she laid her head on it.

"Even better, Mrs. Landry."

CHAPTER TWENTY-EIGHT

Two and a half years later, Kristin found herself right back in Parsons County General hospital. But this time, she wasn't the patient. She was a registered trauma nurse. David was incredibly proud of her. She had transferred the credits from her previous nursing program, graduated from an accelerated one offered through the hospital, and passed her licensing boards a month later. Her life was finally back on track.

She was grateful to all the nurses and doctors who had worked so hard to save her life and who had tried their best to save her son. She felt she needed to be in a field where she could be of service to others. Taking Tiffany's advice, she also started a domestic violence support group at the hospital with the board's approval. The group met every Monday and Thursday evening from seven to nine. She was surprised at how many women and *men*, who lived in the same county, needed the support.

Some stories were so very similar to her own. The first meeting of every month, Kristin gave her own personal testimony of domestic violence to help newcomers feel comfortable sharing their own. She wanted to remind those who were being abused or who had left their abusive partners but were thinking of going back to them that it was never too late to leave. She wanted to leave them with the clear message that no relationship should cause more pain than it does joy.

During one of her lunch breaks, Kristin decided to visit her old hospital room that she had stayed in after the accident. She was amazed at how nothing really changed, but how so many other things did.

She walked over to the window and smiled. There they were again, the two love birds sitting outside, perched on a fragile tree branch.

A knock on the door made her turn quickly. She saw David in the doorway.

"Hey, what are you up to, Mrs. Landry?" David asked, coming up behind her when she turned her gaze back to those little birds chirping away on the branch. He placed his arms around her waist.

"Staring out the window at my friends." She tapped the glass as David kissed her neck.

"That twig is about to give way on them." He pointed at it.

"They'll be fine," she said, and no sooner had she spoken than the branch broke off. The birds moved up the tree to another branch for a new resting spot.

They laughed together, seeing how easy it was for the little birds to make a new branch their home.

"Guess sooner or later, we all reach our breaking point, even those birds," Kristin declared.

David hugged her tighter. "No looking back now. Only forward." He placed his hands on Kristin's small baby bump.

They had taken their time before starting a family, especially with Kristin returning to nursing school. David was more than patient and understanding about it, although he was very eager to have children. Today, she was four months pregnant. It was still too early to tell the sex of the baby. But she didn't mind whether it was a boy or a girl. She just felt blessed that God gave her a chance to be a mother again.

Placing her hands over David's that rested on her belly, she leaned her head back against his chest. "Only looking forward, my love."

DOMESTIC ABUSE RESOURCES

If you or anyone in your family is in a domestic violence relationship, please don't wait. Get help. Below you will find links and contact information for the Domestic National hotline and shelters where people waiting to help you. You can also reach out to your community pastor, a local church, religious organization, or your local state authorities to seek guidance.

National Domestic Violence Hotline:
1-800-799-7233
https://www.thehotline.org/

Find a Shelter:
https://www.womenshelters.org/

ACKNOWLEDGMENTS

Ilike to take this moment to extend my sincere gratitude and acknowledge the Breaking Point team. It has been a true honor to have such brilliantly talented people come together. Thank you for dedicating your time to making this story come to life. All of you have been amazing through this entire process. This would not have been possible without any of you.

To my book editor, Kristen Hamilton of Kristin Corrects—you helped get the ball rolling, and I am forever grateful. To Julie Withaeger, editor and proofreader—from the beginning to end, you were a true blessing to work with on this project. To Calee Allen, who did the final proofread and offered such valuable advice and information on my publishing journey. To Chriselle Tejera, my longtime friend who designed an absolutely beautiful book cover. To Kimberly Peticolas, eBook and paperback formatter—thank you for all your help and recommendations.

In addition, thank you to Anne Mirrop, my social media manager. Your optimism helped carry me through some very rough days. Thank you to Katherine Fleischman, my book publicist, for all the great work you have done and continue to do.

Lastly, to the actors and crew of the Breaking Point Book Trailer: Michael Ezrachi (Cinematographer/ video editor), Chelsea LeSage, Gabriel Hamilton, Andres Castro, Andre Blackwell, Steve Makropoulous, Zack Glassman, Jessica Lyle, Camille Parlman, Thijs Hogenboom, Michael Williams, Alex Tudosie, Matt McQueen and Melissa Williams. Thank you for being part of this project. You are amazing and talented actors and crew, and it was my pleasure to be in the midst of brilliance. You made these characters come to life. To Yangliuhui Jacome, who composed a beautiful score for the trailer. Thank you for bringing your musical talent on board to this project.

To my family, thank you for all your love and support. You believed in me and never doubted that this was all possible.

To my Father in Heaven. Lord, you took me through some rough waters these past few years. But I made it through every storm, with you by my side. You were always faithful. Your praise will forever be on my lips.

ABOUT THE AUTHOR

Who is Cece Reeves? Christian, author, nurse, and mother of two are just a few words to describe this incredible rising talent in the literary world of fiction.

Cece grew up in the Bronx of New York. At the young age of seven, she was inspired by her third-grade teacher to write a story, *The Flying Unicorn*, published for her elementary school paper. From that moment on, she enjoyed producing stories which she could share with family, classmates, and friends over the many years to follow. Writing was always something that came naturally to Cece. Some of her favorite authors as a child were C. S. Lewis (*The Chronicles of Narnia*), Jane Austen (*Pride and Prejudice*), Carol Keene (*The Nancy Drew Series*), and later on, Fredrick Douglas (*An American Slave*), Stephen King (*The Shining*), and Richard Preston (*The Cobra Event*).

Working on her first novel, *The Breaking Point*, has been quite an emotional journey from start to finish. Having had her own personal experience with domestic violence and losing her cousins to a senseless murder that arose from domestic abuse, Cece felt the need to share this story so that readers could have a vivid experience of what it is like to be a domestic violence victim by seeing it through the eyes of *The Breaking Point's* main character Kristin Summers.

With her soon to be released debut book, *The Breaking Point*, she hopes her readers will find a heartfelt story that inspires faith, healing, forgiveness, and spiritual awakening.

www.ingramcontent.com/pod-product-compliance
Lightning Source LLC
Chambersburg PA
CBHW021031130626
46552CB00005B/1788